**In praise of
David Anthony Durham's**

THE SHADOW PRINCE

"Wildly imaginative and thoroughly thrilling,
The Shadow Prince is a Hunger Games for
a big, strange, magical new world."
—Lev Grossman, author of *The Magicians Trilogy*

More praise for Durham:

"David Anthony Durham never disappoints.
I can't wait to read whatever he writes next."
—George R.R. Martin

"Durham is a master of the fantasy epic."
—*The Washington Post*

THE
SHADOW
PRINCE

DAVID ANTHONY DURHAM

Tu Books
An Imprint of LEE & LOW BOOKS Inc.
New York

TU BOOKS, an imprint of LEE & LOW BOOKS Inc.,
95 Madison Avenue • New York, NY 10016
leeandlow.com

Manufactured in the United States of America
Printed on paper from responsible sources

MIX
From responsible sources
FSC® C103098

Edited by Elise McMullen-Ciotti
Book design by Sheila Smallwood
Typesetting by ElfElm Publishing
Book production by The Kids at Our House
The text is set in Garamond

Chapter opener art copyright © by Olga Che
Egyptian Symbols by Good Studio

10 9 8 7 6 5 4 3 2 1
First Edition

Library of Congress Cataloging-in-Publication Data
Names: Durham, David Anthony, 1969- author.
Title: The shadow prince / David Anthony Durham.
Description: First edition. | New York : Tu Books, 2021. | Audience: Ages 8-13 | Audience: Grades 4-6 | Summary: "In this middle grade solarpunk novel set in an alternate Egyptian universe, twelve-year-old Ash must compete and survive to become the shadow-and protector-of the prince"—Provided by publisher.
Identifiers: LCCN 2021012982 | ISBN 9781643794280 (hardcover) | ISBN 9781643794297 (epub)
Subjects: CYAC: Fantasy. | Magic—Fiction. | Gods, Egyptian—Fiction. | Egypt—Fiction.
Classification: LCC PZ7.1.D869 Sh 2021 | DDC [Fic]—dc23
LC record available at https://lccn.loc.gov/2021012982

To the generous readers who read early drafts of this novel. Thank you. Your support kept me going. This book wouldn't exist without you.

DAYS BEFORE

Once a Canal Rat . . .

I saw Merk and his friends before they saw me.

My first instinct was to jump behind something and hide, but I was out in the open now on a flat expanse beside the village, with nothing but sunbaked ground and a few tiny shrubs around me.

My second thought was to drop to the ground and play dead. Not the best plan, though. If they saw me, it would be way too embarrassing. I probably could have leaped back down into the canal next to me, but I'd just been *in* the canal for ages cleaning out debris.

It was one of my jobs—an important one, as my mentor, Yazen, liked to remind me. The village depended on the crops for food, and the crops depended on water to grow. Since we lived in the desert, water wasn't easy to come by. It took a system of canals powered by sunmills to bring it in. Sunmills were a lot like windmills, except the blades of the turbines were covered in suncloth, a thin, sparkling fabric that captured the magic of the sun and transformed it into energy. During the day when the sun was up and shining, we used the sun's power. Then at night, when the south wind blew across the desert, we used the wind for its power. The spinning mills turned the paddles down in the canal, and the paddles circulated water all the way from the River Nile out to our crops. Unfortunately, stuff loved to jam the paddles. That's why I spent way too many afternoons down in the water, digging through canal mud with a little shovel and, just as often, with my bare hands.

When I saw Merk, I'd just climbed out of the canal, dirty, sweaty, and tired, ringing the water out of my linen kilt I wasn't going back in unless I had to. Problem was that I absolutely did not want to talk to Merk. I tried to pretend I was invisible, hoping that somehow Merk and his friends wouldn't notice me. Fat chance. Over the years Yazen had taught me lots of weird skills. Too bad the ability to turn invisible wasn't one of them.

I could blend in pretty well in our village. I was just another soon-to-be twelve-year-old: medium height, skinny and bare-chested. Like all the people I knew, I was dark brown from head to toe, warmed by the sun pretty much every day of my life. My only unique quality was that my bare feet looked a few sizes smaller than they should.

The three boys were headed right toward me.

I checked my hair for debris. It was lumpy and curly in just the right way to trap bits of leaves, twigs and chicken feathers. I wasn't the least bit invisible.

Merk was showing off his new sunboard. Like all solar-powered devices, sunboards ran on the energy of the sun. Across the top of the board was a sparkling surface, similar to suncloth but bonded to a thin sliver of palm wood. Its edges were smooth, all the angles perfect. Merk hovered, balancing on the slim platform. He circled with the board, dipping his right foot down to the ground to swipe himself forward. They said all solar-powered devices worked because Lord Ra, one of Egypt's most powerful gods, joined with the sun each day and shone his magic down onto Egypt. Maybe so. I wouldn't know since I'd never seen any of the gods. They were only stories to me. Incredible stories. Maybe too incredible to believe, even though I wanted to.

Every now and then Merk tried to do a trick, flipping the board up or spinning, but each time he fell off. With my sense of balance, I knew I'd be pretty good at it. But I knew better than to even ask. Merk didn't share. Being the son of the richest merchant in the village, he got all the neat stuff. I don't suppose his father was as rich as royalty or the people who lived in the larger cities, but around here he was top of the heap. Merk loved reminding everyone of that.

"Hey, Dowser!" Merk shouted as they approached me. "Is that a canal rat?"

Dowser slapped his bare belly. Like me and pretty much all the other boys and men I knew, he wore a simple kilt, but otherwise went bare-chested most of the year. "Yeah," he said, "a canal rat." It's kind of a lame contribution, but that's Dowser for you. He's not much of a thinker.

Merk's other buddy, Setka, never said anything. Instead, he just laughed in a way that made his thin shoulders bounce up and down.

"Oh, no," Merk went on, squinting at me, "it's something worse. It's the son of the recluse."

He was wrong again, but I wasn't going to point it out. The "recluse" was my mentor, Yazen. I wasn't his son. Merk knew that, but he enjoyed pretending that he didn't. Truth was, I was an orphan. I didn't even know who my parents were. Sometimes I had vague memories of them, but I might've just been making them up. For as long as I could remember, I couldn't help wondering who they were, what they were like, why they'd left me. I wondered if I'd ever see them again. I wondered if they were alive out there some- where, and I wondered if they ever thought of me.

I did a lot of wondering.

Not that it did me any good. The only parent-like person I knew was Yazen. And it's true, he was . . . peculiar.

"Hi, Merk," I said, wiping the sweat from my forehead. The sun was fierce, as it always was in Egypt. "That your new sunboard?"

It was a stupid question. Of course it was his new sunboard. But like it or not, I lived in this village with Merk. I probably would my whole life—no matter the crazy things Yazen claimed were destined to happen to me. Best to stay on good terms.

"You bet it is," Merk said. He pressed his foot down on the back of the board, lifting up on the front and spinning. It looked impressive, but about halfway around he lost his balance and fell. Dusting himself off, he said, "Pretty nice, huh? Jealous much?"

I had to admit it. The board was pretty nice, and I was jealous. Much. The way it hung in the air, bobbing. It made me want to leap on to it and show these guys how it was done. Not that I knew how it was done. I'd never been on a sunboard in my life. Such things weren't part of my so-called training. Still, I wished . . .

"It's a great board, Merk," I said. "Wish I had one."

"Your old man could never afford it," Merk said.

"No way he could," Dowser said.

"Next year," Merk continued, "my dad's buying me a solar chariot. Can you believe that?"

Not really. I'd never even seen a solar chariot. They had to be seriously expensive, though. What Merk would do with a solar chariot was beyond me. Ride around the village showing off? Probably. "That's cool, Merk," I said.

For a moment he squinted at me, deciding whether he wanted to take that as an insult. I smiled and lifted my eyebrows, sort of a visual way of saying, *I said that was cool, Merk.* He accepted it. He hopped up on his board again, kicked it into motion, carving a few nice turns. He almost ran over Setka, who responded with that shoulder-shaking laugh of his.

Merk tried another trick. I could see what he wanted to do was make his board twirl as he leaped off of it and then be able to land back onto it when it was flat. That's what he *wanted* to do. What he actually did was jump off the board, flail around in the air, and then miss it as he crashed down to earth. The board skittered away and hovered, looking a little depressed.

Dowser didn't have anything to say. Neither did Setka's shoulders.

And that's when I made my mistake. I opened my mouth that I should've kept closed and said . . .

2

. . . Always a Canal Rat

"Don't worry. You'll get the hang of it."

Some people might think that was a nice thing to say, but not Merk. He's an expert at taking things the wrong way. He glared at me. "Who says I don't already have the hang of it?"

I was tempted to point out that he had just landed on his butt, and that I didn't think that was the trick he'd intended to make. Instead, I just pulled a Setka. I grinned and raised my shoulders.

"You always think you can do things better than everyone else, don't you?" Merk asked. "You and your mysterious 'training.' All the important stuff old Yazen claims to be teaching you. As if you're better than the rest of us. You're not, and that old man is just crazy."

"He's crazy all right," Dowser agreed.

"Look, Merk," I began, "I didn't mean—"

"Let's see you do better!" he said. He snatched up his board and thrust it at me. "Do some tricks, canal rat." I tried to refuse, but he leaned in, face menacing. "Now!" He jabbed me with the edge of the board until I accepted it.

I could see only one way to salvage the situation. Get on the board. Try to do some trick. Fail. Make Merk happy. It shouldn't have been that hard. There was only one problem.

Since before I could remember, Yazen had put me through an intense training program. It was mostly done behind the high walls of the compound we lived in. Advanced fighting techniques. Weapons work. Stretching. Palm tree climbing, rope walking, and wall scaling. I could stand balanced on a tightrope and juggle throwing knives. Truth was, I had skills. No one in the village knew the extent of it, but Yazen had, on occasion, let on that some great, noble destiny awaited me. He said he was preparing me for it. He claimed that on my twelfth birthday my future would be revealed, a future that involved demon hunting and all sorts of amazing, important things.

Sounds good, huh?

The problem was that my twelfth birthday was two days away. No sign of anything changing. Nope, just digging in the muck and dealing with the local bullies. That, apparently, was my destiny. Personally, I agreed with Merk. Yazen—as much as I loved him—was a little out of his mind.

The reason my training was a problem with Merk's sunboard was that my instincts and balance were too finely tuned. The moment I stood on that board I felt at home on it. I loved it. I was floating on air! I dipped one leg down and felt the board slip forward. Nice. I did it again. Smooth. Next thing I knew, I was carving ribbons in the air, leaning into turns, spinning and dipping. I sped away down along the canal, snapped out a quick turn, and headed back, zipping from side to side as I carved a squiggly line back to where I'd started. To finish it off, I leaped, catching the board with my toe and spinning it beneath me. I came back down on it perfectly, and then slammed the back end to stop my forward momentum.

I totally forgot that my plan had been to fall. I looked up to see Merk's reactions.

Whack! Merk punched me square in the nose, with

enough force to send me sliding down the bank toward the canal. I snapped to my feet, wiping blood from my nose. For a red-hot moment, I wanted to dash up the bank and tear into Merk. I'd fight all of them. I'd win, too. A lot of Yazen's training involved me learning to fight multiple opponents. I could see just how I'd place a swift kick to Merk's groin, jab an elbow into Dowser's gut, and chop down on both of Setka's laughing shoulder blades. I could've done it so fast they wouldn't have known what hit them. Only . . .

I couldn't. It was the one thing that Yazen had forbidden me to ever do. I couldn't use my training out in the village.

Up on the bank, Merk jumped on top of his board. "I'll take this back now. You're lucky I don't give you the pounding you deserve. You're not worth breaking a sweat over, loser."

"Yeah, loser," Dowser said.

Setka started kicking sand at me, splattering me with it.

"Next time," Merk said, "don't touch my stuff." He turned and boarded away, the others jogging to keep pace with him.

I just stood there, fists clenched, dripping with

muck, watching them go and feeling angry. Seriously angry. I washed the blood from my nose with a handful of water from the canal. At least it wasn't hurt bad. I'd been punched and kicked before by a stronger, more skillful fighter than Merk, that was for sure. Still, it all made me so mad. And I wasn't just mad at Merk. I was mad at Yazen for the strange life we led, one built on secrets and hours spent training each day to fight battles I was never going to have to fight. At the same time, he refused to let me fight the ones that faced me every day.

Trudging back toward the village I was reminded that this place—a nothing town at the edge of the desert—was the only place I'd ever known. It was just a small cluster of buildings and huts, a grain warehouse, pens for our scraggly goats, and a few thin palm trees. I lived with simple villagers who I'd known my entire life. Around our village, there was nothing but a flat expanse of desert all the way out to the horizon. Despite anything Yazen said, I was sure this was going to be the only life I'd ever know. The big twelfth birthday revelation? I just couldn't believe it.

Thinking about it with my nose still aching made me even madder. That's why I kicked open our compound's gate. And it's why I slammed it shut so loudly that Yazen would be sure to hear it.

I stood there glaring at the small collection of huts and training equipment we called home. It was laughable. Yazen was so convinced that I had to be prepared to fight demons that he had built pretend ones for me to battle. They were made out of wood and bound together with reed ropes. He used pulleys and gears to move them around as I sparred. There was one shaped like the crocodile-lion-hippo demon, Ammut. Another one was supposed to be a giant scorpion. There was also a cloak Yazen wore when he pretended to be one of the Wailing Goddesses; the cloak hung on a rack along with the long knives the goddesses wielded.

Over the years, I'd memorized all the evil demons' traits as I'd fought them—or pretended to fight them. Really, it was always Yazen in disguise. When I was little it was exciting. All the seriousness and attention made me feel special. But I wasn't little anymore. Now I realized that Yazen had never once provided proof that any of the stuff I'd spent my life training for was real. It all seemed like one long, cruel joke.

Yazen stepped out from behind one of the huts,

broom in hand. Seeing me, he twirled the broom and held it out to one side in a ready position. I knew what that meant. He was ordering me to attack him. This was part of our training. I was supposed to always be ready to fight. Any time. Night or day. He made sure of it by challenging me at random times, like he was doing now.

Fine, I thought. *You want to fight, old man? Let's fight.* I'd give him what I wanted to give Merk and his friends. I ran toward Yazen, fists tight, legs building up the energy to send me flying through the air, my foot aimed right for his head.

3

Disbelief

That might sound like a mean thing to do to an old man, but Yazen wasn't just any old man. He was a skilled fighting instructor, the one who taught me everything I knew. He was lean and surprisingly strong, with tattoos of hieroglyphs on his arms. They were strange. Even though I'd studied glyphs for years, I'd never been able to read his tattoos. It was like they were a different language, maybe an older and forgotten one. Yazen always ignored my requests to explain them. He was secretive about his past, but he knew lots of things about the wars Egypt had fought with foreign invaders. He told stories so vividly that he must have been in the battles himself, even if he never admitted it.

Now I flew at him, all my force projected through my foot in a flying kick.

Yazen ducked.

I flew over his head, landed at a run, skidded and spun around. I came back at him. I threw a barrage of kicks and chops and punches that would've made quick work of Merk and his goons. Yazen dodged and blocked. His long, flowing pants danced over his smooth footwork. He was bare-chested like me, only with taut muscles that I'd always envied. Every now and then the broom swept up and snapped against my wrist or ankle. His way of giving me little warnings.

Yazen had a puzzled look on his weathered brown face. "Ash, is something the matter? Your attack is forceful, but sloppy."

I snatched a staff from its holder on the compound wall. I spun it, liking the sound of it twirling in the air.

Yazen circled away from me. "Something has upset you, I see."

"You could say that," I said. "Not just one thing, though. Lots of things. Like . . ." In a sharp motion, I brought my staff up and swung it down on top of him. He blocked it with the broom. ". . . how I just got punched in the face by Merk. Insulted by Dowser. And had sand kicked on me by Setka."

"You're having trouble with the village boys again?"

"Yeah, and because of you I can't do anything about it. They make fun of me, bully me, do whatever they want. And I just have to take it." I got near enough to attack again. I feinted a high strike. When he moved to block it, I dropped low and swung for his legs. He leaped above it. The staff scorched by beneath him, just missing his toes. "The whole village thinks we're jokes. And it's all for nothing!"

"You are wrong about that. Your destiny is near at hand, Ash. You have no idea how—"

"Stop! Stop saying that. You've been saying that all my life, but nothing has ever changed or is going to change. I wish you would just admit it!" I swung hard as I said that, hard enough to snap the broom in Yazen's hands.

He leaped back, looking a little sadly at the now useless pieces of wood. "This was my favorite broom." Tossing them away, he stood straight and folded his arms. "I have asked a lot of you. Years of training. Years of asking for your faith in me. It seems I've lost it now, on the eve of your being called."

"Get another weapon," I said.

"No. You may do me harm if you wish, but I will not fight with you in anger, Ash."

"Suit yourself." I hefted my staff and strode toward him. He stood still, watching me come. That's when I felt myself faltering. He meant it. He'd let me hit him just to make a point. In a way, that made me angry. Just the fact that he never let up. He was always kind and generous, fair and giving. He trained me hard and said all sorts of things I didn't believe anymore, but he said them as if *he* believed them. I exhaled an exasperated breath. Truth was, as frustrated as I was, I didn't want to hurt him. He was like an uncle or grandfather to me. He was the only person I had in the world. Sometimes it's easiest to be maddest at the people you love the most.

I still held my staff, but instead of swinging it, I asked, "What do you mean by 'being called,' anyway?"

He bent his head forward and ran his fingers across his bald scalp, the way he always did when he was considering something important. "The time is near enough. You have the right to know. I feared telling you the whole truth before. It was too dangerous, and you were young. It would've been easy for you to speak out of turn to someone. That would have been disastrous." Yazen moved closer to me. "Ash, all the years of study have been for a very serious purpose."

"I know," I said, sarcastically. "I've got some amazing destiny ahead of me."

Yazen's face was grave. "True. You may. It's also possible that you will soon be dead."

Complicated Circumstances

"**W**hat?" Being dead didn't sound like a very exciting destiny.

"It all begins where you began. The circumstances of your birth were . . . complicated."

He began to pace, paying no attention to the staff that I still held at the ready. "There are things about it that are not my place to tell you. I can say that you were born on a very special day. You—and a few other children spread across Egypt—arrived in the world on the same day as an Egyptian prince." I started to interrupt, but he said, "Let me tell all of it, Ash."

I sighed but still listened.

"You are part of an ancient tradition. This tradition declares that children like you, born on the same day as a prince, become shadow candidates. These boys and girls are each trained by a mentor, like me. We teach the candidates martial arts, educate them about demons and their threats, and instruct them in hieroglyphics and such things. Each candidate is raised separately in seclusion, until the time comes for them to venture to the capital and be tested."

There were several things about what Yazen had just said that made it hard for me to breathe. I didn't interrupt, though, wanting to hear it all.

"The testing is hard. And dangerous. Many do not complete it, Ash. That is why when the vessel arrives tomorrow, you will be asked whether you wish to be tested. If you don't, you are free to go. If you accept, you and I will go to the pharaoh's palace in Memphis. You will be pitted against demons summoned from the Duat—"

"Wait." I stopped him. "From the Duat? As in the underworld? The realm of the dead? *That* Duat?"

"Yes, Ash. *That* Duat. There will also be many other trials. Only one candidate can succeed. The one that does will become the prince's shadow. For the rest of his life, he or she will be the prince's close confidant, an ally and friend to the monarch, charged with protecting the young royal from dangers. If you succeed, Ash, you will live the rest of your life involved in the great workings of the empire."

I didn't know what to say. He looked and sounded dead serious, but . . .

"You're joking, right? These are just more stories. I'm not a child anymore. You can't just make me believe anything. If this is true, why has it been a secret all these years?"

"If the enemies of the pharaoh—and there are many, Ash—knew who the candidates were, they would be hunted and destroyed. That has happened in the past. Also, not all the prospective candidates are chosen for the testing. There was always the possibility that you would be found lacking. Then the invitation would never have come, and you would be destined to live a normal life."

"You're saying I wasn't found lacking?" I asked.

Yazen smiled. "Do you remember the old trader that stayed with us a few months ago?"

I nodded. He'd claimed to be a friend of Yazen's, which I'd found kind of strange because I'd never known Yazen to have friends. And I'd thought it even stranger that Yazen had let the guy watch me train. He never let anybody else do that. I'd shrugged it off, though, assuming the trader was just what he looked like—a poor old man who wandered the desert with just the tunic on his back and the few things he bartered with.

"That man," Yazen went on, "was a representative of the pharaoh. He assessed your skills. I'm proud to say he found you acceptable."

For a second I was pleased to hear that, until I remembered that I wasn't really buying all of this. I crossed my arms and smirked. "Prove it."

"You'll soon see for yourself. Tomorrow, an envoy will arrive to see if you're willing. If you choose to accept, we journey to the capital, and your testing begins." Yazen picked up the two pieces of broom. "Come, we should spend a few hours on your hieroglyphs. They need more work than your fighting technique."

"Wait," I called. "What about my parents? Since you're suddenly revealing things, how about telling me something about them?"

Yazen cleared his throat and said, "I'm sorry, but I am forbidden to say any more than I have." With that, he walked away.

A Gathering of Demons

Deep in the Duat and far from Ash's humble village, a very annoyed Egyptian god stood in a gathering of demons.

The god was Lord Set, and he didn't much like demons. In close quarters like the dank underworld cavern he was now in, the creatures were even more unpleasant than usual. Their monstrous shapes crowded the stone chamber, each one of them more beastly than the next. Jaws and claws, glowing eyes and fur and scales and horns. There was no end to the disgusting shapes they took. Set was grateful that at least the light was dim, with only a faint reddish glow. Even his sharp eyes couldn't see them that well. The rank smell of the creatures was almost too much to bear, a mixture of pungent sweat and foul armpit odor and other things Set didn't want to think about. Their garbled grumbling and grunting would, to most people, have been the stuff of nightmares.

Set, however, wasn't most people. He wasn't even a person. He was—in his own opinion—Egypt's foremost god. It annoyed him like nothing else that the other gods didn't acknowledge this. Instead, they had robbed him of his proper place on the throne of the gods and forever punished him for a few small misdeeds ages ago. Youthful mistakes. Nothing more. "It's been a thousand years!" he grumbled. "Really, they should get over it."

It was terribly unfair, in his opinion, and he had every intention of doing something about it. That's why he'd called this meeting of demons. It was part of the plan he'd been working toward since Prince Khufu's shadow testing approached.

Being demons, and not necessarily the cleverest of creatures, they hadn't all arrived on time. Waiting with them had been a tedious affair, but they were almost all gathered now. There was only one that he was still waiting on. When Set heard the loud, reverberating tramp of her footsteps he knew the time had finally come.

"Ah," he said, "there she is now! Devouress of the

Dead, how kind of you to join us." A huge, hulking shape emerged into the chamber, wafting an even greater stink than all the other demons combined. Set held a handkerchief to his snout-like nose and said to the group, "You'll want to know why I've summoned you. I have a task for you." The demons increased their garbled grunting. "Quiet! This is work you'll like. You've been trapped down in the depths for too long. You must all desire to see the world of the living again, to walk among them and do what you do best: bring terror and misery to the human world. Tell me, how long has it been since you tasted human flesh? Young flesh, at that." That silenced them. All around him, the demons crept closer, suddenly very interested in what the god had to say. Set grinned, and flames of excitement kindled in his eyes. "Let me explain what I have in mind. You'll like this. Oh, I'm sure you'll like it very much."

6

A Village Spectacle

I could've died of embarrassment.

Yazen and I stood outside the main entrance to our compound, right where anybody in the village could see us. He had woken me before sunrise in a flurry of motion, saying the day had finally come. I'd never seen him so full of nervous energy. He kept talking about the decision I was going to make. Would I accept the royal offer and journey to Memphis for the testing—which could result in my death? Or do I say *no, thanks,* and settle into a long life in the middle of nowhere? Considering that I'd never been asked to decide anything about my own fate, it was hard to get my head around the notion that it might all suddenly be up to me.

I had moved around half asleep in the early hours that morning, doing the things that needed to be done *if* we were going to be leaving the compound for a while. By the time I was fully awake, Yazen had packed two satchels' worth of clothes and basic supplies. He then led us out the compound gate, closed it behind us, and there we stood, satchels beside us, waiting.

Yazen had added a sleeveless shirt to his attire, which for him was downright fancy. He had an orange cloth wrapped around his head. Protection from the sun, which was pretty important when you're bald in Egypt. I wished I had a headwrap too. I'd tried to comb the knots out of my hair, but it had just made them lumpy in a different way. I shrugged. What did it matter? I was still convinced we weren't going anywhere.

The sun bloomed on the horizon and crept upward. It was going to be hot, but that was no surprise. Yazen bent forward and said a prayer to Lord Ra, asking for his blessing. "Give the boy the wisdom and courage to make the right decision," he said.

Lord Ra—by which I mean the sun—didn't have anything to say in response. He just hung there in the sky, like he did every day.

"Yazen," I asked, "what are we doing?"

"Waiting for a royal barge to arrive."

I smirked. I could see for miles in every direction. I didn't see any royal barge. Nothing was happening out there except for heat waves starting to ripple on the horizon. A few vultures circled in the blue sky. None of it looked special or different in any way.

It wasn't long before villagers began to gather around us. The local strong man was the first to arrive. He dropped the sack of grain he'd been carrying. Stretching the bulky muscles of his back, he asked, "So what's this? You two going somewhere?"

"Perhaps," Yazen said. "Perhaps."

A little later the old storyteller happened by. Leaning on his cane, he said, "Old friend, do I see the makings of a story here?"

Yazen kept his gaze out on the horizon. "Yes, I believe there are the makings of a story here."

The friendly, round baker woman who made flaky pastries joined the other two. She squinted at us for a moment, and then asked, "Yazen, you old fool, where are you going?"

"Perhaps nowhere. Or . . ."

I'd always suspected he admired more about the

baker woman than her pastries, and I could see that he was tempted to say something more. *Don't do it*, I thought. I almost stepped on his toe.

I should've, because after a moment of hesitation, he finished, ". . . perhaps to the pharaoh's palace. Ash is to be a candidate for the office of the prince's shadow."

I groaned. He'd said it! Word of that would spread faster than a stink among pigs.

Sure enough, within minutes the entire village, young and old, stood staring at us. They peppered Yazen and me with questions. Yazen answered cryptically, which just made them more interested. I kept my mouth shut. This had the potential to make me the butt of jokes for years to come. I could hear it already. "Remember that time crazy Yazen and Ash got sunstroke waiting for a summons from the pharaoh? They waited all day and no one came!"

Then it got worse.

Merk, Dowser, and Setka arrived. They squirmed between the adults until they stood right beside me, too close for comfort. Merk held his sunboard gripped to his chest. A grin tilted his lips and grew as he came to understand the situation. For a time he didn't say anything. He just stood there, smiling. I itched to back away from him, but there was nowhere to back away to. He was near enough that nobody but me heard him whisper, "You loser. Nobody's coming to pick you up. You're just a canal rat. A nobody. You will be all your life. I'll never let you forget it."

He pulled away, spun around, and pointed into the distance. "Hey, look," he said with sudden excitement, "is that a sunbarge? It's coming for you, Ash!"

7

A Tale to Tell

"Is it?" Dowser sounded genuinely surprised. He stood on tiptoes to see.

"Where?" Setka asked. "I don't see it."

I couldn't tell if his buddies were playing dumb or just *being* dumb, but I knew what Merk was doing. A joke, that's what I was. He glanced at me, grinning mischievously. To the others, he said, "No, it's out there. I've got really good eyes. Just watch and wait. You'll see it."

You'd think that everybody in the village would know Merk by now. The kids he tormented and teased did. But somehow the adults never seemed to see him for the bully he was. They waited, scanning the horizon. I even felt Yazen stand a little straighter and lift his chin. I half wanted to let them in on the joke, but I didn't have the energy. I hung my head.

"Don't you see it?" Merk asked. He was enjoying himself. "A whole royal barge coming all the way out here just to get Ash because he's so—"

"I see it!" Setka shouted.

For a moment, I thought he'd finally caught on and was adding to the hilarity, but then the baker woman said, "Oh, my. Yes, I believe you're right."

That brought my head up.

"Huh?" Merk asked.

Everyone hushed. We all strained to see. I climbed up on the satchel, gripping Yazen's arm for support. At first, I didn't see a thing other than the squiggly lines that rippled across the horizon. Then something appeared. It was blurry at first. Just a shimmering where there shouldn't be a shimmering.

"It's a sunbarge," the storyteller said. "My eyes are old, but I know the shape."

"Of course it is," Yazen said.

"It's just passing," Merk said. He didn't sound as pleased with himself as he had a moment ago. I didn't know if anybody had noticed that he'd changed his tune. I had to admit, though, that there was a good chance he was right. We'd all seen sunbarges passing in the desert, sailing majestically in the distance, but they never came to our village. Why would they?

"No, it's coming this way," the strong man said.

"Of course it is," Yazen said.

For the first time, I thought he might be right. Amazingly, the billowing, glistening solar sails seemed to be heading toward us. Instead of being filled with wind like a normal sail, the fabric swelled with solar power, glowing with light and energy. The vessel grew larger and more distinct every moment as it floated above the desert. Below its sails hung an ornate, wonderful ship, swaying in the air currents. It really was a sunbarge. And it was heading straight for us!

The closer it got to our village, the faster it seemed to move. It ate up miles of desert at incredible speed, so fast that I began to think it was going to sail right over us. The air around it buzzed with insect life. Even from a distance, I could tell they weren't normal insects like those we had in the village. They were much bigger! Wide-winged dragonflies flew in military formations, darting to change position every now and then. Large scarab beetles wheeled about in front of the prow, dipping and rising like river dolphins before a waterborne ship. Still other beetles crawled across the hull, busy with jobs I couldn't figure out.

At the last minute, the largest of the sun-filled sails disappeared and the vessel slowed. Smaller sails were pulled in one at a time as the massive ship touched down light as a feather at the edge of the village. Figures appeared at the railing. Peering down at us from on high: we must've looked a sad sight. Everyone in the village—including me—stood staring up at them. Merk had let go of his sunboard and didn't seem to notice it floating near his feet. Dowser's mouth hung open. Setka kept blinking and blinking, as if he thought his eyes were playing tricks on him.

Two giant dragonflies carved out from the side of the barge with loud, thrumming wings. Each carried a soldier sitting in a harness. They swept down so quickly that we all cowered back, making space for them to land. Their six, slender legs touched down on the sand and flexed beneath the weight of their bodies. One of the soldiers, a muscle-bound guy with a stern face, surveyed us silently. The other soldier was a woman. She was lean, but looked plenty tough. She gripped a long spear like she knew how to use it.

Soon after, a beetle whose whirring wings seemed

to barely keep it afloat descended from the ship. It flew in an erratic weave, making its way to the space between the dragonfly riders. When it landed, it stood as tall as a person, upright on its two spindly lower legs. Its four other arms moved freely about. One held a board with a sheet of papyrus clipped to it. Another held a writing stylus with which it was marking something on the parchment.

The beetle surveyed us from behind two disks of dark glass, shading his eyes from the sun. His insectile features gave no sign of what he might be thinking about the motley array of villagers in front of him. He spoke in a haughty, clicking voice.

"Who among you is Ash, the shadow candidate? And who is his mentor?" He checked his scroll. "Yazen by name."

8

The Contract

You heard me correctly. He spoke! Never in my life had I seen a human-sized talking beetle, nor giant dragonflies that people rode on. I hadn't even seen a royal barge up close. I guess I shouldn't have been surprised. Our village was just a small spot in the middle of nowhere, yet here they all were standing right in front of us. I was dumbfounded. Fortunately, Yazen wasn't.

"I am Yazen. And this . . . ," he said, indicating me, "is Ash, the shadow candidate."

The beetle's eyes fell on me. With one arm, he adjusted his glasses. His mouthparts shifted around for a moment and then settled down. I had no idea how to interpret that. Was I disappointing? I didn't have a fancy kilt to wear, or any jewelry, and my sandals were worn thin. In pretty much every way, I was an average village kid. Was I what the beetle and these soldiers expected of one of these shadow candidates? I couldn't tell, but it seemed unlikely.

"I am Lieutenant Ruk, of the Royal Army Beetle Corps," he said, "here on the pharaoh's business. This shadow candidate, has he been trained in accordance with the tradition?"

"He has," Yazen said.

"Is he here before me willingly?"

Yazen looked at me. I shrugged. "Yeah . . . I guess."

The beetle studied me a moment. "Are you ready to sign the contract?"

"The contract?"

One of his arms produced another scroll. He snapped it open. A roll of papyrus with hieroglyphs etched all over it poured out. Holding it up where I could see, the lieutenant said, "You'll find it covers all the standard details. Hazards. Responsibilities. Funeral arrangements. Read it over if you like." He thrust it at me.

My eyes scanned the pictographs, but there were so many. They went on and on. I'd never be able to stand there reading the whole thing. Certain glyphs did jump out at me. Dismemberment. Inevitable carnage. Likely evisceration. I didn't know what that meant, but it didn't sound good.

"Ready to sign?" Lieutenant Ruk asked. He held a stylus out to me.

"But I don't understand it all."

The beetle clicked. "It's just standard legal jargon. It says that you agree to all terms and conditions of the shadow testing. You understand the risk of bodily harm and death is great, that few candidates survive the testing, and so forth. You swear that you want nothing more than to succeed and that, if you do, you'll be a loyal servant to the royal family for all your days. Those are the broad strokes, at least. Ready to sign?" He slipped the stylus into my fingers.

Holding the scroll in one hand and the stylus in the other, I hesitated. Was I ready to sign? The hugeness of it all dropped on me all at once. This was really happening. All the years of training had actually been in preparation for something.

It shamed me to think I'd ever doubted Yazen, but it also frightened me to death to imagine what might be ahead of me. Would I really be expected to fight demons? Would I need knife-throwing skills and advanced martial arts techniques? If so, was I ready? I'd always wanted to be far from the village. I wanted to be someplace important doing important things, but now that it was offered to me I wasn't sure I was up for it. What if I failed? What if I wasn't special? I was only a village canal rat, after all. Maybe they'd just make fun of me in the city.

That reminded me of Merk. I looked at him, and at Dowser and Setka. They were staring at me, expressions of dumb astonishment on their faces. I didn't know what awaited me in Memphis, but I knew that if I let this opportunity pass I'd regret it all my life. I'd be making myself exactly what Merk said I was: a nobody. If I stayed his threat would come true. We'd grow old in the same town with him reminding me of how I was a nobody everyday. I didn't want that. I wanted the chance to be somebody, to do great things, to see the wonders of the kingdom. I might die in the process, but at least I had to try. And besides all that, deep down, I knew this was my only chance to find out who my parents were. Maybe they were alive and out there somewhere waiting for me.

I signed my name on the scroll.

When I handed it back to the beetle, I thought I could see amusement in his face. "I wasn't sure you had it in you," he said. "So be it. Climb aboard." He waved two of his arms at the dragonflies. "The sun is strong enough to get the barge back to Memphis before dusk, if we leave now."

"But . . . ," Merk said. "But . . ." He didn't seem to know what to follow that with.

Yazen picked up my satchel and pushed it into my hands. He lifted his, pulling me forward.

As we passed the storyteller, he smiled and said, "This is truly a tale to tell." Others agreed. The strongman did a little dance, which was funny considering his enormous bulk. The baker woman squeezed Yazen's arm and told him to look after me. Some of the kids began to chant my name.

I felt the dragonfly's eyes on me as I approached. Its wings twitched, but the rider flicked the reins and it stilled. He extended an arm and hauled me up on to the saddle behind him. I began to ask, "How do you—"

The rider snapped the reins. The insect's long wings thrummed to life. As it leaped, my stomach dropped inside me. The earth fell away. My adventure—however it was going to turn out—had begun.

9

Above the World

On the deck of the royal barge, people, beetles, and other insects bustled about, preparing the ship to depart. When the captain ordered the sunsails unfurled, the shimmering cloth sparked to life at the touch of the sun. The fabric was so thin it was nearly transparent, but it was strong and hummed with the energy it trapped. The tall, slender masts creaked, and the entire vessel shifted. I grabbed the railing for support as we rose into the sky.

I looked down at the upturned faces of all the people I knew in the world. Those were the faces I'd seen every day of my life. I realized that I'd miss them terribly. Or, most of them. My eyes locked on Merk's. He was staring, his face rigid with anger. He clutched his sunboard like he was trying to snap it in two. It was strange, but from up here, his board didn't look like much more than a piece of wood. A tiny, unimportant thing. While I could still make out his features, I did one last thing. I lifted an arm, waved, and mouthed, *See ya, Merk.*

The barge soared high into the air, and I stayed at the railing watching it all. The world scrolled beneath us as we gained speed. I marveled at the vastness of the desert, and at the lushness of the Nile Valley when it finally came into view. The river was an enormous snake bringing life to the barren landscape. The land on either side of its bank burst with green—tall trees and wide fields of crops. We sailed over crowds of crocodiles and hippos in the river. We flew over towns and cities larger than any I'd ever known. The shadow cast by the barge stirred flocks of pink flamingos into flight. Everywhere I looked, the scenes took my breath away.

"We're really flying, Yazen!" I said. "I'm used to sunboards and sunmills and stuff. I see those every day, but this barge . . . it's amazing. How is it possible? I mean, really possible?"

Yazen thought for a moment before replying, "In Egypt, there are two forms of magic. The first is that of the gods. It's innate within them. Incomprehensible, really. For all I know, they have always walked with magic as natural to them as is the life force inside of you.

"But Lord Ra created a second form of magic, and he made it a gift to all of Egypt. By joining with the sun every day and combining his power with the sun's, Lord Ra transforms its rays into an energy source that we humans have learned to harness. And we'll continue to. Every day, inventors and engineers and scientists are finding new ways to advance our society: new fabrics, devices, machines. We live in a special time and place. Count yourself lucky. All the wide world— and there are many lands outside of Egypt—receive the gift of the sun's energy, but we are blessed to have Lord Ra infusing it with his divine power."

I was starting to feel lucky, but Yazen's words got me thinking. "Shouldn't the whole world have the benefit of Lord Ra's sunpower? Why is it just us?"

Yazen smiled. "That is a generous thought, Ash. Yes, I suppose the whole world would benefit from such a gift. Maybe one day they will." He pointed at something with his chin. "But look. We're approaching our destination."

Memphis, the capital city of Egypt. It was enormous, and just grew more and more impressive as we sailed toward it. Stone buildings painted in vibrant colors stretched out in all directions, along with pillared structures and statues of various pharaohs and gods in all their half-animal forms. Some were life-sized. Some were carved in giant proportions. There were gardens and small palm forests and long rectangular pools of shimmering water. Actually, *everything* shimmered. Everything looked brand-new, like the paint had just been splashed on and the swaying banners had just been dipped in their bright dyes. The skies above the city buzzed with life. Sunskiffs and messenger beetles, dragonfly patrols, and cargo sledges.

Nearing the palace, I noticed other large ships like ours landing and rising.

Yazen saw them too. "Those barges are dropping off the other candidates."

"How many are there?" I asked.

"I don't know. It's better not to think about them too much."

"I can't wait to meet them," I said. I wondered if their lives had been like mine. Had they been as foolish as me, not believing their mentors? That seemed like ancient history already. Had they trained the same way or differently? Did they have skills I didn't? "I have a thousand things I want to ask them about."

"Ash, you may not get to ask them those questions. Though you are all here for the same reason, tomorrow you'll each meet a different fate."

I swallowed. I knew what he wasn't saying. Not all the candidates arriving would live through tomorrow. For that matter, I might not live through tomorrow.

"Tonight, you and I will dine simply," Yazen continued. "It will be a quiet evening, without distraction. You must rest and prepare yourself."

"What about exploring the city? Or the palace?"

"Ash, you aren't here as a tourist. You are here to win yourself a great honor, a responsibility that I *hope* will be yours over a long life. Tomorrow, the testing begins."

The barge began to descend. Something about that scared me. In a few moments, I'd set foot in the city. I'd be on solid ground, and what faced me tomorrow would be more real than ever. Only . . . I didn't even know what faced me. "Yazen, what's going to happen tomorrow? How do you know I'm ready?"

"I know because I've trained you all these years. You have the tools. I've been here before, Ash. I know a strong candidate when I see one."

He seemed to have more to say about that, but he cleared it from his throat.

"All the candidates are tested in the same ways," he said instead. "The morning will be filled with exams, with answering questions and reciting invocations, solving math problems and writing hieroglyphs. You'll be asked to recount the pharaoh's familial lineage, name all the gods, as well as do physical things like running races through obstacle courses, climbing ropes, scaling walls. Through every minute of it, eyes will study each move you make, looking for mistakes.

"Eventually, the results are compiled and all the candidates get ranked. Some will be dismissed right then, but those who scored high enough will be called before the pharaoh's entourage to face demons summoned from the Duat." He paused. "That's where it becomes dangerous. The demons are deadly. Most of the candidates will be disqualified in one way or another. Not all survive. The highest scorers go first. The few who triumph impressively enough win the honor of—"

"Becoming the prince's shadow," I finished.

Yazen shook his head. "I wish it were that easy. The ones who prevail tomorrow proceed to the next stage of the testing. That is carried out over four more days. Each of those days is different, with the testing administered by a different god. I don't know where in Egypt they'll take the candidates, or what the tests will be. So, you see, there is no real way to prepare—except through the training we've already done."

"How many usually make it through all this?" I asked.

Yazen didn't respond immediately. He placed his weathered hand on mine where it rested on the railing. Gravely, he said, "One, Ash. There can be only one."

A Dastardly Arrangement

Lord Set stood on a hovering plank, being pulled through the air by a flying beetle. The insect whirred above the cultivated fields and villages, past the city walls, and over the urban expanse of the great capital of Memphis. Set loved the view. He loved the loud thrum of the beetle's wings. He'd had them clipped to make them louder, with just a bit of sputter.

He approached the palace from the northern terraces, coming to rest beside one of the old gatehouses. He leaped from his board, patted his exhausted beetle on the back, and strode up the stairway.

Prince Rami waited for him on the terrace. At fifteen, he was tall and gangly. He glanced around nervously, making sure they were alone. "My brother's shadow testing is tomorrow," he said. "Is everything arranged?"

Set peeled off his crocodile-skin driving gloves and absently checked his long fingernails. "Everything is arranged," he answered. "I said you could count on me, didn't I?"

"Remember, I want them all gone," the prince said, "every one of those little brats that wants to be Khufu's shadow. You'll put them in the ring with awful monsters, right? With claws and fangs and scales? You'll make sure they all have a horrible fate?"

The bony protrusions on the god's head wiggled. Fire flared in his tiny eyes. "Just as you requested. Only . . ." Set's expression changed to a troubled look. The fire dimmed and his snout drooped a little. "Are you sure you want to go through with this? Khufu is your brother, after all. Harming his shadow candidates will only harm him."

"I don't care!" Rami snapped. "I'm the eldest prince and it's my right to be pharaoh. Why shouldn't Khufu's candidates perish? Mine did. Now everyone's looking to Khufu like he's to be the future of Egypt instead of me. Even my father thinks so! But what does he know? The whole kingdom is in decline. Egypt is getting peaceful and soft. The lowly villagers have too much freedom, and our enemies don't even fear us anymore. My father thinks they can be our friends! What rubbish. We're losing sight of all the things that made us great."

Set grinned. This was exactly what he wanted to hear. "Like war and chaos? Subjugation of the masses? The hoarding of wealth in the hands of the few, with demons roaming the world and . . . well . . . making things interesting for people."

Prince Rami didn't look entirely sure about that last bit, but he said, "Yes. That's it. Anyway, this shadow tradition is out of date and . . ." He seemed at a loss for a moment, but then concluded, "Stupid. That's what it is. Old and stupid."

"Trust me, your brother's shadow candidates will perish on the first day of the testing. So will his prospects of gaining the throne. If neither of you has a shadow, there will be no reason to elevate Khufu above you. You will again be first in line. Just be patient. Play your part. Look like a loyal brother and son. I'll see to everything else." Set's ears rotated, listening for a moment to someone passing on a lower terrace.

When the person's steps faded, Rami asked, "What do you want in return for this?"

Set raised an eyebrow above one of his small, red eyes. "Nothing more than to see you rule Egypt, and for me to rule beside you as your adviser, instead of stuffy old Horus." He grinned so sincerely that Rami marched away satisfied.

"Twerp," Set said once the prince was gone. "He'll be so easy to control. He won't really rule Egypt at all. I will."

THE TESTING DAY ONE

A Peculiar Way to Celebrate a Birthday

The next afternoon, standing in the waiting area inside the palace with Yazen, I couldn't hold still. I paced, thinking of all the tests I'd been through and what was yet to come. I tried to focus on the pattern in the tiles, or the paintings that stretched all the way up to and across the ceiling, or the little canal of water that ran right through the room, coming in from one wall and leaving through the other. It was all impressive, but I had other things to think about.

I watched a boy being led to the testing chamber. He stopped before rounding the corner. Turning, he looked back at me. Despite his brown skin, the boy's face was pale. He swallowed. The simple gesture looked painful. He turned into the corridor and strode out of view.

"He's the last one," I said, "except for me. How many do you think . . . survived?"

"I don't know," Yazen said. His face was lined and tense. I had a sneaking suspicion that he did know, but I didn't push it. "It has been a difficult day. You've done well, though. I'm proud of you, Ash."

It was nice of him to say that, but I couldn't tell if I was doing well or not at most things, and I knew I'd totally made a mess of my hieroglyphics test. I'm the first to admit it: writing isn't my strong point. I could never get my hand to form the symbols and pictures correctly. My mind tried to write one thing, but my fingers wrote something else. The result? I ended up looking like a fool.

At one point a scholar giving the tests plucked up one of my hieroglyphic exercises and studied it. He concluded sourly, "Lord Thoth should look at these."

I groaned inside. The last thing I wanted was for Thoth—the god of magic and knowledge—to look over my scribbled glyphs! As it turned out, my test scores put me dead last of the candidates invited to the next stage. According to my mentor, now was when things began to get serious.

"And my glyphs?" I asked.

Yazen tapped me on the head. "Not 'glyphs.' Say 'hieroglyphs' if anybody mentions them, which I hope they don't. Hieroglyphs never were your strong point. They brought your test scores down considerably. I'm sorry I couldn't instruct you better on them, but there's no use—"

"GROORAAR!"

A bellowing roar echoed from the testing chamber and down the corridor, bouncing off the stone walls. It was a horrible sound, low and guttural. My heartbeat quickened and a film of sweat appeared on my forehead. It was the sound of a cavern demon, one of the very creatures I'd trained to fight, back in the compound. The sound was more terrifying than Yazen had described. Back home they'd been pretend, contraptions rigged up by Yazen out of boards, wood, and imagination. But these cavern demons were the real thing and could come in all shapes and sizes, and . . .

"GROORAAR!"

I'd heard other demons as I waited. Each sounded

horrible in its own particular way. Judging by the sound of this one, it was huge. Whatever it was, the other boy was facing it right now. Maybe quitting and going back to the village wasn't such a bad idea. Merk would tease me mercilessly, but at least I'd be alive.

Yazen wiped the sweat from my forehead. "You remember the demons' powers?"

"I think so."

"And their tricks? They will always favor their tricks. Remember to use them against them."

Sounded good, but only if I managed to guess the demon's identity right. There were as many to choose from as there were stars in the sky. It wasn't like I'd never gotten them mixed up in practice. And I'd never fought a *real* demon in practice—just Yazen pretending to be one. You couldn't summon up a cavern demon for any old occasion.

The sound of weapons clashing cut the air, followed by an impact that shook the foundations of the place. Dust drifted down from the ceiling.

"You remember the demons' weaknesses?"

Some of what Yazen called "weaknesses" I would have called "horrific traits that you might not want to know about." What good was it to know that the Wailing Goddesses' daggers dripped so much blood that they sometimes slipped on the stuff? They were still Wailing Goddesses! With bloody daggers!

A high-pitched scream ripped through the air. The only thing worse than the sound was that it stopped, cut off crisply. A moment later, low, demonic laughter grumbled through the passageways.

"I believe," Yazen said gravely, "the young man came to an unfortunate end. Check your weapons."

I did, trying hard not to think about what had just happened to that other boy. My weapons were all in good condition, sharpened and oiled. One iron spear, good for thrusting during hand-to-hand combat, and three throwing knives. That's what I had.

I asked, "You don't think Ammut will be there, do you?"

"Not likely," Yazen said.

A palace official stepped into the stone entrance-way of the royal audience chamber. He motioned for us to come.

"It's time," Yazen said.

I fought down the sudden urge to throw my arms around Yazen's neck and cling to him, like I had done when I was younger. But I couldn't let anyone think I was weak. The prince's shadow had to be brave—or he had to be good at faking it, at least.

I respectfully turned to the old man, looking him in the eye. "Yazen, thank you for being my mentor," I said.

"I was proud to do it, Ash," Yazen said. He pursed his lips. Almost a smile, but not quite. "You are like a son to me. A much-loved son. Now, we must go."

12

Demon, You May Feed Now

I stepped into the royal audience chamber. For the briefest moment, I saw them: the pharaoh, the falcon-headed god, the goddess with a sun disk headdress, the prince, and the other court officials. I should have been trembling in awe from my head right down to my toes. And I would've been. Really, I would've. I had never been presented to royalty, to the rich and powerful, to gods, even! For a poor villager like me, this should have been an incredible moment. Except for one thing . . .

. . . the cave demon.

He stood in the center of the sparring ring. One glimpse was all I needed to know who he was: one of the nine Jackal-Headed Demons That Feed on Rottenness. No munching on antelope for this guy.

Zebra? Apparently not. He goes for rottenness. I was glad it wasn't Ammut, but still. Cave demons were the stuff of nightmares. Monsters, creatures who had been warped and twisted by the dark magic of evil sorcerers long ago. They were ancient, perhaps even immortal. According to Yazen, they weren't the brightest of creatures either, but being smart wasn't what they were about. Being deadly, that's what they were into.

The demon had a man's body up to the neck. He was strong and muscular, a bit hairier than most. His feet were massive. His toes sprouted curving yellow nails that scratched at the paving stones. No regular jackal had ever had a head as big as his. It was so heavy that he stood straining under the weight of it. His teeth were longer than a man's fingers. His long tongue lolled out the side of his mouth. His red eyes pinned themselves to me. He had only one purpose on this occasion—to make me dead, rotten, and edible. Judging by the look of him, he was ready to get the job done.

"So this is the final candidate?"

I realized the smooth, rich voice belonged to Pharaoh Neferu. I dropped to my knees and bowed, hoping the demon wouldn't take advantage of the moment to bite me in two.

"He doesn't look like much," the pharaoh continued. "I fear he's too thin to survive fighting this demon. Set, I'm not pleased. Your choices have limited my son's chances of securing a shadow. Far too many candidates have perished."

Set? Would that be *Lord* Set? I glanced up.

A figure stood with his arms crossed, leaning against one of the entrance pillars. His body was that of a slim, gray-skinned man, but his head was that of a . . . well, it was a . . . can't say what it was. His head was long and pointy, like an anteater's. He wasn't an anteater, though. He also looked a bit like a striped okapi, and he had two knobs on his head similar to a giraffe's. He was a bit of all these animals, but he wasn't completely any of them. Weird looking as he was, he radiated power. It was like waves of heat rippled in the air around him. He was a god, all right.

Truth was, I'd never quite been able to make sense of the gods. There are hundreds of them. They're immortal. They each have distinct powers all their own. Many of them can change into other shapes at will. They know things no human could ever understand, but they can be just as silly as two kids fighting over who gets to eat the last honey-dipped cricket. They are to be worshipped, and yet they also have to serve humankind. Yazen assured me it all made sense. I've never quite bought it, though.

"The demons have been fiercer than I'd suspected," Set said, answering the pharaoh. His voice made me feel like I'd just stepped barefoot into something soft, warm, and sticky. "If you had voyaged with me to the bowels of the deep caverns—"

"You wished for the assignment."

"I did, yes. My point is only that in those dark, foul places all the demons seem horrific. It's difficult to compare one with another." He glanced at me. His gaze was a hot touch that brushed across my skin. "In any event, we wouldn't want an unworthy shadow for the prince, would we? It might be demons such as these that the shadow needs to defend the prince against someday."

The pharaoh sighed. "All right, let us see what he can do. Young man, this has been a trying day. It is my hope that you will not perish in the next few moments. If you do, I will be truly saddened. But we have traditions to uphold." He raised his voice and pronounced, "Demon, you may feed now."

13

An Unconventional
Fighting Technique

The jackal's eager eyes fixed on me. His tongue slurped. The creature took a lumbering step forward.

I snapped up from my kneeling position, spear in hand. I circled away—I couldn't leave the ring carved into the stone that surrounded us both. It would mean shame if I did. Failure.

The beast didn't rush at me, but he didn't need to. The circle wasn't that big a space.

By the gods, that's a big head!

That reminded me of something that Yazen had said. The Jackal-Headed Demons that Feed on Rottenness didn't just have big heads. They had heads that were *too* big. Their bodies could just barely support them. That was why this guy was moving so slowly. It wasn't just a menacing routine. He was trying not to get exhausted. Realizing this, I changed my strategy.

I ran. I darted around inside the circle. I shifted direction, faking side to side. I was fast and agile; the demon wasn't. For a time this seemed like a good plan. The demon's head craned one way and the next. He stumbled. He slapped his tongue around, getting angrier and looking clumsier for it. That was good, but it didn't make his jaws any less frightening. I needed to attack somehow. *Come on, Ash. You have a spear, do something with it!*

I darted toward the demon, spear held tight in both hands. I took aim and thrust the point of my spear at his throat with all the force I could muster.

The demon shifted to one side. With a burst of speed, he grabbed the shaft of my spear, yanking it toward him—and me with it. Before I could do anything, the creature had me. The spear fell from my hand and clanked down on the stone floor. The onlookers gasped. The demon gripped me under my armpits, making my arms stick out to either side. An embarrassing posture, I assure you. I was so close to his jaws that his foul breath brought tears to my eyes.

Suspended over him in mid air, I remembered

something I wish I had remembered a few seconds earlier. The demon's *weakness* was the size and weight of his head, but his *trick* was luring people into thinking that the size and weight of his head made him unable to launch one sudden, swift attack. Yazen must have been cursing me for a fool. I thought about my daggers, but the demon's grip made it impossible to reach down for them. I had to think quick.

The demon's jaws opened. Saliva dripped from his fangs. There was that tongue again. It slopped around, waving at me from inside with a life of its own. As the demon was about to chomp, I reached into his gaping mouth, grabbed his tongue and yanked. Squirming back as far as I could, I just managed to avoid the teeth that shut right in front of me. The demon's teeth clamped down on his tongue!

He dropped me and howled with pain. He stumbled. His head tipped back and threw him off balance. He careened out of the circle, backing into one of the basins of burning oil that lit the chamber. Instantly, he went up in flames and vanished in a puff of blue smoke. Just like that, he was gone. He wasn't dead, of course, just sent back to the caverns he had been summoned from. But he wasn't here to eat *me*.

I scrabbled back to my feet. I was so surprised to be alive that I forgot not to look directly at the royal court. They didn't seem to notice my breach of rules. After a long moment of silence, Neferu nodded his regally adorned head. His face was strong-featured and proud, with dark, smooth skin. He stroked his chin with the base of his ankh.

Horus did the same, except he had to settle for rubbing the curved point of his beak. The air around him didn't ripple like it did around Set, but Horus managed to look even more powerful. He was dressed as richly as the pharaoh. Though he sat straight-backed and still, just looking at him made me dizzy. It was as if he was diving through the air in flight—and me with him—faster than anything in the world, smashing through clouds, wind whipping at my face. It felt like that, but really he was just watching me calmly.

Then there was the goddess. She sat on the other side of Horus. There was no mistaking who she was: Lady Isis. She was Horus's mother, but her form was completely human. Long, thick locks of hair framed her somber face. A glowing gold sun disk hovered above her head, nestled between two curving horns. It was amazing to think about all the things she'd seen, from the earliest days of creation through the ages since. She'd been a part of battles between gods, triumphs and tragedies I couldn't even imagine. Her eyes had seen so many things. Now they were looking at me.

A boy sat next to her. He wore a smaller version of the pharaoh's crown. It was Prince Khufu, the one all this testing was for. Realizing this made me remember my manners. I bowed my head.

"An unconventional tactic," Neferu said.

"I've never seen the likes of it before," Horus said. His voice was as sharp as the curve of his beak. I could hear his Egyptian words, but the sound seemed mixed with something like the screech of a falcon on the wing or the dry crackling of fire combusting.

Set moved closer to the royal dais. "A farce is what it was! An insult to the demon."

"Insult to the demon?" the prince asked. "The demon was about to devour him!"

"That's true enough, Khufu," Isis said, her voice calm and smooth. "The boy used what he had at hand to stay alive. That's commendable."

Set recrossed his arms and harrumphed, but he didn't seem to want to argue with Isis.

"But . . ." Neferu cleared his throat. "I must admit that tongue grabbing is not an officially sanctioned method for demon fighting. I judge this contest inconclusive."

Khufu began to say something, but Horus cut him off. "Decidedly so," the god said.

"Agreed," Set said. "Let us try again."

"Wait," I said. "What? I have to do that again?"

14

Lucky with Knives

Lord Set either didn't hear me, or he ignored me. He snapped his fingers. Three puffs of smoke appeared in the circle. The vapor cleared, revealing the newly summoned creatures.

Baboons—sort of. Short, bristling with fur, they were like monkeys except with jagged canine teeth lining their long jaws. They looked so much like baboons, though, that for a hopeful moment, I thought I could just find some food to throw at them, and this might not go so bad.

"Ah, I see," Horus said. "The Three Demons of Whirling Vengeance. Unfortunate. Young man, to fight one of these is to fight them all."

One of the baboons smacked the stone tiles with the flats of his hands.

All right, little guy, calm down.

The little guy didn't calm down. Instead, he leaped up into a backward somersault, flipping over and slamming his feet to the floor. His body shook with the impact and . . . changed. His leg muscles bulged. His torso stretched. His arms lengthened and his snout sprouted a few new inches. Just like that, he was almost as tall as me, with a lot more carnivorous jaw and muscle and claws in his favor.

The second one pulled the same move. The third launched himself in a high arc and came down with force enough to shake the foundations of the palace. When the last one's body was done contorting, he was the tallest of the group.

All three chattered in a strange language. It looked like they were comparing their somersaults, gauging which of them had pulled a better move and won the right to attack me first.

"Young man," Pharaoh Neferu said, "you might want to—"

As the first one jumped again, slamming himself to the ground, he grew.

"—act more quickly."

I snatched daggers from their sheaths and threw one in a whip-fast motion. I aimed for the largest baboon who was conveniently standing still. It sunk up to the hilt in his chest. The demon yanked it out and tossed it back toward me without even halting his chattering. I picked it up, thinking, *I should've brought bigger knives.*

The baboons flipped and flipped, growing larger every time. Now that I had seen them change, I remembered that Yazen had mentioned these "whirling demons" before. They egged each other on until they were big enough to devour whatever they were up against. But what was their weakness? I heard Yazen's voice in my head: *Strike while they are in mid-air. That's the only time they're vulnerable to attack.*

That's right! As the big one jumped again, I threw a dagger at the flipping whirl of baboon fur. I watched as the weapon spun end over end until . . . *poof!* The baboon bloomed into a puff of smoke.

Another somersaulted, clearly aiming to land right on me. I sent my second dagger. *Poof!*

The third creature was close to pounding me into the paving stones when I threw the last dagger, the force of the vanishing body knocking me down. I lay crumpled on the stones as the green cloud of vapor rained down on me.

I'd done it! The old guy had been right again.

I glanced at him. Yazen cut his eyes away, but he had been watching.

"Impressive," Neferu said.

"He has a good throwing arm," Horus acknowledged.

"Surely he has proven himself," Isis said.

Set's long nose sniffed. "He's been lucky so far, but I'm not sure he's truly passed the test. Not all of the prince's enemies will be kind enough to jump into knives."

Jump into knives? I was fast concluding the rumors about Set were true. He was as pleasant as a hyena's mangy backside.

Set continued, "I can't tell if it was skill or luck that saved him. Considering that the throne of Egypt depends on this, I dare say we should be sure."

Horus said, "Set does have a point. The boy's victory was surprisingly easy. He should face another."

Neferu grudgingly agreed. Set snapped his fingers again. Another demon appeared in a foul-smelling funnel cloud.

"That reek!" the pharaoh said. "This can only be the Devouress of the Dead."

The title echoed in my head as the cloud cleared to reveal the figure within it. It couldn't be. I shut my eyes, hoping for anyone but . . .

Ammut, a cavern demon so feared she was almost seen as a god. There were lots of reasons to fear the cavern demons, but Ammut was a no-win situation. Consider her parts: massive head of a Nile crocodile, torso and claws of a lion, rump of a hippo. Which way would *you* want to go? Swallowed whole, ripped to pieces, or sat on?

There were no good options with Ammut, since her sole purpose was to eat the heart out of every living thing that crossed her path. So you'll understand why my legs turned to jelly. When you factor in that I had no idea where my spear or knives were, the situation looked rather dire.

Ammut lumbered toward me.

"Wait!"

15

A Short Calligraphy Lecture

The voice came from the entranceway. A figure scrabbled toward us at a run. When he came into view, I saw that he had a human body dressed in a scholar's gown, but atop it sat the slim, regal head of an ibis, a long-necked water bird.

It was Lord Thoth.

"Wait, I say! Is this boy Ash?" He walked right into the circle without the least regard for Ammut. The demon emitted a guttural protest. "Peace, Ammut. I need a moment."

Ammut's crocodile eyes rolled. She puffed her cheeks and plopped back on her hippo bottom. She tapped her claws on the floor impatiently.

When the pharaoh confirmed who I was, Thoth

brandished a sheaf of papyrus rolls. "Boy, is this your work? Are these the hieroglyphs you sketched this morning?"

I was trying to comprehend that I was meeting yet another god. It was so strange seeing the slim bird beak speaking to me that I almost didn't hear the question. And then it registered. My glyphs! Did he expect to have a conversation about my glyphs *now*? I knew they were atrocious, but come on!

"What is this symbol?" Thoth jabbed his finger at the papyrus.

It was my hastily drawn, scraggly version of the symbol for *basket*. It should have been simple. *Basket!* It's like drawing a bowl with a little handle thingy on one side. Mine looked more like a deflated water skin with a worm wriggling next to it.

"A . . . b-b-basket, Lord Thoth," I stuttered. "It's a basket."

"And this?" The god speared another glyph.

"That's an eagle?" It looked more like a duck, but I didn't recall having drawn a duck.

"This?"

"A viper." I was confident on that one. I could draw a squiggling line as well as anyone.

Horus cleared his beak and spoke in his haughty voice. "Lord Thoth, what is the meaning of all this?"

Thoth dismissed him with a shooing motion of his fingers. "Boy, what is this?"

He pointed at my depiction of the power of the sun god Ra as he burst up from the horizon and lit the world. Of course, being mine, it looked nothing like that.

Before I could answer, Thoth did. "It's Ra rising, isn't it? Do you know what's wrong with these, young man?"

"Really, Thoth," Set said, "you're not going to give the child a calligraphy lecture just now."

Thank you, Lord Set, I thought.

Thoth held up the offending papyri, waving them for the royal party to see. "They're sloppy. Nearly unintelligible. But they're unintelligible in a very peculiar way. That's what I must get to the bottom of." He snapped his ibis head around to look at Yazen. "You. Yazen, is it? Why are the boy's hieroglyphs as they are? Did you teach him this?"

Yazen dropped to his knees and pressed his forehead to the stones. "Lord Thoth, forgive me. I instructed him. The fault is mine. I could never get him to write with the proper care."

"No matter what you did, the boy's hands acted with their own intent?"

"Yes, lord," Yazen admitted.

Thoth considered this. "You instructed him to carve his images with care? Slowly?"

"I did, lord."

"And was he tutored in magic?"

Yazen suddenly looked even more uncomfortable than before. "No, lord."

"Why not? All the candidates have at least some basic knowledge of magic."

"Magic, for this boy, was forbidden."

"By whose order?"

"Mine," Pharaoh Neferu said. He looked sternly at Thoth.

Isis added, "The pharaoh has his reasons, Lord Thoth."

Thoth bowed to the goddess. "I understand. But Honorable Neferu, I ask your indulgence. I need to test the boy. It will only take a moment."

Ammut let out a sound somewhere between a groan and a whine.

Thoth walked to me, offering me a thin instrument. "Here, take this."

A stylus? I held it. I had the sinking feeling that this was all heading toward some elaborate joke. Thoth thought my glyphs were so bad that he was going to make me die for it. *Here boy, fight Ammut with a stylus. See if that works for you!*

"Inscribe the glyph for basket. Write it in the air in front of you for all to see. Pretend you are drawing a silly picture on an alley wall."

I blushed. I was good with drawing silly pictures. I did as the god instructed. I fought my hand's impulse to fly through the glyph. Trembling, I drew as slowly as I could.

"No, not like that," Thoth snapped. "Write it as you normally would."

I frowned. *All right, but you told me to.* In a few quick strokes, I had sketched the glyph. It hung there in the air in glowing yellow lines, shimmering with energy like something brought to life.

"What the . . . ?"

Were my eyes playing tricks on me? The glowing image faded almost as quickly as it had been drawn. I stared at the ornate stylus, realizing that it must be magical.

The storyteller back in the village had told lots of

tales of magicians casting spells. He claimed it was possible because of the same magic Lord Ra used to join with the sun. Magicians could use special instruments designed by Lord Thoth. Was I holding one of those instruments right now?

Thoth said, "Now, an eagle."

I drew. The glyph crackled with energy, glowing even brighter than before.

When it faded, Thoth had me draw the symbol for viper and for Ra as the rising sun.

"You know how to draw cartouches?"

Of course. Those were special glyphs drawn inside an oval. It was a way of organizing the symbols to give them a distinct meaning.

"And you finish them with what?"

"A closing stroke." That was the slash that ended the cartouche.

"That's right. It's the closing stroke that makes all the difference. Without the closing stroke the spell fades, as you can see." The god's ibis eyes stared deeply into mine. "Let us complete your testing. Ammut, eat this boy."

16

The Spell

The demon's boredom vanished. She was instantly on her feet. She snapped her jaws together, raked the air with her claws, and waggled her hippo bottom.

Thoth spoke calmly from just outside the circle. "Ash, do exactly what I say." I listened but kept my eyes on the demon. "You will need to draw four symbols very quickly. First, a basket."

Not a basket again!

"Do it!"

I drew a quick, scorching yellow line that pulsed with energy. *There, a basket!*

Lot of good it did me. Ammut lunged right through it. The glyph vaporized. I scrambled back, nearly dropping the stylus.

"Write faster."

Ammut swiped at me with one of her claws. I ducked beneath it, fell into a roll, and came up behind her. As she turned, I shouted at Thoth, "I don't understand! What do you want me to do?"

"Four symbols as fast as you can draw them. You need them all done before the first one fades. Close them in a cartouche, and then—" The god's head drew back on his long neck, his eyes wide in alarm.

Sensing the fetid breath on the back of my head, I darted to one side. Ammut's mouth slammed shut with so much force that one of her teeth snapped off and went whirling away. She howled with the pain of it.

"You finish with a closing stroke," Thoth said. "Make it a strong slash."

"What symbols?"

"Draw them as I speak. Basket."

I backed as far away from Ammut as I could. My stylus carved out the glowing glyph for basket.

The demon yanked out another loose tooth. She glared at me.

"Now an eagle."

The lines of the bird appeared as quick as thought beside the basket.

"Viper."

I slammed the squiggly line and dotted the head of the glyph.

"Ra as the rising sun."

I scratched out the last glyph as Ammut blew air through her huge nostrils and leaned to rush at me.

"Close it in a cartouche!"

I had been fast, but the starting point of the first glyph had begun to fade. I drew the oblong shape around the four glyphs.

"The closing stroke!" Thoth shouted. "The spell will not ignite without a closing stroke. Do it now!"

Spell? Did he say spell?

Ammut's giant hippo legs kicked into motion. She charged.

I slashed in the closing stroke, fearing it was the last thing I would ever do. Nobody in the room was more amazed than me at what happened next.

The glowing glyphs re-formed in the air, twisting into a glowing basket. Its shimmering weave of light and energy hung in the air for a split second and then rushed at Ammut. All of a sudden, the basket burst open. Winged vipers made of the same vibrant essence surged out. Ammut tried to break her run. Her feet skidded on the stones. The viper-eagles shot at her with a blinding explosion of light and heat. For a few moments I saw nothing but burning yellow light.

When it faded, Ammut had vanished. The royal party stared at me in openmouthed wonder. Set wore an almost comical expression of confusion.

Thoth strode into the circle. He placed an arm around my shoulders and faced the pharaoh. "Pharaoh, I make a humble request. I would have this boy as a student. He has a talent such as I have rarely seen before. I could tell from the moment I read his hieroglyphs that they had in them the makings of Divine Writing."

I gulped. Divine Writing? That meant that Thoth, the god of magic, thought that—

"You think the boy has the makings of a magician?" Neferu asked.

"I do. What others dismissed as sloppy I knew to be the work of a gifted hand. Many can write hieroglyphs, but few have the spark of magic in them. That is something innate with the magic user. This boy"—Thoth looked at me and winked one ibis eye—"has potential very different than the other candidates. He could be—"

"No, he can't have him!" Khufu shouted. All eyes turned toward him. "Father, the boy is to advance to the next level of testing. Unless any of you claim he failed today."

"Of course he failed!" Set cried.

"Set, he vanquished even Ammut," Neferu said. "There is no contesting his success."

Set managed to anyway. "Thoth helped him. He was given the spell!"

Thoth kept his voice calm. "I challenged the boy to perform a spell few would have managed even after several years of study."

Really? I thought. Didn't seem that hard.

"I only had him use symbols he himself already knew," Thoth said. "He had all the parts of the spell within him already. I just aided him in putting them together to make something stronger than he imagined. With proper instruction, this boy could learn much that would aid the kingdom."

"He is here to be tested to become my shadow," Khufu said, "not a student of yours."

Thoth nodded grimly. "Prince, I do not deny that. His triumph is yours as well, but he should be trained as a magician. We should see where his talent takes him. It would be a crime to ignore what he might become."

Neferu leaned over and spoke quietly with Horus and Isis.

I stood there unsure what to think. Me, a magician? I had never studied magic, and my glyphs had always been an embarrassment. How could Thoth—the god of all learning, including magic—think I had talent?

The three broke from their huddle. Isis cleared her throat and spoke. "Here is our decision. The boy must complete the testing. Too much depends on it, as you know, Lord Thoth. For now, the testing is all that matters."

The ibis-headed god nodded, gravely.

The pharaoh stood. Along with Horus, Isis, and their attendants, he left the chamber. Prince Khufu's eyes touched on me for a moment, but he turned away without saying anything. Set scowled and trudged off.

Yazen was soon at my side, patting me on the shoulder. "Well done, Ash. That's one day down. Just four more to go."

17

A Promise and a Threat

That evening, Yazen and I ate a dinner of spicy fish soup and fried flatbread. I'm sure the palace cooks were whipping up something a bit more elaborate for the royal family and their friends, but I couldn't complain. The bread was lighter than any I'd ever tasted, with a crisp crust that melted as I chewed. And there was goat's milk with some sort of spice stirred into it. Delicious.

A light beetle crawled in from the hallway. It was shaped like the normal scarab beetles that were all over Egypt, but this one was larger—about a foot long. Instead of having a glossy black shell, it glowed with pure white light. I'd seen one of them last night, but it still surprised me. We didn't have anything like these in the village. When it got dark at night it just got dark. We had a few oil lamps, but mostly we just settled in and went to sleep. Here in the capital, there were hundreds of beetles like this. They spent the day basking in the sun, absorbing Ra's energy. In the evening they lit the palace, slowly releasing the light they had stored. These glowing beetles meant people could do a lot more stuff right into the night. Our visiting beetle climbed up the wall and perched there, brightening the room.

All I wanted was to stuff my belly, and then to crash. Eat and sleep and, hopefully, have no dreams about how I was going to die tomorrow. That would've been about the best evening possible, I thought.

So I wasn't happy when a servant arrived, saying the remaining candidates had been summoned to the queen's anteroom.

"The what?" I asked.

The servant—seeming kind of snooty to me—repeated himself. That didn't help at all.

"It's the room where the queen meets visitors," Yazen explained. He wiped a smudge of soup from the corner of my mouth. He always did things like that. It was starting to feel like he'd still be doing it no matter how old I got. "Be honored, and be quick about it. This lad will escort you."

"You're not coming?" I asked.

"I wasn't summoned. You were. Go. Don't keep them waiting."

The servant walked fast. I had to jog to keep up with him. Down one corridor, into another, across an elevated bridge over an outside water garden full of flowers and shimmering fish, and then inside again through still more corridors and turns. I was lost. I hoped the guy was going to bring me back to Yazen, because there was no way I wouldn't get lost trying on my own.

The moment I entered the queen's anteroom, I was aware of how loud my breathing was in the silent chamber. Before me stretched a long room lit by rows of light scarabs clinging to the high ceiling. Narrow stone pillars supported the ceiling. They were garishly striped in shades of red and yellow and green, with hieroglyphs etched across them in gold. They channeled us in one direction, toward the far end of the room, where the royal family sat waiting. There was already a line of candidates standing before them.

The servant deposited me at the end of the line. I

couldn't help but look the other candidates over out of the corner of my eye. All shapes and sizes. A few looked like they'd be pretty good in a fight. One was huge, with wide shoulders and bulging biceps. No way he's just twelve, I thought. But you never knew. A guy at the other end of the line was half my height. How'd he make it through?

Half of the candidates were girls. I knew that was possible, but for some reason I'd imagined I'd just be competing against boys. I wasn't sure whether to be relieved or more scared. I couldn't help but stare at the girl beside me. She had dark brown skin with hair worn in long locs that were a coppery red. The locs were coated in ochre and oil. I'd heard that people from the south wore their hair this way, but I'd never seen it before. Pretty stunning.

She caught me staring. I smiled sheepishly and said, "Ah . . . hi?"

She smirked. I mean it was a serious, she-totally-despises-me sort of smirk. Rolling her eyes, she looked away.

I realized that the rest of the candidates looked as if they'd dressed for this occasion. A few wore white linen robes and gold and turquoise jewelry, but even the more modest dressers wore sharper clothes than my faded kilt and old sandals. I didn't know where they'd all come from, but it seemed pretty clear that I was the only middle-of-nowhere candidate in the group.

Another candidate arrived beside me. I turned to see who it was and froze. The hairs on my arms stood up and squiggled. This candidate wasn't even a person. She was a lioness! She strode in with such feline grace. The powerful muscles of her back rippled beneath her smooth golden fur. She turned fluidly and bowed to the royal party before sitting down on her haunches beside me. Without so much as glancing at me, she raised her chin and looked serene, calm, and totally deadly.

She, apparently, was the last of the candidates. All told, that made ten of us. Five boys. Five girls.

You'd think that with all the stuff I'd already been through that day I'd not have had any energy left to be nervous, or that the wild beast right next to me would be the main thing I would worry about. But if you'd ever stood before the royal family, all of them sitting in elaborate chairs, garbed in jewelry and crowns and brightly dyed clothing . . . well, you'd know how nerve-racking it can be. Though I tried not to look them in the eyes, I could still see their reflections in the polished marble at my feet. They stared at us. All of them except for Khufu. He was wide-eyed and looking nervous.

One by one, we were called up to speak privately with the royal family. I made sure to remember everyone's name, and I tried to hear what the others were saying. They were near enough, but as soon as they began talking, their voices faded to mumbles.

When my turn came, my feet felt like they were made of bronze. It took all my effort just to clomp forward without tripping. The pharaoh looked down on me. He wore an elaborate crown, the centerpiece of which was the flaring gold cobra head with sparkling red gems for eyes. It seemed to sway hypnotically, as if the gold was somehow alive.

"Hello again, young man," he said. "We won't keep you from your rest long. We are about to attend our dinner banquet. Before we do, though, my wife wished to lay eyes on all those who survived a day of fighting demons—and other tests." Nodding to the woman beside him, he added, "No easy feat, I assure you, my queen."

Queen Heta. Even upside down and reflected on

polished stone she was ridiculously beautiful. She wore a headdress of a falcon with its wings outstretched. Though her arms were slim and shapely, they appeared strong, too, sporting a heavy load of gold rings and bracelets. The wealth from any one of those pieces of jewelry would've completely transformed my village. Here, they wore them like trinkets. She had her arm around a young girl, maybe eight years old. Khufu's sister, Sia, I assumed.

I met the queen's light brown eyes, which I'll admit made me go a bit weak in the knees. When she smiled and winked one eye I nearly fainted. I tore my eyes away and focused on a particularly interesting little swirl in the marble.

Don't look them in the eyes, you ninny!

"And the first day he even defeated Ammut!" Pharaoh Neferu said. He sounded like he still couldn't believe it.

Another voice asked, sullenly, "Are you sure it was Ammut? Perhaps the demon just looked like her."

Wondering if it was Prince Khufu, I glanced at the speaker's reflection. It was a boy a few years older than Khufu and me. His features were jagged and uneven, with creases around his mouth as if he had already spent too many of his years frowning. By his garb and jewelry there was little doubt that he was the eldest prince. He'd been first in line to the throne. If any of his shadow candidates had survived testing, he would have been named crown prince, sure to become pharaoh. But since they didn't survive, the question of who was actually the crown prince was still in doubt.

"Rami, don't begrudge the boy his victory," Pharaoh Neferu said. "His fate affects yours, true, but we all must strive to achieve greatness in our lives."

My fate affects his? I hadn't thought of that before. But it was true. If any of us succeeded at becoming the younger prince's shadow, then the throne would pass to Khufu instead of Rami. I guess in Rami's view, I wasn't just helping Khufu—I was trying to take the throne away from him.

"Of course," Rami said. "I bear no grudge." He smiled. If you could call it that. His lips tilted upward at the sides, but somehow his smile didn't quite look like a real smile. It was more like a snarl. Nobody else seemed to notice.

Pharaoh Neferu said, "And he's a magician. Isn't that right, boy?"

I wasn't sure how to answer. I didn't want to say the

wrong thing. Suddenly, it felt like there could be so many ways to say the wrong thing. When in doubt, try honesty. "Your Majesty, forgive me, but I'm no magician."

"Are you not? Lord Thoth thinks you will be."

"He's very wise. But I don't know a thing about magic. Whatever happened with that stylus was . . . I don't know what it was."

"I like his modesty," Queen Heta said. Her voice honeyed her words, making them sound delicious and tantalizing. At least, that was the effect it had on me.

She then slipped a golden wrist guard onto my forearm. It fit perfectly, molded right to my skin. She motioned for me to draw even closer to her. As I leaned forward, the scent of her perfume wafted over me. It was incredible. It was more powerful and complex than just smell. It carried emotions, too. Adoration. Warmth. Devotion. And sounds. Like birds singing in the night. And entire images. Flowers bobbing in a breeze and bees flitting among them. All of that somehow danced in the air around the queen's perfect face.

She studied me for what seemed like a long time, and then she said, "You have a handsome face. Your skin is the same red-brown as Egypt's. It reminds me of the wet soil by the banks of the River Nile, just as it begins to recede from the annual flood. And you have kind eyes. Kind eyes are rare. What is your name?"

I told her, but it took me longer than it should have to get it out.

"Ash," the queen said. "When this morning began, there were many candidates who might've come to stand where you now stand. Most of them have not. Only you and these chosen few."

Blood rushed to my face. I'd have been embarrassed by such kind words in any event, but coming from the queen? I thought Rami might have something smart to say in response, but I was vaguely aware that he was talking to his father, saying something I couldn't hear.

"Now, I have something to ask of you," Queen Heta said. "I have one command to give you. I command you to live, Ash. Not just for yourself. You must live for my son. You must live for me, and for the pharaoh. Ash, you must live for all of Egypt. Fail at the tests, and you put all of Egypt in grave danger. So tell me. Will you do what I command? Will you live?"

Sure, I'll try, I thought, *but it would be easier if you called off the demons and all that.* When I actually answered, I said, "Yes, Your Majesty. I will live." The words just came out of my mouth. I hadn't known I'd thought them until I heard myself say them.

"Good." The queen's fingers found the pendant on her necklace. She tugged on it as she studied me. "If you do not keep this promise I will be very cross with you. And don't think you can escape me with death. I'll send word to Osiris to make your stay in the Duat . . . difficult." Though her words were sinister, she smiled as she said them. "We have an agreement, then. Our little secret."

Secret? How can it be a secret if we're . . .

The queen drew back, taking the scent and music and emotions with her. The rest of the room snapped back into focus. The conversation between the pharaoh and Prince Rami seemed to have carried on. It was as if the queen hadn't spoken to me at all. Except she had. I knew she had, and the deliberate way she stared at me let me know that she knew it too. Somehow the others hadn't heard the exchange. It was our secret. That perfume—or whatever spell had hidden our conversation—was some strong stuff.

THE
TESTING
DAY TWO

18

The Little Whelps

No god in the Egyptian pantheon worked harder than Lord Set. At least, that's what Set himself believed. He parked his floating platform on a palace terrace. Despite being tired and grumpy after another long night of work, he didn't want to miss the beginning of the candidates' testing. He hopped out of the platform and without so much as a nod to the hardworking beetle that had flown him from Ra's Night Barge, he walked away.

"Sure," he said to no one, "Lord Ra spends all day as the sun, raining light and heat and magic down on Egypt, but how hard is that?" He glanced up at the newly risen sun. He blew a raspberry at the god. With his wobbly snout, he was quite good at blowing raspberries.

"You're just showing off," Set said, knowing that the

god wouldn't actually be able to hear him. "You show off all day, and sleep all night while I guide you through the underworld. I slay the serpent Apep each and every night. I answer all the riddles posed at the gates, stand up to the demons, and fight with this and that goddess. The things I do for Egypt . . ." The god expressed the futility of it all with a wave of his hand. "Soon I'll regain the stature I deserve."

For a moment, Set basked in the warmth of that possible future. He had a selective memory. Truth is, his night work on the barge that sailed Lord Ra through the Duat was punishment for a host of heinous crimes. He was lucky he hadn't been banished completely. He could've been cast out of Egypt forever, stripped of his powers and immortality. His punishment could've been much, much worse, though Set forgot about that. He always forgot about things like that.

He'd barely gone a few paces before Set could smell the boy waiting for him. The god had quite a good snout on him. From the scent of the prince's sweat, he could tell that he'd had pickled crocodile eggs for breakfast, washed down with sweetened coconut milk. He could also smell that he hadn't washed his feet before venturing out of his quarters. Set didn't approve. All princes *should wash their feet daily. It was just the way things were done.*

Prince Rami stepped from behind a pillar and launched right in. "What do you call that business yesterday? A complete failure is what I call it!"

Set wrinkled his snout before he spoke. "Prince, I have a meeting to attend."

"Ten of the peasants! They lived and they're a step closer to being Khufu's shadow!"

"It's just a minor setback," Set said. "Think nothing of it."

"Think nothing of it? There are ten of them trying to win Khufu the throne instead of me! You can't let that happen. I'm older. I'm the rightful heir!"

Who does this kid think he is? *Set thought.* Lecturing a god. *If Rami wasn't a key part of his own plot for grasping power, Set might've squashed him. Instead, he controlled his temper and said, "None of them will survive the testing. I'll make sure of it. They'll die horribly in one way or another. If neither of you have a shadow, you will again be first in line for the throne. That's as true now as it was yesterday."*

"But you're not in charge anymore. Other gods will oversee each day's testing."

"I've got a trick or three up my sleeve." Set tapped the prince's chin with a long fingernail and said, "Worry not; the little whelps will die." He liked the ring of that. The little whelps will die. He repeated it to himself, making a tune of it as he strolled away.

19

And Today's God or Goddess Is . . .

The next day, I stood beside Yazen in the small tiled courtyard we'd been told to wait in. The sun was just getting high enough to tilt warm light into the enclosed space. An obelisk rose from the center—a long, thin wedge of pale white stone that tapered to a sharp point capped with a gold pyramid. I'd seen lots of obelisks, but this one was different. The hieroglyphs covering the stone looked like they were carved into it, but each time I studied them more closely, the glyphs would scroll across the surface. It was like they were alive, anxious to be read and dancing for my attention.

I recognized some of the symbols, but most I'd never seen before. Beneath the moving glyphs, silver highlights flickered within the stone, some at the surface and some deeper in. If I was alone, I might've gone over and touched it.

Carved scarab beetle symbols also crawled across the stone. They were each a reminder of the rising sun. Like the regular beetles that could be found all around Egypt working hard, they represented the rebirth of each new day. Each was a continuing gift of life.

Or, in my case, another day to be tested . . .

But I wasn't alone. The other nine candidates were there, too. They each stood beside their mentor, whispering, nervously checking out the competition while pretending not to. I did my best to look calm, though I probably wasn't fooling anybody.

Yazen eyed the sunlight, which had almost reached the point of the obelisk. He spoke softly: "When you see whatever god or goddess accompanies the pharaoh, greet them with calm respect. Show no surprise. Let them see that you are in control of your emotions. Unafraid of whatever they might throw at you."

"You mean *pretend* to be unafraid." I fiddled with the sheaths of my throwing knives.

"We don't know which god will oversee your testing," Yazen said, "not today or any of the subsequent days. It could be anyone. Do your best to recognize them quickly, though. Gods can be vain. They all want to be recognized."

"Everybody wants to be famous."

"Listen carefully to everything they say. If they instruct you, absorb the knowledge like a sponge." Somberly, he added, "Your life may depend on it."

I didn't have anything to say to that. Just a few days ago, I was a village kid living in the desert. My biggest worries were Merk and company, boredom, sunstroke, and stepping in goat dung. Now, I'd spent a day fighting demons, casting magic spells, talking to royalty, and staying in the capital of all of Egypt. And that was just the beginning. One day down. Four more to go.

Pharaoh Neferu entered the courtyard, his posture as straight and upright as a statue. His crown seemed to float just above his head. Prince Khufu walked beside him, looking a lot like a smaller version of his father: the regal posture, his chin held high, the same full nose. His eyes were different, though. Neferu's were so dark they almost looked black. Khufu's were a light brown. *Just like the queen's*, I thought. Behind them came Lord Horus, Lady Isis, and Lord Set. Something about what Set saw in us candidates made his snout wrinkle.

Well, good morning to you too, I thought, making the words as sarcastic as I could—even though nobody but me heard them. I was starting to not like Set much.

Another figure entered last. She walked in on all fours, long and lithe. At first I thought she was a feline goddess, but when she rose to stand on her hind legs, I saw that she wasn't a cat. She was a mongoose. She wore thick bracelets around her wrists, and her large ears sported several golden loops.

I blurted out, "Lady Mafdet!"

So much for looking calm and collected.

I heard Yazen sigh. Other candidates turned to stare at me. Horus clicked his beak in disapproval.

At least Mafdet looked pleased. She cleared her throat and held her chin a little higher. She wasn't one of the more famous gods, but I had always admired her. Back in the village she was called upon for protection from scorpions and snakes. Little statues of her adorned every hut. Children who were sent on errands that took them out into the bush wore tiny pendants of her mongoose form on strings about their necks. I was thrilled to actually meet her.

Yazen tugged on my arm, reminding me to bow to the monarch and the gods.

"Candidates, welcome to day two of your shadow testing," Neferu said. "We are gathered here in the Cherished Ka's Courtyard. He was the last king of a still divided Egypt, but his vision for a unification of all the lands of the Nile was carried forth by his children. They erected this obelisk to commemorate him." He gestured toward it. "We honor him not because he was able to achieve his vision, but because he instilled that vision within his children. They created what he had dreamed. You cannot read the magical inscriptions upon it now, but maybe, one day, when it deems you worthy, it will reveal its secrets to you."

He left that prospect hanging in the air a moment, and then cleared his throat and got down to business. "From today forward, when you candidates fight demons or face other dangers, you're completely on your own. Neither I nor any of the gods are allowed to intervene. The tests will no longer take place in the palace. You will meet with a new god each morning—assuming you've managed to stay alive—and they will transport you to their chosen testing area. As Ash enthusiastically proclaimed, Lady Mafdet is in charge today."

The goddess studied us with her light brown eyes. Her gaze didn't simmer and heat my skin like Set's did, but there was an electric intensity to it. "Are you all ready to begin?" she asked.

I half wished I could say I hadn't managed to get much breakfast down. Maybe I could come back after some honeyed raisin bread? No chance. A chorus of voices said, "Yes, Lady Mafdet."

"Then let's begin. Prince, as this is the testing of your possible shadow, you will accompany us. It is customary that you observe the candidates' performance. Give me your hand." She extended a paw toward Khufu. He stepped forward, looking a little nervous. "And you, candidates, link hands with us."

Once we were all connected, she said, "I assume you've all traveled through a light portal?" She made it sound like a statement and a question at the same time. Nobody answered, which made me feel slightly better for having no idea what a light portal was. "Really? None of you?" Lady Mafdet seemed amused by our astonished faces. "Well, this will be a day of many firsts. It's simple. I'll open a gateway of sorts.

We'll step into it and travel at the speed of light to our destination. Here, let's try it."

She stepped lightly forward, tugging us with her. She whispered something. The next instant, the world went completely, brilliantly white.

20

The Corridor of Cages

An instant later, the light vanished as suddenly as it had appeared. In the blink of an eye, the world had snapped back into view, only it was a different view than before. We weren't in the courtyard anymore! Before me stretched a dimly lit subterranean corridor lined with cages. I couldn't see into the cages, but I could make out bulky shapes moving within them. I heard something that sounded like the clicking of scales grinding over each other.

"Where are we?" I asked.

"Beneath the desert near Saqqara," Mafdet said. She smiled. "Just a quick trip for your first journey through light, and a good place for the creatures we'll be dealing with."

I didn't love the sound of that.

Before I could ask anything more, a man stepped out from the shadows, making me—and several others—start. He was a small guy, but he looked tough. He wore a metal plate over his chest and a helmet. "Good morning, Lady Mafdet. They're ready for you."

Mafdet greeted the man with a nod. "This is the keeper."

The keeper of what? I wanted to ask.

Mafdet was on to another topic already. "During the ancient days," she said, "a queen called Nedeti had twin sons. One day they were sleeping in their cribs, safe within the palace. Who can tell me what happened to them? Any of you may answer."

I had no idea. Another candidate did, though. It was the lioness. "Both of them were stung by a scorpion," she said. Her voice was soft and youthful, sounding pretty much like any girl our age.

"What is your name, young lioness?"

"Seret."

"You are exactly right, Seret," Mafdet said. She pulled on her whiskers, looking troubled by the tale. "Stung over and over again. They cried out. Guards rushed to them, but they, too, were stung. A good portion of the household died that day. Nedeti herself lived, but she lost her mind in grief and was never the same again. How was it possible that one scorpion could kill both the princes and many household guards?"

I scrambled for an answer. Frankly, it didn't seem possible. I hated scorpions, but they were fairly small things. If they surprised you they could give you a nasty sting, but a bunch of guards? Any one of them should've been able to just step on it. Or squash it with the butt of a spear. It didn't make sense that one little creature could do so much damage. Unless . . .

"I think," Seret said, sounding tentative, "that the scorpion was quite big."

That's what I was going to say!

Mafdet gave a curt nod. "Right again, Seret."

The lioness beamed, her eyes twinkling and the corners of her mouth lifting just slightly. She was going to be hard to have around, especially if she was right all the time.

Mafdet continued, "The scorpion was not a regular scorpion. It was one of these."

The cages—now that we were walking past them and seeing into them—contained massive, many-legged, scaly shapes. Scorpions the size of camels, with jagged pincers that snapped at us as we passed. One lunged with its tail. The wicked point of its stinger slammed through the bars, stopping just inches from Mafdet. She didn't even flinch. "Imagine the victim's terror in the moment that one of these beasts attacks. If you are to protect Prince Khufu from such a horrible fate, you must be lightning fast. You understand?"

I nodded. We all did.

"I hope so," Mafdet said. She turned and led us out of the corridor of cages and up a few steps onto an elevated platform, a ring of smooth sand. "Who among you considers him or herself fast?"

I had always considered myself quick. I was the fastest kid in my village by a long shot. Yazen had often commented on the speed of my footwork when we sparred. Considering that, I opened my mouth to say so. Someone else beat me to it.

He stood with his chin jutting out, like he was posing for a sculptor. His head was shaved to the scalp except for one ponytail of hair that sprouted from the back. In my village, Merk would make fun of anyone with a haircut like that, but somehow I suspected that this kid wasn't any old village peasant. He also had a pretty spiffy-looking sword in a scabbard at his waist. "Lady Mafdet," he declared, "in my province I am considered to be the fastest for my age." He let his eyes slide over the rest of us, looking smug.

"Your name?" Mafdet asked.

"Sutekh," he said, proudly. "You may recognize the name. My father's the governor of Abydos."

Great. Not only did he know who his father was, but he was a governor! As far as I was concerned, that practically made him royalty. We hadn't even started yet, and I was already feeling a bit out of my league.

"It's good to hear about your speed, Sutekh. You'll need it. Let me show you what you'll be doing." Raising her voice, she shouted, "Keeper, send one my way." She put her hands on her hips and rocked her torso around, stretching. "You might all want to back up a little. They tend to come out in pretty—"

The locks on one of the cages clicked. The door banged open, as if propelled by the hissed roar that accompanied it.

"—bad moods," Mafdet said, finishing her sentence and her stretching.

The scorpion demon came raging from the corridor, up the steps and onto the platform. It was even larger than I'd imagined. Its legs pierced the sand with each step. Its claws snapped open and closed. And worst of all: the curved barb of its stinger rose up behind it as if it had a mind of its own. Hissing, the demon attacked Mafdet.

The fight that ensued happened with such blurred speed that I could barely keep track. The scorpion darted forward, its claws snapping and snapping, swiping at Mafdet, trying to get a hold of her. The goddess darted and danced, all fluid motion. The scorpion couldn't touch her. That didn't stop it from trying, though.

"As you can see," Mafdet said, speaking calmly even as she moved with mongoose-goddess speed, "it's just a matter of efficiency of motion. Never a wasted gesture. Precision in every defense—"

I gasped as the scorpion's stinger cut through the air, directly at Mafdet.

The goddess snapped her wrist up. The stinger point slammed into her golden bracelet. The scorpion pressed down, the bulbous body of the stinger sloshing with venom. Mafdet strained beneath the pressure. "—and precision in every . . . attack," Mafdet concluded.

In an amazing burst of speed, the goddess spun around, grabbed the stinger with both hands, and yanked. The scorpion flipped into the air. She slammed it down on its back, knocking it unconscious. Wiping the dust off her paws, Mafdet climbed onto the demon's segmented belly. She leaped up and down, furiously, until . . . poof! The scorpion exploded into a cloud of green vapor. Just like with the demons at yesterday's testing, this one returned to the realm of the dead.

Mafdet said, "So, that's the way it's done. One of the ways, at least."

In a hushed, impressed voice, Khufu spoke for the first time that morning. "Hey, if you ever want a job at the palace . . ."

"Thank you, prince, but I have many responsibilities. Protecting you from such beasts will have to be another's duty. Okay, it's time to get on with the testing."

She slapped her paws together. "Right! Sutekh, ready for your turn?"

21

Tough Luck

Yeah, Sutekh was ready. The kid may have been a bit full of himself, but he had reason to be. When a scorpion surged onto the platform, Sutekh didn't hesitate. He drew his sword and ran toward it. The demon looked as stunned by this as I was. Sutekh ducked and slid under the creature's belly. He came out behind it, leaped up, grabbed onto its stinger, and clung to it until he could strike with his sword. The scorpion looked up just in time to see the sword pierce it between the eyes. Instantly, it turned to vapor.

"Well done, Sutekh!" Mafdet called.

He wasn't the only one with a stellar performance. One of the girls, Mery, was wicked fast with a pair of short, curved daggers. She sliced and diced with a confidence I certainly didn't feel. The muscle-bound boy, Tau, who I still thought was older than twelve, went at the scorpion like a veteran brawler. He got right in close, swinging his fists fearlessly. In the end he caught the demon under the chin with an uppercut and vaporized it.

"Wow. Did you see that?" the boy beside me asked. He was the small one. Unlike Tau, he could've passed for nine or ten instead of twelve. His face was round, his eyes large, and his mouth a bit small—until he smiled. Then everything seemed to fit together perfectly. His black hair was wavy instead of tightly curled. He twirled some around his finger and tugged on it as he said, "We've got some stiff competition. I'm Gilli, by the way."

"Ash," was all I said.

Kiya, the girl who had smirked at me in the queen's antechamber, stepped onto the platform twirling a wooden staff. She leaped toward the scorpion, tilted the staff to the ground, and used it to pole-vault, flipping end over end above the demon. Her red locs fanned out into the air. It was a beautiful move, like a dance or an acrobat's trick. At least, it was until she landed behind the scorpion and broke its legs one by one with her staff. She finished by cracking it a good one on the head. The beast was probably glad to turn to smoke. At least it got spared the headache. She walked from the platform, tossing her staff into the air and catching it as she did so. A few of the candidates cheered for her. I wondered if they were forgetting that we were all in competition *against* each other. Not that I wanted the others to fail or get hurt or anything, but . . . it was all kind of confusing.

"She's good, isn't she?" Gilli said.

"Yeah, she's good," I agreed.

"I know what you're thinking," Gilli said. "Yeah, she's cute."

"I wasn't thinking—"

Gilli cut me off. "But you have to ask yourself if you want a girlfriend that could crack you over the top of the head any time she wanted to."

"I don't want a—"

"She comes from a famous clan of warrior women from the far south. I overheard some guards talking about her. They were placing odds on who was most likely to live through the testing. You and I aren't high in the rankings, if you were wondering. Kiya's another story. Fighting is in her blood. Her great-great-great-great-grandmother was the Shadow to Merneith, the first pharaoh-queen of Egypt. Only thing is that she's a second daughter. Her older sister is going to be the head of her clan. So Kiya's out of luck as far as that goes. And you know what that means, don't you? It means she's highly motivated to prove herself. I'm kinda hoping to just stay alive. I don't think she's like that. I think she wants to win. Nothing else matters. So, like I was saying, you'll want to think twice before asking her to take a ride on your magic carpet or something."

"I don't want to do that! I don't even have a—"

"Whatever you say, Ash." Gilli rolled his eyes. "Truth is she's a bit out of your league, anyway."

That I couldn't argue with.

"I hope my training was good enough to prepare me for this," Gilli said. "I'm not so much on the hand-to-hand fighting. More of a spell guy myself." To demonstrate this, he scratched out a quick, invisible glyph with his finger. I couldn't tell what he'd drawn, but he did seem pretty fast. "All this fighting is kind of barbaric, if you ask me."

As if to prove his point, the next candidate—a kid all the way from the Nile Delta—got tripped up by a scorpion's claw. A second later he was dangling above the demon's mouth. And then he was gone. One minute he was there, thrashing around trying to get free. The next he was swallowed whole. Quick as that.

I couldn't believe it. It hit me like a punch in the gut: we can really die here.

I'd known it, but it was different seeing it happen right before my eyes. I could tell the others felt it too. A few of them gasped, and we all fell into a stunned silence as the scorpion lumbered away. I wondered if the athletic kid was already in the Duat, standing before Lord Osiris and having his soul weighed against a feather as his fate in the afterworld was determined. Death, and the mysteries it involved, had never before seemed so close.

"Now that's a bit of tough luck," Sutekh said. "I feel sorry for the kid." The words were right, but something about the way he said them made me think he meant the opposite.

"The dangers here are real, as you see," Mafdet said, sounding grave. "Such is the code of the shadow testing. It has always been this way. Be brave and let us continue."

Seret fought with her claws. She looked almost as

fast as Mafdet. She dodged and twisted, punched and scratched. In the end she took out her scorpion by diving under its belly, twisting onto her back, and kicking him with all the power of her hind legs. That did the trick.

Unfortunately, one of the other girls made the mistake of trying to circle her demon opponent. She didn't expect it to be able to swing its tail like a club. It swatted her against the wall and devoured her a moment later. I was glad the scorpion's bulky body blocked the view, but still it was horrible to know what was happening. I felt queasy.

From then on I watched in a terrified trance. I forgot to care that we were competing against each other. I just didn't want to see anyone else die. I was glad when the rest—including Gilli—made it through safely. I didn't know the kid, but he seemed nice enough. Relief washed through me as he stepped off the platform, smiling after having jabbed his demon with a spear.

My relief didn't last long, though. I was up next.

22

The Problem with Cages

Lord Set had arrived silently to the scorpion testing. He simply appeared through the traces of the solar portal left behind when Mafdet transported the candidates. Not just any god could do that, but Set had had lots of practice sneaking around behind his fellow deities. Hidden near the mouth of the cavern, he'd been able to watch a portion of the testing. He wasn't pleased by what he saw. It was nearly over, but only two of the candidates had died so far? Rubbish. Next time, he'd have to arrive earlier and do what he could to see that the body count was higher.

"As in all of them," he grumbled.

He crept toward the cages. He kept his ears pricked to catch any sounds. He heard the commotion of a candidate's fight with a demon, the disgruntled rustlings from the cages, and he also heard a tune. The latter came from the keeper, who leaned against the corridor wall a little distance away, humming to himself as he awaited further instructions.

Set didn't like the look of him. Humming? *he thought.* While on duty? The lack of discipline is appalling!

Before the keeper noticed him, Set closed the distance between them in a few rapid strides. He snapped his fingers, and a brass tankard of beer appeared in his hand. Just as the keeper turned to see who was there, Set struck him on the head with the beer mug. The man crumpled to the ground, unconscious.

Set murmured, "Humans really are a feeble species." He settled the tankard into the crook of the slumbering man's arm. "That'll make you think twice about drinking on the job. Now, to cause a little mischief . . ."

He heard the poof of a demon vanishing from the ring and knew he had to work fast. Stealthily, he tiptoed over to one of the cages. The scorpion in it hissed at him and thrust a claw through the bars.

"Oh, hush!" Set shot back. "I eat insects like you for breakfast. Deep-fried, with a honey glaze. If you want to take out your frustrations on someone, aim for the young whelp on the fighting platform. Here, I'll help."

Set snapped his fingers again. The lock on the demon's cage clicked and the door swung open. Out came the lumbering demon. It glared at Set, but the god didn't show the slightest concern. He pointed down the corridor toward the platform. "That way," he said. "Kill the remaining boy and I'll reward you later. Go on. Be quick about it."

The scorpion grumbled. It snapped its claws, but then turned as instructed. As it skittered forward on its many legs, Set said, "The problem with cages is that they don't really work if they're unlocked."

The god snapped his fingers again, louder this time. With one unanimous click, all of the cages opened. Insectile shapes crept out of them, eyes flaring in the dim light.

Set wished he could stick around to watch the show, but it wouldn't do for Mafdet to spot him. So he slipped back onto the trail of solar light and vanished.

23

A Stinger or Two

"**A**s I told the others, Ash," Lady Mafdet said, "once your testing begins I cannot intervene on your behalf." She paused. "Ash, what are you doing?"

What I was doing was unlacing my sandals. I tugged them off and tossed them away. Rising, I said, "I like to fight barefoot."

"Barefoot?" Seret asked, twitching her whiskers. "What if somebody steps on your toes?"

"His little toes, you mean," Gilli said. When I glared at him, he added, "What? You've got small feet!"

"Anyway," I said, "it's just . . . I trained this way back in my village."

"What strange customs villagers have!" Sutekh said. He looked around as if asking the others to agree with him. To me, he asked, "Can't your parents afford training sandals? If not I could loan you a pair."

Sutekh had a way of saying nice things while twisting them into insults. I'll admit it; it hurt. I had to clear my throat before I could say, "No, it's fine. Like I said, it's what I'm used to."

"Well, I hope . . ." Mafdet's voice trailed off. A look of concern wrinkled her brow. Her mongoose ears snapped around, pointing toward the corridor of cages. "Oh, no! How could that have—"

A demon lumbered up the steps and into view. Its stinger swayed from side to side, sloshing with venom. Its whole body trembled with excitement. Its eyes, for some reason, focused only on me. That was bad enough. What was worse was that another scorpion appeared behind it, and still another after that.

Lady Mafdet hissed a curse that would've made me blush if I hadn't been terrified. She grabbed Khufu and pulled him away from the platform. She ordered the others to stay back. I almost followed them, but Mafdet shouted, "The rules must be followed. It's your turn, and you have only one choice. Fight, Ash! Fight for your life!"

The first scorpion thrust out a claw as it surged

forward. I jumped. The claw snapped shut just beneath me. I landed on it and vaulted off. I somersaulted in the air and landed on the back of another scorpion. I used the natural bounce to leap into the air again. Kicking out to either side, I avoided the scorpion's stinger, which sliced through the air between my legs. Way too close for comfort! I crashed down amid the chaos of stingers and claws and jointed legs. I scrabbled on all fours beneath the bellies of the demons. How was I ever going to survive this? I only had four knives.

As I emerged from underneath them, the scorpions jostled each other as they searched for me. One of them sideswiped his neighbor with a claw. Another ran over the scorpion in front of him. Two exchanged a quick barrage of claw snaps, hissing as they did so. Three more scorpions lumbered in to join the confusion, and I could make out the moving bulk of more following behind them.

I glanced at the people at the side of the fighting ring. Prince Khufu's face was pale. By the look of it, he didn't think I stood much of a chance. The smug amusement on Sutekh's face indicated he had come to the same conclusion. Only *he* was happy about it!

Strangely, realizing that helped me to snap into focus. I'd trained for this, hadn't I? All those years with Yazen had to count for something, even if we were only rural villagers.

I yanked two knives from my belt. I took aim at the nearest scorpion and flicked my wrist as I released the blade. It twirled end over end until it pierced the scorpion's side. The creature's body shuddered at the impact. The next instant, it disappeared in a plume of putrid yellow smoke. I grimaced as the stuff blew over me.

My next knife landed right between the eyes of the largest scorpion. I pulled my third knife and pinned the demon's claw to the side of its face. This didn't kill it, but spun it in chaotic circles, trying desperately to yank the claw free. It so jostled the other scorpions that I ran in among them. I snatched up my last knife from my belt and stabbed another scorpion, vaporizing it.

I had just started to think I had things under control when a claw swiped my legs out from under me. I landed on my back, hard. Breathless, I rolled to one side as a stinger slammed down into the sand beside me. The scent of venom tinged the air. Scurrying forward on all fours, I felt a scaly underbelly slide across my back. Definitely gross. I dove between two legs, only to have one of them rise and press down on my shin. The sharp point of it pierced my flesh. For a moment I thought that was the end, but I still had a knife in my hand. I slammed it into the creature's belly, and was rewarded with the rotten-egg gas dropping down on me.

After that, things got chaotic.

There must have been a dozen demons left, and they all converged on me. Snarling mouths and snapping jaws and thrusting stingers and stomping legs. I dodged and darted, moving as fast as I ever had. I kicked and twisted and jumped. I popped out punches. I swatted claws away. I sliced and diced with the knife.

"Ash," Gilli called. "You're doing it!" A few others cheered for me. I doubt Sutekh was one of them.

One by one, I sent the demons back to the underworld. Sweat stung my eyes. My muscles burned. The knife got harder to hold in my sweaty hands. That's why I lost my grip on it as I jabbed it into yet another scorpion's scaly side. The knife fell from my hand as the demon trickled away, another yellow cloud.

"Ash," Seret cried, "behind you!"

The hairs on the back of my neck stood up and squiggled. I spun around and came face-to-face with one last scorpion, the ugliest one I'd ever seen. Or smelled. The thing exhaled a foul breath and said something in what must've been Scorpion. Its stinger reared up into view, a vicious point that looked needle-sharp. Distracted by the sight of it, I forgot about the demon's claws. They converged on me from both sides, snapping closed in a painful double grip across my torso, trapping my arms to my body.

Once it had me, the scorpion seemed to get giddy. It lifted me into the air, spinning around as if showing me off. Its mouthparts clacked and clicked grotesquely. I could see right into its moist, pulsing throat. It was too disgusting. I tore my eyes away.

That's when I saw it—one of the throwing knives I'd tossed earlier lay on the sand just below me. As the scorpion lifted me about, the knife bobbed around in my view. A couple of times when I got near it I tried to reach out, but it was no use. The scorpion was holding me too high up. I tried to grab the weapon with my toes, stretching a leg out, but I only managed to brush it. It spun away.

The demon spoke again. I couldn't understand a word. I knew the cadence, the relish with which it spoke. It was monologuing. Probably bragging about its prowess, explaining all the horrible things that were about to happen to me. Come to think of it, I was glad I couldn't understand.

And then the moment came. The scorpion laughed, a low clicking that vibrated through its scales. It lowered me, opening its mouth and preparing to shove me into its gob.

I turned toward where the others watched. Mafdet's mongoose face was grave, her whiskers twitching. Seret and Gilli and some of the others stared, mouths gaping. A few of the others chose to look away. Not Sutekh, though. His eyes shone with amusement. Pulling my gaze away from his, I saw Khufu.

The prince didn't look sad or guilty about my fate. Instead, he was dancing a strange jig, gesturing with his hands, pointing at something. For a moment I couldn't make any sense of it, but then I understood what all the gestures were telling me to do. I stretched a foot down. My toes felt around on the sand for a moment, and touched something solid. The knife! The scorpion had moved directly over it!

I got ahold of the blade's handle and gripped it between my toes as hard as I could. Just as the scorpion began to shove me into its mouth, I kicked him with everything I had, piercing him with the blade between my toes. For a sickening moment, I thought I hadn't been fast enough. I felt the inside of the creature's hot, foul mouth. Its wet mouthparts were closing around my head. I could feel its jaws beginning to crush—

Poof! My knife completed its work. Instead of being crushed inside a wet mouth, I found myself, and my knife, floating in midair inside a cloud of vapor. I dropped through the yellow mist and landed on the sand. I sat there, stunned, breathing hard.

Lady Mafdet exclaimed, "Barefoot fighting, indeed! Rather impressive. Wait here a moment." She scurried down toward the row of cages, hopefully checking that there were no more demons coming our way.

Others rushed to help me up, congratulating me. Gilli made another joke about my nimble little toes. Tau slapped me on the back with enough force to nearly knock me over. Seret said, "I suppose you planned that bit of toe-dagger work all along, right?" She said it teasingly, but not meanly. There's a difference. Maybe she was all right.

I grinned. "Yeah . . . well, I had to put on a good show for everyone, right?" Glancing at Sutekh, I added, "Peasant-style, of course."

Sutekh mumbled something under his breath.

Prince Khufu hung back, acting aloof as usual. I only glanced at him for a moment. I felt like I should thank him, but I didn't get the chance.

Mafdet returned. Her mouth puckered as if she were considering a mystery. "Strange," she said. "Very strange. I'll have to discuss it with the other gods. Come, young ones, let us join hands and return to Cherished Ka's Courtyard. We have news of victory and loss to share."

"Before we go," Sutekh said, "I have to question the fairness of this. The rest of us only got to fight one scorpion. But Ash unfairly got to fight more." For half a moment I thought Sutekh was going to say I should get higher marks for that, but that wasn't the way he worked. I should've known better. "He had the unfair advantage of multiple foes." He looked around at the others for support. "Any of us would've welcomed the challenge, wouldn't we?"

Most weren't so sure, but a few mumbled their vague agreement.

"I certainly would have," Sutekh continued.

"That's not possible," Mafdet said. "As you can see, all the demons were vanquished."

"Then Ash got special treatment. I thought the testing was supposed to be fair." Sutekh pouted.

The worst part was that Mafdet seemed to believe he meant it. "You make a good point, Sutekh," the goddess said. She brushed her whiskers with a paw as she considered. "Ash performed in a very impressive manner, but the strange occurrence offered him outsized potential to shine. I assure you all it will not be weighed to his advantage. I'll mark him as if he had faced a single combatant. That seems fair enough."

Not to me. I *hadn't* faced a single combatant! I didn't even know how many I'd fought. It went by in too much of a blur. Sutekh was pleased, though, and nobody else argued my side—including me.

Sutekh got in one final jab. "Not to mention that the prince gave Ash help. Very kind of you prince, but . . ." He let his voice trail off, like he was too humble to go on.

"True," Mafdet said. "No others had the prince's aid. I'll factor that into my scoring."

By the sounds of it I was going to end up with the

lowest score out of everyone. I still didn't speak up for myself, though. What could I say? Khufu *had* helped me. Truth was, I owed him my life. I looked at the prince, meaning to thank him. But instead my eyes met Sutekh's. He had managed to position himself beside the prince, smug and pleased with himself.

24

Banquet

Back in the courtyard, two mentors faced the most horrible of news about their candidates. One looked from one candidate's face to another over and over again, as if she'd find her mentee if she just kept looking. The other one broke down and had to be led away. I wanted nothing more than to run to Yazen and tell him everything and hope that he'd find some way to make it all seem better. I'd survived another day, but I'd ended up feeling less in control than I had when I arrived. But the gods weren't ready to release us just yet. The remaining candidates were to receive a second wrist guard.

Lady Mafdet reported on the testing. Pharaoh Neferu, Lord Horus, and Lady Isis listened with stern, attentive faces. Lord Set stood just behind them. He kept wrinkling his snout as if he smelled something unpleasant. Considering how many times his eyes touched on me, I must've been the source of the smell. I half wanted to sniff my armpits to see. I just stood there until we were each presented with our wrist guard, just as beautiful as the first. This time, Lady Mafdet slipped them into place.

Then we were dismissed.

I arrived back at our room tired and sore from the fighting. I washed and got changed and was ready to plop onto my mat and pass out. But when I came out of the baths I found a black cat waiting for me. He stood upright beside a padded table, looking mildly impatient.

"Apparently," Yazen said, "you are to be treated to a massage."

"A . . . cat massage?"

The cat said, "There's no better kind, really. Up on the table, kid."

I glanced at Yazen. He gestured that I should do as the cat said, so I did. I was skeptical at first. Sure, the cat could talk, but otherwise he looked like a normal house-cat. What kind of massage could little cat paws give?

I soon found out. I lay on my belly. The cat climbed up onto my back and went to work. Those cat paws squeezed and pressed and chopped and kneaded. He felt a lot bigger and stronger than I'd expected. I even tried to crane around and see him, but a paw held my head in place. "Please," the cat purred, "just relax yourself." After that I was putty in his paws.

By the time the cat packed up his table and headed out, I was a relaxed sack of mush. I would quite happily have stayed that way, except that I got summoned to the royal banquet hall. Apparently, the pharaoh thought it was time to show the candidates off to the court.

A servant marched us into a massive room, dotted with low tables piled with roast duck and fried fish and fresh-baked bread, with melons and dates and bunches of grapes and honey-drizzled cakes for dessert. It all smelled delicious. The room's light scarabs glowed with a soft light that pulsed in time with a tune being played on harps and tambourines. People lounged on cushions or reclined on couches. The royal family and several gods dined in a special elevated area.

In addition to the testing gods, Lord Ra was in attendance. Normally, he would be resting after his long day's labor of casting magical light down on Egypt, preparing himself to do it all again tomorrow. But I guess even gods like to attend a good party every now and then. He wore his falcon head, but he shone with a different sort of radiance than Lord Horus. Ra glowed from the inside. He looked like his body had the power of the sun trapped inside it, barely able to contain it.

I stood with the other candidates in the center of the hall while everyone gawked at us. They pointed and chatted. We were each announced by our names and our parents' names. Sutekh wasn't the only one with highborn parents. Kiya had her warrior-women ancestry. Another girl, Neema, was from a family of rich merchants. Seret could trace her family lineage back to the goddess Sekhmet. I guess that explained how she could be a talking lioness. The point was, each and every one of them had parents. Everyone except me. When the announcer got to me, he had to consult with his assistant before saying, "Ash . . . parentage unknown."

A lady nearby gasped. The whole crowd leaned forward, peering at me. I was mortified. Now they all—including my fellow candidates—knew just how much of a nobody I was. They stared at me like they weren't sure if I belonged here. I wasn't sure either.

Eventually, we were allowed to mingle as we wished. I headed for the farthest ring of tables, hoping to hide at the edge of the room. I hunkered down on an amazingly plush cushion and tried to be invisible. After a few minutes, I was pretty much forgotten.

I took the time to look around the room. I'd never seen so much of everything: food and jewelry and headdresses and fine clothing. Every one of the guests looked to be richer than any person I'd known in my life. Instead of regular servants, glowing figures moved around the tables. They were people, but small ones, about knee height and made entirely of light. They shimmered in shades of green and blue and purple. They refilled glasses and popped grapes onto plates and brought out new platters of food.

For some reason, taking it all in made me think fondly of my village. I almost missed the simplicity of life there. We never had much, but with hard work we got along all right. All the excess and riches of the capital made me wonder what could be possible at home if the pharaoh decided to spread more of the wealth around.

Sutekh worked the room, chatting with people. He made it look like everyone was an old friend his. Kiya stood at the center of a circle of admirers. I couldn't help but stare at her and wish that I was standing next to her, saying something to make her laugh, having a good story to tell. I wasn't even sure why I cared. It was just that my eyes seemed to always want to find her, and the thought of making her smile gave me butter-flies. Of course, I hadn't made her smile, and didn't expect I ever would.

Seeing how much she and Sutekh seemed to belong there made me feel more down. There was no way I was ever going to feel as comfortable with all this courtly stuff.

One of the glowing servants leaped up onto my table. He bowed and looked at me expectantly. He had a small mustache. He held one arm across his abdomen, with a tiny cloth dangled over it. He tapped his foot impatiently.

I realized he was waiting for me to request some-thing. With my stomach so tied in knots, I couldn't imagine eating. "Could I have a glass of water?" I asked.

The little figure darted away.

I looked over to where the royal family dined. Wow, the prince looked different than he had before! His skin glistened and his eyes shone with energy. He looked taller and older. A brand-new version of himself, as if all his features had been polished. His entire family could have been living stone, too perfect to be real. The hue of their skin was too rich. Their jewelry sparkled too brightly. Their eyes were large and piercing. When something amused Princess Sia, her laughter sounded like music and birdsong blended together.

"They look spectacular, don't they?" a voice behind me asked. It was Seret. She and Gilli sat down at my otherwise empty table. "Mind if we join you?"

"I thought we weren't supposed to talk to each other."

"That was just the first day," Seret said. "It's allowed now."

Gilli sloshed liquid around in a chalice. "Look, I've got my own personal glass filler." He pointed at the glowing servant that had followed him to the table. Instead of a towel on his arm, this one carried a small vase made of the same glowing energy he was. Gilli took a sip and then said, with the deep voice of an old aristocrat, "Top me up, old boy."

The glowing servant did as requested, though his expression said he was getting a bit tired of it.

"Isn't magic wonderful?" Seret asked. "That's why the royal family looks like it does. It's a radiance spell. Makes them look . . . well, radiant. It wears off in a few hours, and they'll look normal and mortal again."

"Is there anything you don't know?" I asked. I didn't exactly say it unkindly, but I didn't exactly say it nicely either. I couldn't help it. I just wanted to be left alone until I could slink back to my room and worry about tomorrow.

Seret raised an eyebrow. "There are plenty of things I don't know. But I'm young yet. Give me time."

Gilli, having just had his chalice refilled yet again, sighed and looked around the banquet hall. Wistfully, he said, "I could get used to this." He tilted his chalice and drank.

I hope that's not wine, I thought.

"Hey," Gilli said, leaning closer and lowering his voice, "you ever wonder what happened to the pharaoh's shadow? I tried asking about him, but nobody will say a word."

"Well, you should start by asking about *her*, since she was a woman," Seret said. "But that won't help either. No one speaks of it. All I know is that her name was Aniba, and that something horrible happened. It's probably better not to ask."

The servant I'd sent away returned with my glass of water. I wasn't thirsty, but I thanked him and took a sip anyway.

Seret perked up and said, "Today went well."

I frowned. "For you, maybe."

"Are you kidding me?" Gilli asked. His large eyes got even bigger with excitement. "You did great. The way you fought all those demons at once." He mimed slashing and dodging and punching, making facial expressions that would've made me laugh if I was in a better mood. "Didn't know you had it in you, kid."

Who was Gilli to be surprised by *my* performance? He was half my size! Part of me wanted to point this out, but it wasn't the nice part of me. I knew neither of them was making fun of me. I could tell already that they weren't like Sutekh. Or like Merk, for that matter.

Seret studied me for a moment. Her golden eyes were large and thoughtful. "Ash, it might be better for me if I don't say anything, but . . . you shouldn't give up yet."

"I'm not—" I began, but she kept talking.

"You look like you've already decided the contest is over. It's not. You've got skills. Everybody saw that today. Don't let Sutekh make your victory seem like a failure. It wasn't, so don't sell yourself short."

"I guess," I said.

Leaning forward, Seret spoke confidentially. "Do you know what? After the testing, Sutekh pulled me aside and said he and I should partner up. We could help each other knock out the competition."

"You mean us?" Gilli asked.

Seret nodded. "He had some whole story about how only he and I was worthy of being the prince's shadow, but nobody else was. So why not team up? He's a jerk and I told him so. A little later I saw him whispering with Kiya, probably giving her the same line."

Something about the thought of Sutekh talking secretly with Kiya bothered me. It must've shown on my face. Gilli said, "Oh, don't worry, kid. I've had to revise my earlier opinion. I'm pretty sure Kiya has a thing for you, after all."

25

A Question of Fear

"**W**h-what?" I sputtered.

"Seriously, I know you keep looking at her. What you don't notice is that when you're not looking at her, *she's* looking at you."

"No way," I said, but I thought, *Really? You sure about that?*

Seret asked, "And why are you looking so carefully at her, Gilli?"

Unflappable, Gilli just grinned. "I'm the observant type. That's all."

Seret looked amused, but she didn't press it. "Anyway," she said, "it's obvious they're up to something."

I glanced over to where Sutekh was bragging to a group of people. He was dressed richly for the occasion, in robes I could never afford. He kept running his hand over his shaved scalp and down his ponytail. Little scarab beetles clung to the ends of his hair, pulsing with golden light. What a showoff. His audience was eating up every word he said.

"It looks like we're the only ones that know that," I mumbled. "Look at him; he's virtually the prince's shadow already."

"No, he's not," Seret said. "Listen, he's got it all wrong. He acts like only one candidate—preferably him—will get out of this alive. Why can't we all live through to the last day? The gods would just have to decide between us then. I say that we can and should all fight to survive this thing. We should be *trying* to help each other."

"You're right," I said. She was saying things that deep down I already believed. I'd just been spending too much time feeling sorry for myself to see it.

"Good," Seret said. "Then it's agreed. We help each other when we can. Same goes for the others. I don't want to have anybody's death on my hands."

Sounded good to me. It was the first thing all day that really had.

"Hey," I said, feeling like the moment was right for

asking, "when you met the queen yesterday, did she say anything strange to you?"

Seret looked puzzled.

Gilli asked, "Like what?"

"Oh, I don't know. Anything that seemed secretive?"

"How could she?" Gilli asked. "We were all standing there together."

"Yeah, I know. I just thought . . ." This wasn't going well. "Forget about it. I think I'm just tired." I thought of something else to ask. "What do you two think about being here? About risking our lives to be the prince's shadow?"

Gilli shrugged. "It's an important job, right? I was lucky enough to be born on the right day to have a shot at it, so pretty much all my life has been training for it."

"Wait," I said. "All your life? You knew?"

Gilli looked confused. Seret asked, "Sure, we all did. We've all trained for this. If I'm chosen, I'll be the first lioness to be the prince's shadow. In all of Egypt's history. Imagine that! That's something I'm proud to risk everything for. What about you? What's this all mean to you?"

I didn't know how to answer. For that matter, I

didn't *know* in general. I didn't want to say that all of this had only been revealed to me a couple of days ago. Why was I the only one who hadn't known?

Was it because Yazen didn't believe I was up to it? Or that I could keep the secret?

I felt my face flush with shame. I supposed in some way I hadn't quite realized, I had hoped that being the prince's shadow—being important—would lead to finding my parents. Maybe they were out there, and would be proud of what I'd become. But I didn't want to reveal all that.

"I . . . um . . ."

I didn't notice Rami until he stopped in front of us and cleared his throat. The radiance spell had transformed him. Before, I'd thought his face was gaunt and a bit irregular. Now it was still gaunt and irregular, but he made it look like the definition of handsome. The girls at the table nearest us—some Libyan princesses, I think—swooned. One of them fainted right into a platter of fish. She wouldn't be happy when she woke up.

Rami seemed to take pleasure in ignoring the princesses. Holding his chin out, he looked down at our table. "One of you is Ash. Am I right?"

I nodded, not exactly happy with the admission. "That's me, Your Highness."

"I hear you tried to outshine the other candidates today. Cheaters never win, you know."

"I didn't . . . ," I began, but then thought better of disagreeing with him. I said, "You're right, prince. Cheaters don't win."

"You won't do it again, I'm sure." He looked away, scanning the crowd. I hoped that meant he was going to move on. No dice. "Fighting all those scorpions . . . were you scared?"

I answered honestly. "Terrified."

This brought Rami's full attention back. "What else is the mighty Ash afraid of?"

"In this world, Prince Rami," Seret said, "there are many things to fear."

"I want him to name one," Rami snapped.

I hesitated. What did this guy want? Anybody with a bit of common sense was afraid of things. Spiders, scorpions, snakes. Poverty, disease, death. Take your pick. Big or small, the world was a scary place to hang out in. Everybody knew that, except maybe princes glowing with radiance spells.

"Drowning," I said.

"Drowning?" Rami scoffed. "Don't peasants know how to swim?"

"My village is in the desert. We've got a well for water and some irrigation channels, but that's about it." Rami kept staring at me. "No place to swim, I mean." There was more to it than that, but I didn't need to tell him how I used to have nightmares about falling into the village well and being stuck down there, sinking slowly into the black depths.

"I've been swimming off the royal river barge since I was seven," Rami said, projecting his voice so the girls at the other table heard him. Cue more swooning. "It's easy! If you expect to be a shadow, you better learn. We travel the Nile on barges, don't you know. Sometimes, at least, when there's a reason not to fly *The Mistress of Light.*"

I wanted to ask what *The Mistress of Light* was, but I didn't want to give him anything more to make fun of.

Rami stared at me a moment, and then got bored. Absently, he said, "Afraid of drowning. How provincial." He wandered away to enrich someone else's life with his pleasant company.

When he was out of earshot, I grumbled, "If

Khufu turns out to act anything like him, I won't envy whoever becomes the shadow."

Gilli's eyes slid away from me and found Khufu, who sat sullenly among his shimmering family. "Khufu's nothing like him," he said.

"How do you know? We've only heard him say a few words."

Gilli said, "I just have a feeling about him."

"I think you're right," Seret said. "The only thing that worries me is how he would turn out with someone like Sutekh as his shadow. Imagine having to spend every day for the rest of your life with *him*."

Gilli grimaced. "That would be awful!"

"I guess we just have to make sure that doesn't happen. Right?" I asked.

Seret smiled. "That's the spirit. And on that cheerful note, I think it's time for me to go to bed. Just one more thing, Ash. You can swim."

"No, I can't."

"Yes," she said, "you can. Every living creature can, even elephants. It's true. Nothing is more natural than swimming. Humans just overthink it is all. It's not the water that drags them down; it's their fear.

Swimming is wonderful. It's like flying in the water. Think of it that way."

"Lot of good that does me! I can't fly in air any better than I can swim in water. Anyway, I thought cats hated swimming."

"Naw," she said, standing and stretching. "We like it all right. We just don't love the way we look wet." With a wink, she turned and wove her way through the crowd, all feline grace.

Gilli pushed himself upright. He yawned. "I'm going to call it a night too. See you tomorrow. And, hey, try to stay alive, will you?" Just him saying that kind of choked me up a bit. Before I could respond, he did a little dance, a familiar one. "I think I drank too much," he confessed. "I need to use the bathroom."

After he left, I whispered to the empty table, "Hey, you try to stay alive, too." I meant it. I meant it for Gilli, and for Seret, too.

THE
TESTING
DAY THREE

26

Call Me Cranky

Rami hated waking up early. When he was pharaoh, he planned to do away with morning meetings and such. No state business before lunch! That would be the rule. He would have lots of rules, but only ones that pleased him.

This morning, however, he was eager to speak to Lord Set. Nothing was going right with the god's plans. Something needed to be done. The sooner the better. That was why he'd placed himself on a couch near the corridor he knew Set was likely to pass through on his way to the start of the day's testing. He lounged there, bored and impatient at the same time.

When he spotted the god, Rami called, "Lord Set! I'd have a word."

Set moved at a brisk pace. He showed no intention of stopping to chat. "Prince, I'm in no mood to talk," he said. "Call me cranky, but I've been up all night piloting the old glow-hard through the underworld."

Rami leaped up from the couch and trotted to keep up with him. "You do that every night, as you have done for thousands of years."

"So you can see why I'm feeling a bit sleep deprived. Makes one testy. Even a god."

"It's about the candidates," the prince whispered, glancing around to make sure they couldn't be overheard. "A bunch of them are still alive, in case you haven't noticed."

Set quickened his pace. "I don't need you to inform me of that. As I said before, I'll handle it."

Rami was running out of breath. He grabbed the god by the elbow and pulled him to a stop.

Set spun on him. The flames in his eyes flared. "Prince," he said, his voice low and menacing, "you seem to have my arm gripped in your fingers. Are you sure that's wise?"

Rami, looking sheepish, let go. "Sorry. It's just that I want to know what you're going to do."

"I'm going to take care of everything."

"You didn't yesterday."

"The whelps got lucky. It won't keep happening."

"Why don't you do it yourself? Just get it done!"

The flames sputtered out. Set's regular small eyes returned, looking a tad astonished. "I could ask the same of you. You want them dead; do it yourself. Or have your little brother meet an unfortunate end, for that matter. A spot of poison would do the trick in a jiffy. Royals do it to their siblings all the time. It's gone on for centuries. Donkey's years."

"If it comes to that, I will." Rami crossed his arms and squeezed his lips together in a bitter line. "But the point of our little arrangement is for you to do the work. It wouldn't do for me to get caught strangling my brother's scrawny neck. Though how I'd like to . . ."

"Neither of us can afford to get caught," Set said. "If our plans are to come to fruition, neither of us must be suspected of doing anything devious. That's why I will make it look like an accident."

Rami let his puzzlement show on his face. "Fruition?"

"Patience, that's all I ask," Set said. "Today's another day of testing, after all."

"Take me with you when you follow them. I want to see for myself." Set began to protest, but Rami cut in. "I demand to go. You failed two days in a row. I deserve to see with my own eyes that you're really trying."

Set thought about it a moment. Eventually, he sniffed. "Fine. I'll collect you when it's time." He began to move away.

"Wait!" Rami called. "One other thing. Last night, one of them . . . Ash, that's the one. He admitted that he couldn't swim. He never learned, desert villager that he is. Isn't that pathetic?"

Set spun back slowly. His jaw hung open slightly as he considered this. He ran his tongue along his small, jagged teeth. "Considering who is overseeing the testing today, a fear of drowning could prove most beautifully problematic."

Watching the god continue on his way, Rami scowled. He hadn't liked the way Set's eyes had flared at him. The cheek of it! As if he was calling the shots.

It reminded him that he had quite a list of things to get sorted once he became pharaoh. He'd likely have to arrange for some unfortunate accident to befall his brother. Something deadly. That would be the easiest way not to have to worry about the upstart trying to do the same to him and steal his throne. Khufu didn't actually seem that ambitious, but still . . . you could never be sure.

There was Set to worry about, too. Rami might try him out as his godly confidant, but if he didn't do as he was told . . . "I'll dismiss him," he said. He could do it. That was the thing about being pharaoh—even the gods had to obey the pharaoh's every wish. Once he took the throne, he could order Set around. If he found him lacking, well . . . "I'll send him back to the Night Barge."

He grinned at that. It was going to be good being pharaoh. Very, very good.

27

That's What a Snout's About

Day three of the testing was about to begin. Last night, it felt like I'd found friends in Gilli and Seret. But now, waiting nervously in Cherished Ka's Courtyard, I was more aware of the fact that I might be about to lose them. I didn't know what today would bring, except that it would be full of danger. I watched the hieroglyphs slink around the obelisk, unreadable and yet calling to me. Was our fate somehow written there?

"What I want today," Yazen said, "is for you to forget that this is the third day of testing. Forget what came before. Forget that there are other days to come. Keep all of your mind here, in this moment. If you do that, nothing can stop you, Ash."

Yazen was good at pep talks. I appreciated them. I just didn't always believe them. It seemed to me that I could do my best all I liked, but if some demon's best was better than mine, then . . . the end of Ash. A one-way trip to the Duat.

Plus, there was the competition to worry about. Worrying about getting beaten by them *and* worrying about something bad happening to them.

My gaze drifted over the other candidates. Each of them whispered with their mentor, probably hearing the same sort of stuff Yazen was telling me. Yesterday, there had been ten of us. Today there were eight: Seret, Gilli, Sutekh, Kiya, Tau, Neema, Mery, and me. After the testing, how many would be left? Only two days down. Still three to go, and I didn't like my chances. I also wondered who today's testing god was going to be, where he or she would take us, and what we'd face when we got there.

"Are you listening to me, Ash?"

"Yeah," I said. "I always listen to—"

The pharaoh, Prince Khufu, and the gods arrived. Each of them emerged through an opening in the wall that enclosed the courtyard. Lord Horus was as stern as ever. Lady Isis took us in, her chin raised and lips pressed together. Lord Set yawned and looked bored. Lady Mafdet nodded to us, seemingly wishing us luck. I guessed the old mongoose really did care about us. Khufu looked as nervous as I felt.

The last to enter was the day's testing god. The first part of him to appear was the tip of his snout. A gnarled bulb of a nose. As he walked through the opening, the snout grew longer, lined with large, jagged teeth. About halfway down the snout's length I knew what kind of animal it was—and what god it belonged to.

"Lord Sobek," Pharaoh Neferu said, "will be performing today's testing."

I hadn't known whom to expect, but I'd have preferred to hear anybody else's name. Sobek was the god of the Nile. He regulated the annual floods that brought rich silt from the River Nile into the valley to fertilize the farmlands. His work was incredibly important to all of Egypt, but he was also incredibly dangerous. He could take complete crocodile form. As the tales say, he was in this form when he rose up out of the Mediterranean and single-handedly destroyed an invading Hittite navy. His jaws had snapped ships in half, devouring the screaming crewmen whole.

Fortunately, he was only in his crocodile-headed

form today. Below the neck, his body was that of a tall, green man. His bare, heavily muscled chest glistened. It was said that if need be, he controlled the flow of the Nile with his own sweat. Considering how vast the Nile was that was hard to believe. Though I did have to admit the god's green skin did look . . . moist.

"Prince Khufu," Sobek said, "are you and the shadow candidates ready?"

His voice was a deep rumble that I didn't so much hear as but feel. It made my bones tremble. The sound was still reverberating in my head when Khufu answered, "Yes, Lord Sobek. My candidates are prepared for whatever test you choose to offer them."

Hey, don't overdo the confidence, I thought. Wouldn't want the god deciding to make the test any harder than it had to be.

Apparently, the answer satisfied Sobek. He said, "Then let us go. Into the portal, candidates. We have a great distance to travel."

28

The Headwaters

It might've been a great distance, but the journey by light was over in the blink of an eye.

As I stepped out of the portal, two sensations hit me full in the face and ears: wetness and sound. Moist vapor floated in the air, instantly soaking me. We stood on an island surrounded by a massive, raging river. Water poured over ledges. It billowed around stones and smashed into cliff walls. Currents of froth churned. Waves rose and exploded. Sinkholes swirled into existence one moment, and vanished the next. Gusts of wind grabbed at us, like wet hands trying to yank us into the river.

It was a world of water, all of it rushing toward a precipice. Downstream from our island, the world dropped off into nothingness. Far below, behind the billowing clouds of mist, I could barely make out the distant tumble of a great canyon. There was no way to tell how far the water fell. One thing was certain: it was a deadly drop. No living thing could survive such a fall, not with the currents to drown you and the rocks to smash you to pulp.

"The source of the Nile," Sobek said. "This is where Egypt's life blood bursts into being."

Gilli—who didn't seem the least bit nervous talking to a god—pointed and asked, "What's that?"

We all looked to see that he was pointing at a mountain that loomed up out of the mist in another direction. The chaos of the current made my head spin, but the mountain felt like silent tranquility, floating on a blanket of cloud. Its bottom slopes were thick with lush vegetation but the mountain turned more rocky as it rose to the sky. Streams of water plunged down through a crisscrossing network of crevices. Its peak was snowcapped, a white pyramid of ice.

Sobek turned his massive crocodile head in its direction and stared for a long moment at the peak. Misty eyed, he said, "That is the mythical mountain of Bakhu. My home."

Squinting, Gilli prodded him. "What's mythical about it?"

"It is a place of legend. The true source of the Nile. No humans have ever reached it. None even know where it is. It is a place of myth."

None know where it is? Was he kidding? I was looking at it. We were all looking at it! I began to point this out. "Uh, Lord Sobek—"

Seret jabbed me in the ribs. She gave me a warning look. I kept my observation to myself.

"It is a sacred place to me," Sobek went on. "When I am away from it, my heart is rent in two. I keep a temple there, made of carnelian. A place of such beauty . . ." The big croc looked like he was about to tear up.

"What's carnelian?" Gilli asked.

Sobek didn't answer. He said, "Enough questions. Let us begin. The Reheptah Dynasty reigned many years ago. A powerful clan. They might now be ruling Egypt, if not for an unfortunate accident. One day, while on a diplomatic mission to Lower Egypt, the royal barge attempted to navigate a cataract. The barge capsized, throwing the entire family into the swift waters. With no one to rescue them, they all perished.

It was a grave day for Egypt. I never wish to see its like again. That is why I've brought you here. Many members of the royal family were aboard that tragic day, along with many friends and trusted servants and guards. You, candidates, must be prepared should something similar ever happen again. For your vessels, behold!"

He gestured to one side with a sweep of his long arm. A whole area of mist cleared, revealing a calm cove sheltered from the main current. In it, tethered to the shore, floated the kind of gear that Merk would've killed for: solar kiteboards. I'd never seen one before, but Merk had rambled on about them at home, saying how he was going to get one once he left the village and joined the real world. I guess I beat him to it.

The boards were like oversized sunboards. Long, thin ropes stretched up from the boards, angling high in the sky. At the top of the ropes, sunkites billowed with solar energy, pulling the ropes taut. The sunkites looked similar to solar sails on a sunbarge, only smaller. On the kiteboard itself were two loops to hold your feet. A rider was supposed to stick their feet into the loops, grip the handle at the bottom of the rope, and hang on as the sunkite pulled them forward. There were eight of the boards. One for each of the remaining candidates.

"We each get to ride one of those?" Gilli asked, sounding excited.

"Excellent," Sutekh said. He looked pleased. "I've got one at home. This should be easy."

"Easy, you say?" Sobek asked. "Let me make it a bit more challenging, then." The god raised one of his long, green arms. A tangle of writhing cats dangled from his fist. Caracals. Normally, caracals were fierce hunters. They're smaller than big cats like lions and cheetahs, but larger than domestic cats.

Instead, these caracals had left all their hissing ferocity behind. They looked like they'd rather be someplace—anyplace!—but here. The smallest of them fixed me with a pleading gaze. Its large, kittenish eyes begged for release. Pathetically, it tried a drawn out, "Meeeoow?"

As if that was the cue he'd been waiting for, Sobek spun around and hurled the cats into the air. They flew far upstream, spreading out as they twirled and spun. They plopped down into the froth at various points in the river. They came up clawing for dear life.

Their eyes grew even larger as they realized the current was rushing them toward the waterfall.

Sobek's low voice rumbled, "Shadow candidates, save them. Save them if you can."

29

Drowning on Dry Land

The other candidates rushed to the kiteboards, but my feet wouldn't move. Save the caracals? How could I possibly save them? All that water! And I couldn't swim. I was the worst person in the world for this challenge. Even though I was standing safely on the island, I couldn't breathe. I tried to, but my chest wouldn't obey me. I was suffocating where I stood, paralyzed by fear. It was worse than the nightmares I used to have about sinking down into the black water of the village well.

The caracals cried out for help. I watched one claw at a stone as it swept past it, leaving long scratch marks behind. Another surged down a flume of water and disappeared into the froth. When it came up again, its eyes were wide with terror. They were all sliding past the island and on toward the waterfall. I had to do something. But I couldn't.

Seret's feline face appeared in front of me. "Ash, let's go. We have to save them!"

I tried to, but when I moved I started to sway. It took all my effort just to stay on my feet. Why couldn't the test have been something other than water? I could've faced anything else bravely, but not water.

Seret grabbed me by both arms and shook me. "Ash, you're not breathing! What's wrong with you?"

Gilli appeared beside her. "Let's find out." He hauled off and smacked me on the cheek.

"Ouch!"

"He can feel pain, at least," Gilli said. "That's a good sign."

I gasped. "What was that for?"

"To get you breathing again," he said. "See, it worked. Let's go!"

I couldn't dispute that. I stood there sucking in breaths, feeling life rushing back into my body. I'd been standing there drowning on dry land, drowning just because of fear. Out of the corner of my eye, I saw several of the kiteboards carve out of the cove into the raging current. Their sunkites pulled them with startling speed, but I wasn't moving.

"What's wrong?" Gilli asked.

"It's because of the water, isn't it?" Seret said. She kept glancing over her shoulder at the river. She wanted to be there, not here. And yet she was here, trying to help me.

Gilli's eyes lit up. "Here's the plan, then . . . Ash, don't fall in. Can't swim? Well then, don't swim. You'll be fine. Just stay on your board, kid."

He was right. It was so simple. Just stay on the board. I could do that!

As we ran for the kiteboards, I realized there had been somebody else standing nearby. I glanced back. Prince Khufu. He must've seen and heard the whole thing. I ran that much harder, not wanting to think about what he thought of me now.

I reached the sheltered cove just as the others pulled up in front of me. The sight before us wasn't what we'd expected. Sutekh had been the last to take off from the cove into the current, and the three remaining kiteboards followed behind him. They were riderless, but the sun's energy was filling the sunkites and pulling them forward. We watched, helpless, as all three careened into the current, out of our reach.

"That rat!" Seret shouted.

"He cut them loose!" Gilli said.

Without thinking, I was running toward the shore. There were stones just beyond the riverbank. I shouted to the others, "Come on! Use the stones!"

At the water's edge, I leaped with everything I had. I just barely reached a shelf of rock, awash with splashing water. I jumped from it to another rock, and then picked my way farther and farther out, using the rocks like gigantic stepping stones. The kiteboards were up ahead. I tried not to think about the surging flumes of water rushing between the rocks. The spray soaked me and the water's roar was deafening. I kept my eyes focused on the next slab of solid stone as I jumped. Jumped. And jumped.

Finally, I caught up to one of the kiteboards. As the kiteboard floated by, I vaulted for it from the rock I was perched on, aiming my feet for the foot loops. My arms cartwheeled in the air, but my feet found their targets, slamming home into the loops and nearly flipping the kiteboard over. Trying desperately to keep my balance, I fumbled to get a grip on the handle attached to the ropes controlling the sunkite.

As soon as I had the handle tightly in my fists, I felt the pull of the sunkite high above, thrumming with solar energy. It was amazing! I glanced back to see the others leaping over the stones in pursuit of the other kiteboards. My board surged forward across the water.

30

Good Little Fishy

"That old gator has a one-track mind," Lord Set muttered. "All mythical mountains and sweat of the Nile and such foolishness." Set had arrived to the testing site well prepared, having anticipated Sobek's location. He pulled his rain poncho tight around his shoulders.

Rami crouched beside him, looking miserable. He hadn't thought to bring a poncho. "Set, you didn't say I'd be getting"—a splash of water slapped his face—"wet."

Set shrugged. He reached beneath his poncho and produced a visor of tinted glass. Balanced on the bridge of his snout, it protected his tiny eyes from the spray. Hidden behind a rock, he and Rami both peered over at the unfolding scene in front of them.

Lord Sobek and Prince Khufu were standing on an island in the raging current. In the distance, the mythical mountain hung in the sky. Set sniffed. "Bakhu," he whispered disdainfully. "What a backwater. Palace made of carnelian? Sobek always overdoes things."

Rami squinted as he studied the action on the river. Kiteboards zigged and zagged through the raging current, cutting between rocks and riding over waves. There were creatures flailing in the water, but Rami didn't know if they had anything to do with it. "Sobek calls this a test? Looks like joyriding to me."

"Look at that fool boy," Set said. "He has no idea what he's doing!"

He was talking about Ash. His board twisted first this way and then that way, his control lines all tangled together. He was heading right toward a jagged boulder that sawed up out of the current.

"Smash him to pieces," Rami whispered.

Ash must've seen the boulder at the last moment, because just before he hit it, he pulled down on his sunkite lines and crunched his knees up to his chest, lifting the board out of the water. He scraped across the stone, the board bouncing and sliding as it went. When he reached the stone's end he pulled himself airborne, whirling around like a top. His lines untangled and the sunkite spread and billowed into place. When he landed on the surface of the water again he wobbled but found his balance. His kiteboard raced forward. He leaned back and curved the kiteboard downstream. He slipped between two angry backwashes until he found a clear tongue of water.

"The peasant boy is a fast learner," Set said. If he hadn't been so disapproving, he might have sounded impressed.

Despite himself, Rami had to agree. "Do something, Set!"

Ash gripped the handle in one hand and thrust an arm down into the water. He pulled out a thrashing, sputtering, miserable-looking caracal. He plopped it on the board behind him. A moment later, he scooped another cat as he circled around the boulder it clung to.

"I see," Set said. "This is a reenactment of that Reheptah debacle. They have to rescue those poor creatures."

"Well, stop them! Look, the others are snatching them up, too!"

"Worry not, prince. I know just what to do."

Hidden behind a barricade of rocks, the god climbed down to the river's edge. He darted a hand into the water, felt around a moment, and came up with a tiny catch. A minnow, just big enough to fit in the palm of his hand. He showed it to Rami. "I'd hoped for something a little more impressive, but this should do. Just a little puff of a spell."

"Just a puff?" Rami asked. "Why hold back?"

"My breath is rather strong, prince. A puff will be enough."

Conjuring a spell, Set lifted the fish to his lips. The fish wriggled, but Set's snout closed around its mouth and held it firm. He exhaled, blowing the spell into the fish's billowing body.

Rami agreed that Set's breath was strong, but he didn't see any reason to take it easy on the candidates. The stronger the spell the better, he figured. So he gave Set a firm pat on the back, just enough to push a little more air out of his lungs. The fish rolled its tiny eyes in crazy circles. When Set released him, the fish coughed, sending a puff of foul-smelling spellsmoke into the air.

Set scowled at the prince. "This is why you shouldn't come on these little ventures. No sense of subtlety. You really should trust me on matters of magic." Turning his attention to the minnow, he said, "Now be a good little fishy and do my bidding." Set dropped the fish back into the water. It swam away.

Within a few strokes its tail began to lengthen. Its body bulged and contorted.

"Let's go," Set said. "It wouldn't do to be seen here, considering what's about to happen."

Rami desperately wanted to watch the show to come, but the god was right. Better to be prudent.

31

Sink or Swim

I was starting to get the hang of kiteboarding. I had to surf, dodging rocks and gauging the flow of the currents while controlling the sunkite high in the air above me. I also had to locate the caracals in all the commotion and churning of the river. And I had to beat the other candidates to them, while avoiding crashing into them or getting tangled in their lines. Honestly, if I'd had to think about it all I would never have managed it. I was functioning on pure instinct.

With two cats clinging to the back of my board I figured I was doing all right. I snatched a third caracal out of the water by the tail. "Sorry," I said, depositing her behind me with the others. Seeing another one, I turned toward him. I angled my sunkite to better catch the sun. As the kiteboard sped up, my arm muscles strained from the increased pull. The water fizzled as the sunboard skimmed over it. Why had I ever worried about drowning? Standing on the board, the surface of the water held me up with no problem.

As I closed in on the caracal, he turned toward me, frantically clawing at the water. It was the kitten, the one that had meowed. The little guy was round-eyed with terror. He had realized something that was only just dawning on me. The edge of the falls was perilously close. Too close! But I couldn't turn away now. The kitten's eyes pulled me in. I gripped the handle in one hand and reached out with my other, watching the frightened kitten through my fingers. I grabbed him and felt his claws dig into my forearm. I would've tried to shake him onto the board, but there was no time. I pressed the kitten against my chest. The edge was—

—It was too late. I shot out over the falls, right into midair. The entire river dropped away, falling straight down into a billowing tumble.

Time slowed. I hung there for a stretched-out moment, realizing that the sunkite's sail was great for pulling us skimming across the water but wasn't strong enough to suspend us in the air for long. It wasn't going to be drowning that did me in after all. It was going to be a fall from an enormous height and the impact with the boulder-strewn riverbed that was probably hidden beneath the foaming mist, waiting to smash me into pieces. I accepted my fate. I closed my eyes and held the caracal tight, sorry that I hadn't managed to save him or myself.

But then a great breath of air shot up from the turbulent churning of the falling water. It filled the sunkite like a sail and blew it—and me, the board, and the caracals—high into the sky, carrying us back upstream in the process. All I could do was hang on as we flew and watch the scene pass below me.

Seret was clearly having a hard time with the kiteboard. Her paws couldn't get a good grip on the steering handles, and her feet were too large to fit into the foot loops. I could see her frustration building. A caracal bobbed past her, twirling in the current. She watched with large frantic eyes as the smaller cat sank below the surface.

"Come on, Seret," I whispered. "You can do it."

She couldn't. But she could do something else. She threw the handles away and yanked her toes from the foot loops. She leaped onto a rock, jumped from it to another one, and then plunged, head first, into the raging river. She came up clawing against the current, with the caracal clenched—gently, I hoped—in her jaws. She clawed her way up onto a rock and began leaping toward the shore.

Gilli had saved a caracal, but was in trouble for it. The cat had clawed its way up onto his head and clung there. Gilli was trying desperately to convince it to come down, getting tangled in his guide ropes in the process.

Kiya tried to help him out. If you could call it that. She roared past him, sending a wall of water splashing over him. When it cleared, the cat was no longer on Gilli's head. It was on the back of Kiya's kiteboard instead. I cried out that she had cheated, but my voice got lost in the roar of the river.

Kiya wasn't the only one cheating. As my kite-board began a slow descent toward the river, I caught sight of Sutekh. He knew how to kiteboard, all right. He held his steering line in one hand, but still managed to weave through the rapids with ease. I realized he was also holding something in his free hand, but I didn't figure out what it was until after he'd used it. He cut in behind Tau, who was using all his strength to control his board—and wasn't being very successful at it. Sutekh zipped by him, his free hand darting out as he did so. A moment later, Tau's kite twirled into a death spiral. He lost all momentum. The current grabbed him and dragged him toward the waterfall. He went over. Unlike me, his kite didn't catch the gusts of air. The fabric flapped uselessly in the mist from the falls, and I watched—sick to my stomach— as it sank out of sight, dragged down by the weight of the boy's falling body.

"Sutekh cut one of his lines!" I shouted, as my kiteboard touched down and started surfing again. "He's cheating!"

I doubt Sutekh heard me in all the commotion, but as he rounded and headed back upstream, he scanned the scene, no doubt checking for witnesses. His eyes found mine. I could tell by the way his face hardened that he knew I'd seen what he had done. I should've headed straight for the island to report what I'd seen to Lord Sobek and Prince Khufu. Surely, cheating was cheating. And Sutekh's style of cheating was deadly. He would be disqualified. That was my hope. But . . . it didn't happen. Unfortunately, something else intervened. Something monstrous.

32

In the Drink

A grotesque shape rose from under the water, moving fast, squirming, growing larger with each passing moment. *Is that a fish?*

It was thick and scaly, with bulging eyes and a mouth so wide it could've swallowed a kid whole. I'd never seen a fish this big. It churned through the river, dodging boulders and smashing through waves. Its tail thrashed behind it, taking it right toward Neema, who didn't see it approaching.

"Hey!" I yelled as I surfed toward her. "Behind you, look!"

She looked over her shoulder at me. I pointed to the fish. Horror spread across her face. She yanked back on the steering lines and dodged behind a rock. She skimmed across the tops of several waves, cut a sharp turn, and zipped along beside a rock wall.

The monster bore down on her. It got closer no matter what she did, knocking a boulder the size of an elephant out of its way and sending it rolling down-stream and over the falls. And then—when Neema cut behind a small island—the fish leaped out of the water. It arched through the air, massive mouth gaping open.

"No!" I cried. I didn't want to see any more death. "No!"

My shouts did nothing to save her. The fish crashed down, mouth closing over her. It dove into a great splash of water and vanished.

"No . . ."

I felt like crying. I hadn't really known Neema. I didn't know if she was a good person, or if she was crooked like Sutekh. Now I'd never know.

Sobek bellowed from the large island, announcing that we should return. The testing was concluded. I barely cared. It seemed wrong to count how many caracals we'd saved, to compare numbers and get our scores. Still, I got the caracal kitten to retract his claws. I set him on the board with the others. Cutting a turn around a large boulder, I headed back toward the island.

That's when Sutekh slammed into me—sending me flying.

I should never have taken my eyes off him. Glancing back, I saw Sutekh snatch up one of my caracals by the scruff of its neck. Then I hit the water face-first, plunging down into it. I'd thought the river was loud from above the surface. Below it was even worse. Such a complete inundation of sound and motion. It felt like it was attacking me, so I fought back, kicking and thrashing. But I was powerless against the force of the water. The current yanked my legs and arms around, twisting me whichever way it wanted to go. It was horrible to feel such raw power, and yet to have my arms and legs just pass right through it, useless.

I tried to scream, but nothing came out. Instead, water rushed in, filling my mouth and nose. I slammed into a rock. That knocked the rest of the air out of me.

Part of my mind feared the monster fish could be anywhere, but it was the river itself that terrified me the most. I already felt exhausted. My lungs burned. I didn't know which way was up. With my eyes open all I could see was the chaotic fizz of the water and rocks. I had to get to the surface to breathe. And soon, before the river swept me over the waterfall. At that point, it would really be all over.

And all because of Sutekh. That cheater. That low-down, despicable cheater!

The thought of him getting away with it filled me with anger. I didn't want to die and I didn't want Sutekh to win by cheating. My lungs cried out for air and I began to feel my consciousness slipping. What had Seret said about swimming? We overthink it? That's it! We drown because we're afraid and confused. All mammals can swim. Maybe, if I thought like a caracal . . .

With images of the soaking, unhappy cats in my mind, I tried to find the surface. A rock skimmed past my face. Right, rocks are at the bottom. I flipped over. I tried to mimic the motions the cats had made. Paws paddling rhythmically at the water. I figured they'd been kicking their hind legs, too, so I did that as well. I felt the water slipping between my fingers, but I realized I was able to claw my way through it. With my legs kicking beneath me, I felt myself rising.

I saw the surface. The world of air and life was just there, almost within my grasp. I reached for it. But as the light of the sky was getting nearer, my inner light was fading.

Finally, my fingers punched into the air. My head burst through just after. I sucked air into my lungs, greedily. Nothing had ever been sweeter. Each breath blew life back into my body. It was like being born. But where was I? Was I about to plunge over a waterfall to certain death?

This wasn't over yet.

I kept clawing and kicking, still barely believing that I was actually swimming. I rode up and down on the waves, sometimes sinking below the surface, but always able to climb back up again. For a time, I was terrified of the rocks, the way they rose like obstacles running at me. But they weren't moving—the current was. I was. I didn't need to fear those rocks, I needed to get a whole lot friendlier with them!

The first time I tried to grab a boulder I bounced off it. The second time I managed to slow down, but couldn't stop from sliding around it.

I caught glimpses of the plumes of mist rising from the falls. The edge was so, so close.

A smaller rock came into view. I splattered it with my whole body, plastering myself to it, arms wrapped around it. It stopped me. I clung there for a long moment as water billowed around me. *Yes!*

I only said it inside, but still, I'd spoken too soon. The added pull of my weight made the rock come loose and roll over, spilling me over the top of it and closer to the edge of the falls.

There was only one other slab of rock within reach. I paddled across the current toward it. The roar of the nearby falls was incredible. I grabbed for the rock. My hands slid down the smooth, slick stone. I dug in with my fingers, trying to make them claws. Gradually, gradually, I slowed. I was all the way at the end of the slab. The water was slower behind it, but still it tugged at me. I lay there, half submerged, hugging the rock with all the strength I had left, knowing that it wouldn't last long.

The falls still wanted me. If I was going to survive, I needed someone to rescue me, and soon.

33

And My Savior Is . . .

Someone did.

When I saw a hand reaching toward me, I grasped for it with what little strength I had left. The hand swung me up onto the kiteboard just as it surfed over the edge of the waterfall and caught the updraft of air. As we rushed up high above the falls, I realized who had come to my rescue.

Sutekh.

I couldn't believe it. It didn't make sense. Just being so near him made my skin crawl. I nearly rolled back into the river. The only thing that kept me clinging to the kiteboard was the possibility of splatting on one of the numerous rocks below me. That and pure anger. Indignation. Resentment. The second we reached the others I was going to let him have it. I'd reveal him for the scoundrel that he was.

Sutekh touched down with ease. He brought the kiteboard into the cove and parked it neatly. He hopped off and then reached back to give me a hand. "Careful, Ash," he said, loud enough for the others to hear. "Let me help you—"

"I can do it myself!" I snapped. I leaped off the board. Landing awkwardly on the stones, I twisted my ankle. I limped toward Sobek and the others. I opened my mouth and—

"That was quick thinking, Sutekh," Sobek said. He strode right past me and clapped one of his massive arms down on Sutekh's back. "Not only have you safely returned with an astounding seven caracals—"

Seven! "But wait," I tried to cut in. "He stole some of them from—"

"—but you've also saved one of your peers from certain death. Well done, young man."

Well done? No, that was all wrong! "But Lord Sobek—"

The god turned toward me. "The moment Sutekh spotted you clinging to that rock he rushed out to rescue you. Not even a moment's hesitation or concern for his safety."

"But he—"

"The others didn't even know you were in danger, but Sutekh here was already in motion. It's uncanny. Almost as if he can smell danger in the air!"

"But that's because—"

"I don't suppose you would've been able to hang on much longer." Sobek crossed his arms and looked at me gravely down his long snout. "I believe thanks are in order," he prompted, none too subtly.

I couldn't believe it. He was ordering me to *thank* Sutekh? He was the reason I'd been in the water in the first place! I was about to spill it all, now that Sobek was finally giving me a chance to speak. Only . . . the god and the other candidates all looked at me expectantly. Prince Khufu craned his head forward. Waiting.

All the words I wanted to shout died on my tongue. I realized I couldn't say them. I wanted to, but I could tell that in all the moving chaos of the rapids none of them had seen what I'd seen, not even Seret or Gilli. They hadn't witnessed Sutekh take out Tau. They hadn't watched him knock me into the water. All they had seen was Sutekh looking the hero.

I could try to deny it, but who were they going to believe? Me, the one who was sopping wet? The one they just saw get plucked from the edge of the falls? The guy who had been slipping slowly toward his death? Or . . . Sutekh.

Judging by the smug way he watched me squirm, he knew the answer. He reached behind his head and casually wrung water out of his ponytail, watching me through triumphant eyes.

"Well, Ash," Sobek said, "don't you have something to say?"

Oh boy, did I! But I couldn't say it. Instead, I mumbled, "Th—thank you . . . Sutekh."

Sutekh grinned and said, "It was nothing." Looking at Prince Khufu, he said, "I'm sure he'd do the same for any of us." Somehow his tone managed to say that he really thought the opposite but was just being generous to me. Kiya guffawed and tossed her locs. Just like that, I was sure that all the people looking at me thought I *wouldn't* do the same thing for any of them. But I would! My head wanted to explode with all the things I couldn't say trapped inside it.

I felt something brush my leg. The caracal kitten. He looked up at me with his massive round eyes. I couldn't help but reach for him. Cradling him to my chest, I rubbed his fur. He nuzzled against me. At least somebody knew what had really happened. That counted for something.

Back at Cherished Ka's Courtyard, I stood listening to Sobek's final tally of the testing. Sutekh brought back the most caracals. Kiya was next with four. Seret had managed to save two. Gilli and Mery saved one each. And me? Dead last. I may have been holding a sleeping kitten, but I didn't get credit for saving it. I felt my chances of becoming the prince's shadow fading fast.

Sobek described my pitiful state and Sutekh's daring rescue of me. By the time he was done, I almost believed that was really the way it had happened. He became more somber on the subject of the two candidates who had perished. Tau, he announced, had gone over the falls to his death. He must have surfed too close to the edge and lost control. He was right about that, if not about *who* was responsible for it. He had seen Neema get swallowed by the monster fish. That seemed to trouble him. He contemplated it for a long time, before commenting in his boulder-grinding voice, "That was a peculiar fish."

The other gods agreed, but none of them seemed to know what to make of it beyond that. None except Lord Set. He said, "Well . . . we are talking about the headwaters of the Nile. What do you expect, Sobek? That backwater is so far south it's barely even Egypt! Of course there would be all sorts of nastiness to contend with."

I didn't really know either candidate, but I got choked up about their deaths. Tau's mentor fell to his knees and banged on the stone tiles with his fist. Loudly, he blamed himself for not having been a better teacher. The merchant girl's mentor was stoic. Only the glazed look in her eyes and the trembling in her lower lip betrayed the emotions she was keeping hidden. Lady Isis tried to console them, saying none of it was their fault and soon they would understand that things were not as dire as they now thought. They were respectful, but neither mentor seemed to take much comfort from the goddess's words. Eventually, they were both led away.

As everyone filed out of the courtyard, I noticed Sutekh and Kiya lingering near the obelisk, whispering. That reminded me of my unfinished business with Sutekh.

34

Speechless Once Again

"You're still sopping wet," Sutekh said as I approached them.

"Thanks to you."

He laughed. Glancing at Kiya, he said, "Can you believe this kid? After I plucked him off a rock at the edge of the falls!"

Kiya grinned. "You'd think he'd be more grateful, but some people can't help being sore losers." She turned on her heel and strolled away. I couldn't help but watch her go, imagining how amazing it would be if she said something nice to me.

Once we were alone, Sutekh jutted his chin at me and snapped, "Well, what do you want?"

"I want you to confess."

"Confess what?"

"That you're a cheater! That you cut Tau's sunkite line. Confess that you knocked me into the water and snatched my caracals. Just confess everything! If you don't, I'll tell on you myself." Okay, I already knew I wasn't going to do that, but I figured a bluff was worth a try.

Sutekh didn't look nearly as troubled by this threat as I would've liked. He pursed his lips. "Go ahead," he said. "Tell on me. Before you do, though, consider a few things. Nobody saw me cut that boy's line. It's your word against mine. Nobody saw me knock you into the river. We were conveniently hidden behind a boulder, you see. Again, your word against mine. What did they see? Oh, me returning with seven—that's *seven*—caracals. They saw my act of compassion in surfing out to save you." He looked past me to where his mentor had stepped back into the courtyard. He nodded to him, holding up a finger to buy a little more time. When his mentor stepped away again, he lowered his voice and said, "If you really must, go ahead and tell on me. See if they believe you . . . or if they believe me. Personally, I like my odds."

I hated the kid. I really, really despised him. He was so . . . grr. I don't even know the word for it. But he was right. I was in no position to make accusations. He was leading. I was trailing way behind. It would look like I was a bad sport, trying to blame someone else for my own failures. It was totally unfair, but for the time being there was nothing I could do about it.

"Why do you even want to be the prince's shadow, anyway? If you win it by cheating—"

"I'll be keeping up an old tradition," Sutekh cut in. "Come on, Ash. Don't be so naive. The world is a harsh place. Any advantage you can take, you should take it."

"It doesn't have to be that way."

"But it *is*," he said. "Maybe if you'd had real parents they'd have taught you that."

Have I said already that I hated the kid?

"As to why I want to be the prince's shadow," he went on. "To make sure the right people stay in power."

"The right people?"

"*My* people. My father says Neferu is too welcoming of village folk into our society. What's the use of being rich if there isn't a class to serve us? It's maddening! Khufu would make it even worse. But in *my* Egypt, the one thing I'll whisper into the prince's ear each day is that the rich shall stay rich and"—Sutekh smirked—"the peasants will stay in their place."

"Khufu would never let you do that!"

"Khufu's a weakling! He won't have a word to say about it. No, I know exactly why I want to be the prince's shadow. The real question is, why do you?"

He peered at me as if the question were a threat. I tried to think of a response. Something harsh, something as angry as I felt, something righteous and good and totally the opposite of everything he stood for.

I wanted to be the shadow to help the prince, not to control him. To be his friend, to protect him and be there when he needed me. We'd do amazing things and work for the good of all Egypt. Power wasn't about controlling things for your own benefit. It was about feeling a responsibility to others, about being as smart and wise and generous as you possibly could. That was what I would try to be. I knew it now. And what was more, I wanted to know that I belonged somewhere, that I mattered, that I had a family . . .

Wait. As soon as I thought it, I knew that was the truest of all my reasons. I was an orphan. A boy without parents who didn't know where or how I belonged, who I'd come from. If I didn't know those things, how could I ever know who I was meant to be in life?

I realized, standing there in front of Sutekh's arrogant face, that from the moment Yazen had revealed the opportunity, I'd wanted to become the prince's shadow so that I would have a family. I'd be virtually part of the royal family. I'd make Yazen proud. And maybe I'd get to ask the pharaoh who my birth parents were. I'd put that mystery to rest and I'd know. *I'd know.* My mind raced.

All this family talk reminded me of the queen. *Live,* she had said. I wondered if the secret-seeming conversation she'd had with me had been unusual. Had she told the others to live in the same way? Had she said *they* were important to Egypt's future? Or was it just me?

Sutekh stared at me, chin raised as if waiting for me to answer his question. I couldn't say any of what I was thinking to him. He'd find some way to use it all against me. I wouldn't let him do that. But considering his reason for wanting to be the shadow, it was now way more important that I—or one of the other candidates—win the testing.

After all that thinking, all I said was, "You wouldn't understand." I turned and walked away, ignoring the sound of his laughter at my back.

35

Games Played in a Skiff

All I really wanted to do the rest of the day was hide in our room and pour out everything to Yazen. I knew I could tell him about the horrible stuff that had happened. He'd believe me. I didn't think he could do anything to make it better, but I still hoped he'd try.

When I arrived back at the room, Yazen stood waiting for me. He was all smiles. The moment I stepped in, he pointed at something laid out at the foot of my bedroll. It was an ornate, polished piece of armor. A chest plate. Radiantly golden, with a scarab beetle carved into the center. I ran my fingers over the glinting metal and the green jewel set in the carved scarab's back. It was magnificent. It was treasure beyond anything I'd dreamed of back in the village. And also great protection from jaws, claws, stingers and probably even river rocks.

"What is this?"

"It's yours," Yazen said, "for completing the third day of the trials. Congratulations, Ash."

I started to strap it on to test the fit, but just then another royal summons came. Apparently, Prince Rami had invited the candidates to join him for a sail in his sunskiff.

"Really?" I asked, puzzled. That seemed strangely generous of the elder prince.

Yazen explained. "I think that the pharaoh and the gods wish to keep you candidates occupied, to keep your spirits up, as it were."

I joined the others in yet another inner courtyard. No obelisk in this one. Instead it had flowering peach trees that stretched up the walls, branches twisting and twining like dancing snakes. If I could have, I would have climbed them, perched somewhere high, and taken in the view. I'd have munched on delicious fruit surrounded by rippling leaves. I would've loved to have done that right then! But just as soon as we arrived, a guide led us away, deep into the maze of grand structures that was the royal palace.

We came out from under the pillar-supported roof and onto a raised stone platform. I was already completely lost and overawed by the riches of the capital. The view of the surrounding palace grounds was still as stunning as it had been on the first day: gold-capped pyramids and sparkling obelisks, barges, lush gardens with fish ponds, paths beneath the shade of tall palm trees, and dragonflies and beetles zooming through the sky. It was the sort of view I'd never get tired of. Never in a thousand years.

"Hey, look!" Seret said. She pointed a paw toward a long, wide thoroughfare lined with massive statues. They were far away, but I could tell they were enormous when compared to the tiny people that walked by beneath them. "It's the Avenue of the Gods."

She was right. I could make out Anubis, the god of embalming the dead. His statues always looked so stern, like he was angry about something and was just about to let you have it. I guess I'd be grumpy, too, if I had to spend day after eternal day with dead people. The plump hippopotamus goddess, Taweret, stood posed on one leg, her arms held out to the sides as if she was caught in the middle of a dance routine. Wadjet was there in full cobra form, head raised high and her hood spread in threat. I recognized a few others as well: Anukis and Isis, the moon god Khonsu, and the short, stout half-lion god Bes. He was posed with a tankard held up in one hand. According to the rumors, he had a thing for strong beer. Egypt's gods—I'd learned about them all my life, but they still seemed strange and unknowable in so many ways.

A horn blew, announcing the passing of an hour.

"Watch this!" Seret said.

While the sound of the horn still reverberated over the city, the statues shuddered into motion. The stone came alive, and they moved as smoothly as if they were made of muscle and bone. Anubis crossed his arms and looked off to the side, chin raised high. Taweret stood on her tiptoes and tented her arms over her head. Wadjet suddenly sprouted wings. She maintained her cobra head, but her body took on a vulture shape. *Bes?* He just brought the tankard to his lips and tossed back his head. He froze like that. They all did, coming to rest in new positions as the sound of the horn died.

"They move like that every hour," Seret said. "Cool, huh?"

Prince Rami stood waiting for us in his floating skiff, one leg up on the railing, looking bored to death. He nibbled on his fingernails as we approached. Beside him, Prince Khufu watched us intently.

The skiff was lean and sharp. It looked fast as an arrowhead and light as a feather. The sail was furled, but the suncloth fabric shimmered as it caught the rays of the late-afternoon sun. It looked like one fast ship. A pretty small one, too.

Prince Rami took his position near the tiller and began loosening the ropes that secured the skiff to the dock. "I can only take four passengers," he said. "More than that is too dangerous. Someone could fall out." The way he glanced at us when he said this made me think he might not mind if we did. But he finished with, "Some of you will have to wait."

Before I could even think to do it, Sutekh called firsts. A second later, he, Kiya and Mery were all aboard. They stood on the bobbing vessel, looking pleased with themselves. Sutekh made a show of offering Khufu the seat with the best forward view.

The prince looked awkward for a moment, stuck between accepting the offered seat and something else. I was as surprised as Sutekh when Khufu said, "I think

I'll let you have this first ride. I'll stay with the others and go along next time." Sutekh started to protest, but Khufu jumped from the boat to the solid stone dock. "You all go ahead. I'll just stay here and . . . chat."

It was the most I'd heard the prince say in one go. I was a bit mystified.

Sutekh could barely hide his annoyance. He did so only by plastering a smile across his face. "So right you are, prince! How rude of me to jump at the chance to go first. Just honest enthusiasm, though." He began to climb down. Kiya and Mery were right behind him. "As a matter of fact, I insist Ash, Gilli, and Seret go first. It's the least I can do, especially since they performed so poorly today. You could use a bit of cheering up, couldn't you?" he said, looking at us with his fake smile.

Once all three of them were off the skiff and back on the dock, Sutekh pushed and prodded me toward the skiff. "Go on," he said, giving me a shove that pushed me a little too close to the dock's steep drop-off.

"Suit yourself," Seret said, and leaped aboard in one powerful motion.

Gilli jumped in and called the bow seat, right up at the front of the skiff. Shrugging, I joined them.

"What sort of game are you all playing?" Rami asked, squinting at us.

I nearly told him I wasn't playing any game at all—Sutekh was. And it turns out, so was Khufu.

36

Memphis at Sunset

Khufu put on a thoughtful expression. He set one hand on Sutekh's shoulder. "A point well made, Sutekh. Very generous of you. And since—as you said—these three had a disappointing day, it's the least I can do to help cheer them. So . . ." He jumped back into the skiff.

"But . . ." Sutekh didn't get any further than that.

"Let's go, Rami," Khufu called. He slid onto the bench beside me. "Take her up and away!"

And that's just what Rami did. He threw off the docking lines and tugged the sail up to its full height. The sunskiff rose. Any fatigue I felt from the long day vanished. As the sleek skiff emerged above the level of the nearby buildings, its sail caught the direct rays of the low sun. The skiff kicked forward, straining against the one line that still connected it to the terrace.

"Ready?" Rami had the tiller jammed under one arm. With his other hand he untied the last line. Grinning, he tossed the line free. The skiff surged forward. Below us, I watched Sutekh's angry face drop away. I enjoyed that, I don't mind admitting. For once, Sutekh had been outmaneuvered. And it was the prince who had done it. I didn't know what that meant, but I was pleased.

Before long, the speed of the sunskiff captured all my attention. I had never felt such power. I grabbed for the railing, white-knuckled with fear and exhilaration. The wind tore at my face with a physical force I hadn't imagined it could have. Beneath us, the palace grounds fell away. We zipped across them, rising higher. This was nothing like the trip on the sunbarge.

"Look down there." Khufu pointed over the railing, continuing to be talkative. "See that triangular shape?"

I did. It was a small structure at the center of a smooth field. Workers and all manner of sunsail machines were crowded around it.

"It's the model for the new pyramid design," the prince said. "It's just a small one, but the architects have almost perfected the measurements. My father hopes to have one built in his honor, but it might take so long that it'll be in *my* honor instead."

Just then, the sunskiff heaved over to one side. Suddenly, instead of there being a boat beneath me, there was nothing but air and the world far below. I tried to grab for something, but I was already over the railing. And Khufu was over with me. I could see him out of the corner of my eye. His arms whirled like windmills. We were both on our way back to earth, fast.

Something caught one of my arms. I felt a searing pain and then I was yanked back into the skiff. I landed in a confusion of arms and legs and lion parts. The sunskiff righted again. I realized that Seret had grabbed both Khufu and me with her lion claws. As we untangled ourselves, Seret retracted her claws. She plucked the curved barbs of her fingernails from our flesh one by one. Looking a bit embarrassed, she said, "Sorry. I just . . . didn't want you two to fall."

"My mistake," Rami called from his post at the tiller. "The, um . . . tiller slipped."

"Well, don't let it happen again!" Khufu shouted. "You almost got us killed. If it wasn't for Seret here, we'd be"—he glanced down at the world far below—"pulp."

Rami scoffed. "Don't be overdramatic. It was just a little bump. And by the way, if there's ever to be a great pyramid it's going to be the Great Pyramid of Rami. Just don't forget who's oldest, younger brother."

"How could I," Khufu said, "with you always reminding me?"

I couldn't shake the feeling that Rami had tipped the boat on purpose. I wasn't sure why he'd do that, though. To make us scared, I guess. He was that sort of person. I could tell he liked to have power over people.

Even though Rami made me nervous, he also kept the ride thrilling enough to distract me. In no time at all we were beyond the palace compounds. We sailed over the mazelike alleys of the city of Memphis. The people were so tiny. Many of them stopped and gazed up at the sunskiff. I tried to be cool, but before I knew it I was waving down at them. I hooted and called to people. I would've been embarrassed, except that Khufu, Seret, and Gilli were right there beside me, doing the same.

As Rami carved into a long turn and began to

head back toward the palace, Seret and Gilli jumped to the other side of the skiff to take in the western view. I began to do the same, but Khufu grabbed my elbow. "In the testing this morning," he whispered, "the others helped you. Seret and Gilli, I mean."

I wasn't sure if that was a question or a statement. I nodded. "Yes, prince, they did."

"Why did they do that?"

"Because," I said, "we're friends."

He looked surprised. "Are you?"

"I mean, yes, I think so. I don't know them well, but I'd like to think we're friends."

"I see. I guess one should look after their friends."

"It's more than that, though. They're good people, prince. We all want to win, but Seret and Gilli know that's not the only thing that's important. They think we should work together, stay alive, and wish each other the best."

"And you?" Khufu asked. "Do you think as they do?"

I nodded. "Yes, prince, I do."

He looked at me for a long moment. Long enough that I started to wonder if I'd said the wrong thing. It was what I believed, but what did princes believe? Were they like Sutekh, all cold calculation and self-interest? Would I seem like some silly country boy to someone who had grown up surrounded by the intrigues of the royal court, with assassinations and demons and rivals to constantly worry about? Maybe I sounded naive. Maybe I *was* naive.

"I see," was all Khufu said in response. Then he joined the others, falling right into the loud conversation as if our whispered one had never happened.

THE
TESTING
DAY FOUR

37

The Vulture Queen

"**H**ave you given that creature a name yet?" Yazen asked the next morning.

I sat in the Cherished Ka's Courtyard with the caracal kitten in my lap. I stroked the cat's soft fur, loving the feel of it, listening to the low rumble of his purr. He'd spent the night curled up beside me on my cot.

"No," I said, "not yet. I don't want to get too attached."

Yazen chuckled. "Looks like it's too late for that! That little guy is yours for life, I think."

I almost groaned. *For life?* How long was that likely to be? I mean, there were two more testing days left. Yesterday, two more candidates had died. What would the body count be at the end of today? There were only six of us left: Seret, Gilli, Sutekh, Kiya, Mery, and me.

The caracal looked up at me with his large, green eyes. I tipped him over on his back and rubbed his belly. I tried to sound casual. I said, "Well, if I survi—"

"No," Yazen cut in. "Not *if*. *When*. Ash, you must have confidence in yourself."

"I do, but—"

"There can be no *but*! Even a small bit of doubt is too much. Think how close you came to failing yesterday. Your doubt stopped you on the river. It froze you and would have conquered you had not your friends been there with you. They may not always be, so let no doubt into your heart. Now, tell me again what you were about to say, but say it correctly this time."

"Fine," I said, a little testily. He may have been right, but that didn't mean I had to like being lectured to. "When I get through all of this and become the prince's shadow, then I'll name him. Is that better?"

Yazen didn't get to answer. The pharaoh, the gods, and Prince Khufu arrived. My eyes darted from one to the next, eager to spot the new god.

And spot her I did. It would've been impossible to miss her! A baldheaded vulture, with enormous eyes and a curved, frightening beak. Her body was squat, with black feathers that looked as sharp as razor blades. She walked in with her head held high, blinking, and looking about as if she was on display for an adoring public. Her neck was hung with jewelry, most of which appeared to be elaborate necklaces with pendant images of herself.

"Rise, candidates," the pharaoh said, "and meet Lady Nekhbet."

I bowed my head and kept my face as vacantly awed as I could.

The goddess stared down her beak at us. "They're not much to look at," she said. "Are you sure these are the surviving candidates?"

"They are," Lord Horus intoned.

"They've all done marvelously so far," Mafdet added.

Good old Mafdet. How I wished I was going to be spending the day scorpion fighting with her. That was not to be, though.

"Well . . ." Nekhbet didn't look convinced. "They won't need those weapons. Leave them here."

"No weapons?" Mery asked. The very idea seemed incomprehensible to her.

"Exactly. Leave them here." The goddess draped one of her large wings over Khufu and motioned him forward. She cautiously extended the tip of her other wing toward the candidates, as if she knew she had to make contact but found us repelling.

I handed the caracal to Yazen. He clawed at me until Yazen tugged him away. "I'll be back soon," I said, hoping it was true. I set aside my spear and throwing knives.

I reached for the goddess's outstretched wing, touching a feather along with the others.

38

A Factory Job

A factory. Lady Nekhbet took us to a factory.

She called it the Temple of Sahure at Abusir. "Dedicated to myself, of course," the goddess added. She walked along ahead of us, wafting a scent of decay in our direction that was only slightly more over-powering than her perfume. After a few inhalations, my nose burned. My head swam, though I tried not to show it.

If this was a temple, it was about worshipping the production of all things Nekhbet. Crowns, bracelets, necklaces—all of them were stamped with the goddess's image. Stonemasons carved her profile into obelisks. Teams of sculptors worked on massive statues. One room was piled high with little wooden Nekhbets.

Toys for children? In another, leather workers put the finishing touches on Nekhbet sandals. *Who would want to walk around with bobbling vulture head tassels on their feet?*

The goddess led us through massive rooms crowded with elaborate contraptions: pulleys and conveyor belts and vats of bubbling liquid and steaming, groaning, whirling gadgets of all shapes and sizes. We passed goods being loaded on to sunpowered transport sledges. The heavily laden vessels floated into the air when slats in the roof opened, letting in the sun. As the sledges rose up on Ra's rays and slid away, they were replaced by others that drifted in to be loaded.

Workers paused and bowed to Nekhbet whenever she passed near them. They gazed upon her with blissful eyes and slack jaws, as if they'd never beheld anything more beautiful.

On several occasions, Nekhbet stopped to look at her reflection in the polished bronze mirrors that ran along the walls. Many of the rooms had them. She would study her beaked face from several angles, pose with her wings outstretched, shuffle a few steps with her head held high. She'd even turn and look back over her shoulder, considering the view of her tail feathers. Every time, she concluded her examination with a satisfied grunt and said, "I've still got it."

Finally, we stopped in a warehouse at the far end of the temple, away from most of the bustling activity. As in the other rooms, a large, complex puzzle of machinery filled this space. But instead of being surrounded by workers, short, squat birds toddled about. Baby vultures. Dozens of them.

When they saw Nekhbet, they rushed toward her. I almost bolted. There's something really disturbing about having a stampede of baby vultures waddling toward you, cloth diapers around their bottoms. They swarmed around her, squawking excitedly. They thrust their beaks at her, looking like they were trying to bite her to death. Apparently, that's what passed for a vulture greeting.

"As you can see, we've been using this wing of the temple as a nursery. These," Nekhbet said, looking lovingly at the hideous little vultures, "are my grand-children."

"All of them?" Sutekh asked. He looked a little green.

"Yes, yes," Nekhbet said. She fluttered her eyelids. "In my youth I had many mates. I won't go into the details." Was that a blush that turned her cheeks pink? "The result was many children. They, in turn, have had many offspring of their own. All of them are welcome here until they're old enough to sail into the sky. I'm sure you'll agree that there's nothing more lovely than the sight of a vulture in flight?"

She asked the question wistfully, but as soon as she said it she cocked her head to one side and studied us with one of her bulging eyes. We fell over ourselves agreeing with her.

"Nothing so grand as a vulture on the wing!" Sutekh said.

"The sight of them soaring always brings tears to my eyes," Seret claimed.

Kiya said she prayed to one day be transformed into a vulture, and Gilli did a strange little dance, flapping his arms like wings and thrusting his head forward and back. I did my part as well, which was mostly pretending to be the wind that lifted the vulture version of Gilli up into the air. Not sure that went over that well with the goddess.

"Candidates, your task is simple. These machines produce just one item." With a wing, she gestured at the contraption upon which several of the baby vultures climbed and banged, pecking at it with their beaks. "A wonderfully flattering and very protective necklace in my image. Anyone wearing one of these carries my blessing, a small sliver of my strength."

Oh, that made sense. Her necklaces were like the tiny pendants of Mafdet that kids wore back in the village to defend against snakes and scorpions. Nekhbet's were probably a bit more expensive, though.

"As an added bonus," she said, "anybody wearing one can't help but look gorgeous. Behold . . ."

We stepped up to one of the conveyor belts. On it was a long line of pendants shaped like a vulture with her head turned to the side and wings flaring out, with a ring so that they could be attached to a necklace chain. They looked to be solid silver inlaid with colorful gems and highlighted with metal-flecked paints. Each pendant was large enough to cover a person's entire chest. Whoever wore it wouldn't so much be adorning themselves but walking around as a free Nekhbet advertisement for all to see.

"They're in great demand in Buto," Nekhbet said. "Candidates, you will spend the day working the production line. You will each have your own conveyor belt to manage."

We were going to spend the day working in a factory? Making vulture necklaces? Was she serious? I was starting to think nobody had told her why we were spending the day with her. Did she think we were just looking for jobs? Well, of course we were, but not *this* job.

"Here's how everything works. Listen carefully and don't interrupt."

She explained that once she turned the machine on, molten silver would feed down from the vat in which it bubbled. The silver poured into molds to make vulture-shaped pendants, which were then dropped onto another conveyor belt. That was where our job started. We had to inspect each pendant for quality and inlay it with various colored jewels. We had to get the pattern just right, setting each glimmering stone into the slot prepared for it. "No improvising," she said. "It's perfection already. No need to attempt to improve upon it."

Before I knew it, we were all standing with smocks on, a pouch of precious stones in one hand and a small jeweler's hammer in the other.

"I'll leave you all to get on with it. The prince has asked to see my temple at Buto."

"I have?" Khufu scratched his head.

"Yes, yes. You'll love it. We'll come back and check on their work later." Then, as if it were a casual afterthought, she added, "And do look after the young ones for me. A factory can be a dangerous place, but I trust you'll keep any harm from befalling them. They'll be no bother. They're wonderfully well-behaved."

I looked from the goddess to the vulture toddlers. *Well-behaved?* The chicks doddered about, completely uncontrolled. Several bounced on the conveyor belts. Still more climbed high up on the machines. Some jumped into the air, careening toward the floor despite the frantic flapping of their little wings. One of them pecked up jewels in its beak, tossed them into the air, and swallowed them!

The goddess didn't seem to find any of this disturbing. She took hold of a lever in the wall and cranked it. The ceiling opened, letting a flood of light cascade down onto the necklace-making contraption. It rumbled to life. The cauldron began to bubble. The belts began to move. Gears and levers jolted into action.

After Nekhbet left, dragging a reluctant Khufu along with her, Kiya mumbled, "Is it just me, or does this kinda suck?"

"It *definitely* sucks," Sutekh said sourly.

Gilli pursed his lips, considering. Then he grinned. "Look on the bright side."

"What's the bright side?" Seret asked.

"It's safer than fighting cave demons!"

Good old Gilli. He had a point. I said, "Yeah, you're right. I mean, what's the worst that could happen?"

Into the Cauldron

From a hillside upwind of the Temple of Sahure, Lord Set watched as Lady Nekhbet rose into the sky, carrying Prince Khufu. He had arrived alone this time, having slipped away before Prince Rami could pester him. Nekhbet had keen eyes, and that nose of hers wasn't to be taken lightly, so Set waited as she moved away. Truth was, Set was a bit afraid of Nekhbet. They'd had a little disagreement a few hundred years back. Set still remembered the beak lashing she'd given him.

The goddess flew on wings that grew larger and larger as she circled on thermals of heated air. She turned her bald head toward Buto. Set had little doubt that she was on her way to show Prince Khufu her other temple.

He leaned back, using a long fingernail to pick at bits of food stuck between his teeth. Nekhbet flapped her wings every now and then, covering miles with each slow stroke.

Deciding the coast was clear, he strolled inside the temple. He knew from experience that Nekhbet's minions had eyes only for her, so he strode through the bustling factory with no regard for the workers. He ignored them; they ignored him. It wasn't until he located the candidates that he resumed being stealthy. Crouched atop a sledge piled high with Nekhbet jewelry boxes, he took in the scene from a short distance away.

She has them working like common peasants, *he thought.* Well . . . some of them are dusty villagers. *The candidates darted from point to point along the conveyer belts, working furiously with a flock of vulture babies under their feet and flitting about.*

This wasn't at all ideal, Set thought. Not a demon in sight. No wild animals to enrage. Nothing more frightening than a bunch of little vultures in diapers. He considered a spell that would bring the factory roof crashing down, but . . . if he got caught he'd have Nekhbet as an enemy for at least a thousand years. The thought of that made him shudder. He needed to get a closer look at their work if he was going to figure out a way to turn this ridiculous test against the candidates.

The god leaped from the sledge as it began to rise with the power of the sun. Landing lightly on his feet, he slipped through a maze of crates, squeezed under a partition, and quickly passed a group of workers, sucking in his snout and tufts to momentarily blend in. With the candidates distracted by their work, he dashed into the shadows of the warehouse. He climbed silently up the back of the scaffolding at the far end of the necklace machine, then headed for its upper reaches.

His long arms and legs made quick work of it. He came to rest on a platform beside the cauldron of molten silver that fed the machines. The precious metal slowly boiled within it.

"Nekhbet and her love of silver," Set mumbled. "Silver and jewels. Jewels and silver."

A thought stopped him midsentence. "Silver, huh?" he mused. "What if . . ."

And then he had it, a spell that just might take out all the remaining candidates at once. It was incredibly simple. Any novice magician could create it. He spun the spell in his mind and felt it take physical form in his mouth. He hocked it up and, with a pucker of his *rubbery lips, spat it into the vat. The spell hit the liquid metal with a fizz and a small puff of smoke.*

"There," he said, "good luck dealing with that."

40

Keep Your Diapers On!

At first, the relentless oncoming motion of the conveyor belt was unnerving, necklace pendant after necklace pendant sliding toward me, each one with a new one appearing just behind it. I started tapping the jewels into place with the hammer. It didn't seem possible to place all the jewels into their little slots before the pendant would tumble off onto the waiting sledge, especially not with the way my fingers trembled.

The important thing was to be quick, efficient, nimble, and precise. I was trained for all those things. I just had to adapt them to a production line. If I set the stones as carefully as I'd aim a throwing knife, they fit right into place. If I tapped them with the hammer like I was releasing a knife, I could hit them just right. My fingers loosened and I let instinct take over. I knocked the last scarab emblem into place just as the first necklace tipped off the end of the belt onto the waiting sledge. *There. Done!*

I glanced around at the others. Kiya had finished her first necklace and was already on the second. Mery was just a few seconds behind her. Sutekh had a vulture toddler trapped under one of his feet as he worked. I thought Seret might have a hard time with the delicate work, but she pinched the jewels between the sharp points of her claws. She slotted them into place with precision, and then slammed them snug with the flat of her paw.

Gilli had ended up with a different job: trying to grab a restless flock of toddlers that were swarming around, bouncing up and down on conveyor belts, climbing on and over pretty much everything. He had his hands full, that was for sure.

One after the other, piece by piece, I tapped gems into place. Pendant after pendant tipped off the conveyor belt. I was starting to think I'd actually pull this test off—maybe all of us would. We could all survive. I gently tapped a ruby into place, admired my work, and then stretched to set another stone into the vulture's wing tip.

Blink. *Did that emerald eye just blink at me?* No way. I figured it was a trick of the light as it flashed off the pendant's emerald eyes.

Nope! The pendant's head rose and darted forward. Its beak opened and clamped onto my wrist. I heard a snap. Pain seared up my arm. I cried out. I wanted to yank back my arm, but I was pinned motionless, in agony. My arm, I knew, had been broken.

The silver vulture looked as surprised to be alive as I was watching him move. As the conveyer belt inched along, devious thoughts seemed to whirl behind the jeweled bird's eyes. They flicked from my face to my wrist. The bird's head lifted from the conveyer belt and opened its beak, not to let me go, but to snap down that much harder. I pulled my arm away just in time. The vulture's sharp beak scythed together, making the ear splitting sound of two blades sliding over one another. The first bite had been just a peck. The second would've cut my hand clean off.

"It's alive!" I yelled, scrabbling backward across the floor.

"Stop trying to distract us!" Sutekh shouted. He

had two wriggling vulture chicks under his foot now. Not the guy to employ as a babysitter, that was for sure.

"I mean it. One of the necklaces is actually alive!"

The flat crest of a necklace freed itself, peeling up from the conveyor belt. It stood there a moment, jiggling along, staring at me. Its eyes flashed with malice. It leaped to the floor, then lifted one foot by tilting over, wobbling there a moment, and swinging the upraised leg around. That was one step forward. It leaned over the other way, a bit more steadily this time, and swung through another step.

I slid farther back, barely managing to get to my feet. It was hard, with only one good arm. "Hey, everyone?"

"Hey, put that diaper back on!" Gilli yelled. He obviously wasn't talking to me. Or even looking at me. "Everybody, keep your diapers on! Don't fling that at—"

By the wet thwack that cut off his words, I had a pretty clear picture of what the diaper had been flung at.

Kiya shouted, "This one's alive, too!" Seret growled. Mery shouted, and Sutekh danced away from his conveyor belt, trying to kick free the silver vulture that had clamped down on one of his ankles.

I tried to keep my eyes on the shiny vulture in front of me. I was cornered. When it opened its beak and hissed, I thought I could use some diapers myself. With its wings outstretched, it bore down on me, beak yawning open and closed.

We had our hands full, and me without my knives or spear—with only one good arm!

41

A Quick Plan

Just as the silver vulture was in my reach, I leaned back and planted a solid kick right across its middle. If I'd kicked a person like that, they'd have hunched forward in pain. Not so with the vulture. It was still metal. The creature knocked back a few paces. Its eyes flashed with anger, and it came at me again.

I bolted. Not the bravest thing to do, but I needed time to think. I ran toward Gilli so fast that I crashed into him, almost knocking the chick out of his arms. He said, "Hey, watch it!" He didn't turn to face me until he'd finished tying the toddler's diaper back in place. "What are you doing here? You're supposed to . . . Your arm! Did the machine do that?"

"No!" With my good arm, I pointed at the marching silver vulture. Behind it, another jumped off the belt, and still another rose up from it.

"No way," Gilli said, finally realizing what was happening.

The first of the silver vultures was getting close.

"Let's get out of here." I grabbed Gilli by the wrist and started to pull him into motion.

"But we can't! The chicks." Gilli motioned behind him to where the oblivious youngsters still waddled about. "We can't leave them."

"All right," I said. "You round them up and get them on a transport sledge. I'll keep those things distracted until we can all get away."

"Not with that broken arm, you won't!" Gilli said. "You can't do anything with it dangling like that. Here, let me at least bind it."

He reached down and tugged loose the knot of the nearest chick's diaper. He snapped it in the air with a flourish that, I think, was meant to empty it of any contents it might hold. The vulture squawked with delight at being free of it. I squawked in protest as Gilli wrapped it around my chest, pinning my broken arm in place.

"Quit your shrieking," he said, knotting the free ends of the diaper snugly. "It's for your own good. Now go!"

The first silver vulture was near enough that I could hear its metal talons scratching across the stone floor. It nipped at my heels as I darted away, biting down on the stone instead of my flesh. As it screeched out in frustration, I watched another silver vulture spring to life from the conveyor belt and focus its emerald eyes on me. That gave me my first proper idea yet. I had to turn the machine off, which meant I had to get to the lever on the far wall.

"I know what to do!" I shouted as I sprinted past Seret, who was in the thick of it, surrounded by pecking vultures. "Help protect the chicks!"

"I'm having enough trouble protecting myself!" She swatted one silver vulture away, kicked another.

Darting and dodging to get through the silver vultures, I tugged on a wingtip and knocked another flat with a leaping two-footed kick. For a moment I slid across the floor on top of that one, grinding silver against stone. I leaped off when I saw the vulture take aim at one of my big toes. Then I sprinted past the conveyor belt to the lever on the wall.

I hadn't noticed before how high it was on the wall.

I jumped. Missed. Jumped again. Nothing but air. It was just a little out of my reach.

Clicking and scratching across the floor, the silver vultures were getting closer.

I took a few steps back, ran forward, and planted one foot on the wall. I pushed up off it, and *just* got a grip on the lever. My arm went taut, my full body weight pulling down on it. Nothing. I just hung there. I tried yanking, twisting, squirming.

Nothing worked. I wasn't heavy enough! *Why isn't anything ever easy?* I wondered, dangling dejectedly. Where was everyone else?

I spotted Gilli trying to herd the baby vultures onto the sledge. Seret had joined him. The chicks weren't making it easy for them. One or another of them would leap away, or slip between their feet, or just go into a full-on tottering run, looking delighted in the way that only little kids can at causing mischief. Maybe they weren't so bad after all.

Pain seared up from my toe. First the right leg, then the left. The silver vultures had me by the toes. They pulled. My grip was failing. My good arm didn't feel so good anymore. It felt like rope, floppy, muscle-less. I was just about to let go and drop into the silver misery below me.

But then the lever shifted. Another vulture clamped onto my ankle, and the weight of it was enough to drag the lever down. I heard the conveyor belt shudder to a halt. The entire contraption stopped, just like I wanted. That would put a stop to it producing new little metal bird monsters. Perfect. Except . . .

The lever snapped. I fell down into the silver vultures gathered beneath me.

42

The Fallen Girl

I hit the floor hard, flattening one of the vultures beneath me. The collision knocked the others back, spinning across the floor. I was in a world of pain, with my broken arm at the center of it. The impact knocked the air from my lungs. I banged my head as well. The factory ceiling twirled sickeningly above me. That was when I saw Sutekh, who was perched on top of one of the conveyor belt frames, smiling as he watched the show going on beneath him. I was about to shout at him, but I had a more immediate problem to deal with.

A silver vulture climbed on top of me. It was heavy, wings outstretched, its head off to one side in profile. When it turned to look at me straight on, sunlight flashed from its jeweled eyes.

The creature drew back its beak to strike. I didn't let it. Instead, I levered my legs back and sprung to my feet. The vulture fell to the floor.

Once upright, I kicked furiously at the mass of silver beasts. Every which way, crazy combinations of snap kicks and roundhouse kicks and back kicks. I still held the snapped-off lever, and I swung it like a club. I couldn't tell how many of them there were, but a few more must've climbed from the conveyor belt before I turned the machine off.

I managed to keep the metal vultures back, but I couldn't do so for long. My feet were taking a pounding, and the vultures were unrelenting. I wasn't hurting them at all. It didn't seem possible to hurt them. They were metal, after all. I could pound on them all I wanted to. They just kept coming back for more. I had to get away.

I smacked one vulture after another, knocking them back until I had an opening. I dashed through it, then down and around the other side of the machine to get a view of the others. I prayed Seret and Gilli had all of the chicks on a sledge by now. If they did, I'd yank down on any lever I could find until the roof opened up, charging it with power. We'd float away, leaving the silver menaces behind. Assuming they couldn't fly, that was.

Please, don't let them be able to fly! I thought.

As I passed the long mirror that Nekhbet had preened in earlier, I turned to see Gilli and Seret. The scene I beheld took my hopes and tossed them off a ledge. Try as they might, Gilli and Seret couldn't control the chicks. As quickly as they tossed one on the sledge, another two of the little rascals leaped off and wandered away in another direction. Our plan was never going to work.

Especially not without everyone helping! I looked around for the others. Sutekh was still atop the scaffolding of the necklace machine. Kiya was now climbing up to join him. Perched high above the chaos, neither of them was in any danger. The vultures couldn't fly. They couldn't climb either. Sutekh grinned and slapped his knee, busting up about all the trouble Gilli and Seret were having.

Kiya shouted something down to the factory floor. I looked over to see Mery starting to climb up toward her. The floor beneath her thronged with silver vultures, more even than had gathered below me. "Climb!" I whispered. I hadn't ever talked to Mery. I only knew her name. But there were so many vultures below her.

Kiya's ochre locs dangled as she looked down. She swiped them to the side and stretched out her arm. I breathed a sigh of relief when Mery reached up and clasped Kiya's hand. All Kiya had to do was pull her up. Kiya held her as the girl strained to reach the top, her feet slipping and losing traction with every passing moment. And then . . . Kiya let go of her. Mery fell, her arms and legs wheeling in the air. She dropped right down into the swarm of vultures and disappeared among them.

Kiya looked at Sutekh. He nodded and bowed respectfully, congratulating her on a job well done.

I shouldn't have been shocked. I had seen Sutekh's treachery already, and I knew Kiya was in league with him. But still, seeing someone betray another person like that drained all the hope out of me. I swore right then and there never to be foolish enough to like Kiya, or believe that she liked me. So what if she had the prettiest eyes I'd ever seen? So what if the way she fought was awesome and I kept wanting to ask her stupid things like, *So Kiya, what's your favorite color?* None of that mattered now.

If only Lady Nekhbet was here! Or the prince! But they weren't. Sutekh and Kiya had no witnesses but me, and just like before, it would be my word against theirs.

Cradling my busted arm against my chest, I slumped back near the smooth mirrored wall. I was out of breath and soaked in sweat. The silver vultures fanned out in front of me, trapping me. Their beaks snapped in anticipation of carving me up. Their heads swayed side to side menacingly. I closed my eyes, trying to focus, to think of any way to defeat these things, but I came up empty. What a way for it all to end, sliced to pieces by living jewelry. At least I'd lasted until the fourth day. That was a good showing. I could be proud. All I had to do now was fight with the last drop of my strength. Nobody would be able to say I was a quitter. I straightened as tall as I could and opened my eyes, ready to go out swinging and kicking with everything I had.

I chose the nearest vulture to attack. Lifting the lever, I prepared to swing and . . .

And nothing. I didn't get any farther than that. The vulture wasn't attacking. Instead it shifted to the side, trying to see something behind me. All of them were doing that. They stared behind me, transfixed. What was so interesting?

I stretched my good arm backward, wondering if there was some new horror there. My fingers touched the smooth surface of the wall. It was just the wall. Or . . . not just a wall. It was a mirror. They were looking at themselves! Slowly, cautiously, I began to slide along it. They still didn't attack, just moved with slight aggravation to see past me. A few steps, and I was out of their way, which was just what they wanted.

As soon as they had an unobstructed view, they fanned out, each fascinated by its own reflection. New ones arrived to join them. They posed. They postured. They lifted their wings and studied their profiles. They shifted so that their jewels flashed, delighted by the effect.

"Why is it so quiet over here?" Seret approached cautiously, Gilli just behind her.

"Ash, you got them to stare at themselves!" Gilli exclaimed.

Seret put a paw on my shoulder. "That's brilliant, Ash! Great plan!"

"Well, it wasn't exactly a . . ." Then noticing how

complete the silence was, I asked, "Why are the chicks so quiet?"

"They fell asleep," Seret said. "Just all of a sudden. They all dropped where they stood. Tired out, I guess."

"Hey," Gilli whispered. "Ah . . . something's happening."

One of the silver vultures must have heard us. It turned and looked at us. And then a few others did. One of them snapped its beak, as if remembering how tasty we were.

"This isn't good," Seret said.

Gilli looked around. "If I had a stylus . . ."

The silver vultures began to converge on us again. This was going to be a full-on brawl. I lifted the lever, which was bent and warped from use.

"Hey!" Gilli called. "Let me have that!"

He jumped up and grabbed the lever.

43

Strike a Pose

Before I could ask him what he meant, Gilli began drawing in the air with the lever.

"What are you doing?" Seret asked, claws out and ready to fight.

Then we saw. Hieroglyphs sparked. They glowed, dimly, but they were there. Somehow Gilli was using the lever as if it were a stylus. The snapping of beaks and clicking of metal feet on the stones were all around us.

"Gilli . . . ," I began.

Gilli finished a set of glyphs. He circled it and slashed in the closing stroke. The spell shot out. The nearest of the silver birds froze. It had just opened its beak and thrust its head forward to bite Seret. But that was as far as it got. It stayed in exactly that posture, completely still. The energy faded from its eyes. Instead of living gems, they became regular gems. One by one, the others did the same. Each of them froze, each in a different pose. Whatever energy had animated them vanished. They became statues of themselves.

When it had sunk in that we weren't about to be sliced and diced by silver vulture beaks, I asked, "What just happened?"

"I had a hunch," Gilli said, holding up the lever, "that since this was from a god's magical factory maybe it would have magical properties. So I made up a spell for stillness. I guess it worked."

"Good hunch," I said.

Gilli shrugged. "Like I said, magic is my thing. I mean . . . I want it to be, at least."

Just then, Nekhbet arrived at a swift waddle. Khufu jogged to keep up with her. "What's going on here?" She made directly for the collection of motionless figures. The goddess craned her long neck around, taking in the silver vultures from various angles. "This is most irregular. Most irregular, indeed."

"Ah . . . ," I began. "You wouldn't believe this, Lady Nekhbet, but—"

"Why, these aren't even necklaces anymore! You've made them into statues."

"That's because they came to life and—"

"And in such varied poses! Perfection yet again. It's to be expected, though. They are images of me, after all." She glanced at me, her one eye cocked and waiting to hear my affirmation. After I'd agreed with her, she squinted at the impromptu bandage Gilli had wrapped around my broken arm. "Odd way to use a diaper. Just goes to prove what I always say—'There's no accounting for what the youth call fashion.' Now, where are my young ones?"

"They're here, Lady Nekhbet," answered Sutekh. He and Kiya approached the group. I couldn't believe it. Both of them cradled sleeping chicks in their arms! "No need to worry. They were safe with us all along."

"Safe with *you*?" Gilli snapped. "Why that's an outright—"

"Look at my beauties!" Nekhbet gasped. "What's lovelier than such a sight? Nothing in the world, I tell you. I haven't seen them sleep so soundly in some time."

Khufu followed all of this with a perplexed expression on his face.

Sutekh gently brushed his nose across one chick's beak. "I have a way with children. Just a gift, I guess. And Kiya sung them lullabies."

"A gift!?" Gilli exclaimed at the same instant that I shouted, "Lullabies!?"

Seret began, "Lady Nekhbet, that's not the way it actually—"

"Now, now," Nekhbet said, snapping her beak in disapproval. "You can't dispute the obvious facts. While you were amusing yourselves with statue arrangement or something, these two were caring for my grandchildren. I find that highly commendable. I'd ask you to reflect on it. Now, let us return to the courtyard and report to the pharaoh." Pausing, she asked, "Weren't there more of you?"

"Yes, Lady Nekhbet," Sutekh piped up, "but the other girl fell to her death." He glanced at me, his eyes sharp.

The goddess made a tutting sound with her beak. "That is indeed a shame. Industrial accidents are one of the hazards of the business. On we go, then."

"But what about her"—I swallowed and said the word—"body? Shouldn't we get her or something?"

"Oh, there won't be any body," Nekhbet said. She

added, "I mean, don't worry yourself over it. Everything's being taken care of."

And that was that. She zipped us back to the courtyard. She announced Mery's death like it was a minor detail, and then she proclaimed the testing largely a failure. "Not one of the candidates succeeded at the task I'd assigned them. The statues are beautiful, of course, but I'd specifically asked for necklaces. As a result, no points will be awarded."

I wasn't the only one who groaned at that. I guess if no points were to be given my score at least didn't get any worse for it. That was something to be—

"Except"—Nekhbet squinted her large eyes nearly closed—"for Sutekh and Kiya. They did no better than the others in the manufacturing department, but they did look after my grandchildren. I saw with my own eyes the gentle care they gave them. For that, let them both be rewarded. One point for Sutekh! One point for Kiya!"

"So be it," Pharaoh Neferu said.

Lady Nekhbet conceded that since we'd survived we deserved a reward. This time, it was an armband to be worn above the biceps. Looking at mine, I wasn't surprised to see an engraving of the goddess herself.

I had to admit, it was pretty stunning.

But still, I was angry. Sutekh and Kiya had gotten away with it again! Just like last time, I couldn't see any way to reveal them that wouldn't make me look like a sore loser with no evidence. Seret and Gilli would back me up, but they hadn't actually seen what I had. We'd probably end up having points deducted.

There was one thing I had to say, though. As Kiya walked past me to leave, I whispered, "I saw what you did."

She stopped and turned those large eyes on me. My face flushed, and not just with the anger I felt. "I know you did," she said, leaning close so that nobody would hear her. "And yes, I'd have done the same thing to you."

"Don't you care about anyone?" I asked.

"I do," she said, "but . . . I have to win this."

"We all want to win."

"But I *have* to! My mom . . . You don't know what she's like. She'll disown me if I don't win. She's all perfect and famous, and my sister is going to inherit her position in the warrior clan. I've got nothing without this."

I nearly told her she was lucky to have a mother at

all, but the words stuck in my throat. Some things, maybe, are too true to say out loud.

Kiya's face softened a bit. "Ash, if we'd met in a different time and place . . ." She seemed at a loss for what to say next. "Things would've been different. But they're not."

She spun away and was gone before I could respond, before I even knew what to make of what she'd said.

No Bouncy Balls!

That evening, the remaining candidates were called to Prince Khufu's section of the palace. There weren't that many of us. Just Seret, Gilli, Kiya, Sutekh, and me. All of us a day away from the final testing. Who knew what that would be?

I should have been more curious about the prince's quarters. If I became the prince's shadow I'd be living right in the palace, surrounded by luxury and riches. I should have wanted to know all about it, right? I wish I had, but I was tired. Tired of seeing kids eaten by monsters and pecked by jewelry. Tired of worrying about the few people I could truly call friends. Tired of not knowing what was coming next. Tired of becoming more and more certain that either Sutekh or Kiya was going to beat me, Gilli, and Seret.

I was also late arriving. One of the royal physicians had treated my arm. It was a clean break, he said, likely to heal as good as new. He splinted it with a cast made of molten gold. Must've been magic, because he poured it right onto my arm. It wasn't hot, but it was liquid enough for him to shape it. He let it set for a moment, and there I was: the boy with the golden forearm. I kinda liked the look, even if it was still sore.

I was escorted as far as the last long hallway that led to the prince's quarters. I hurried down it. It was lined with statues of various gods, and of members of the royal family. They certainly liked to make statues of themselves. I wondered if anybody had ever made a statue of a shadow? Probably not. We were only shadows, after all . . .

"You're late." Prince Khufu stepped out from behind one of the statues.

"Sorry, prince," I said, bowing my head. "I . . . I had to get this taken care of." I waved my broken arm.

"Of course," he said. "How is it?"

"Sore, but it could've been worse."

He frowned. "Yes, I know." He looked uncomfortable for a moment, and then he perked up. "Come,

I'll show you around myself. The others have already begun the tour."

He began to lead me down the hallway. I immediately felt awkward. How do you speak to a prince? He wasn't a normal kid, after all. Suddenly, I couldn't think of a thing to say.

"So how did you get to be such a good fighter?" Khufu asked.

I wasn't sure that I was such a good fighter, actually. Sutekh was stronger. Kiya was faster. Seret had all sorts of lioness skills. Gilli was more impressive than he looked and knew more magic than me. I probably didn't need to point these things out. I was here for a job, after all. "Just lots of practice," I said. "My mentor never lets me off easy."

"That's good. I knew the testing was going to be hard, but I didn't know how hard. I guess your mentor knew how to prepare you."

I guffawed. "Prince, I barely feel prepared at all."

"But think about all the things you've done so far!" he said, growing more animated. "The way you tricked the Jackal-Headed Demon into biting his own tongue. The way you threw knives at the Three Demons of Whirling Vengeance. All those scorpion demons. I doubt any soldier from my dad's royal guard would've done better against them. And that trick with using your toes to wield your knife . . ."

I blushed. "That's nice of you to say. I just wish I had the points to show for it."

"Yes, there's that. Doesn't seem fair, does it?"

For a moment, I thought about telling him what had happened today—and on the other days. He'd believe me, I thought. He'd do something about it. But I hesitated. What if he didn't believe me? That could make everything worse. I didn't get the words out, and then the moment was gone.

"Show me some fighting moves!" Khufu stopped in the middle of the hall, suddenly excited by the idea.

"Right now?" I looked up and down the empty hallway.

"Yeah. My father keeps promising me that I'll get military training, but he keeps putting it off. Too afraid of something happening to me. Possible heir to the throne and all that. Let's spar a bit. I don't mean really fight, with your busted arm and all. Just show me a few things."

"Shouldn't we get to your rooms first?" I asked.

Khufu glanced to the door at the far end of the

hallway. "It's probably better to do it here. My servants are kind of overprotective. Just show me a few techniques. Pretend I'm an enemy assassin. You've just found me. I attack you . . ." The prince made some vague motions with his hands. "What would you do?"

I demonstrated a few kicks, some blocking moves, how to swipe a person's legs out from under him. At first I was cautious, worried both about my hurt arm and about the prince. But Khufu was a quick learner. Before long we were dancing through a choreographed fight routine. I forgot how tired I was and started to have fun. Things were going great, until I accidentally jabbed my elbow into Khufu's side. The prince let out a cry and went over.

I said, "Sorry, I didn't mean to—"

That was as far as I got before the door to the prince's quarters slammed open. With a speed that amazed me, round figures erupted out of the room. They bounced from ceiling to floor, wall to wall.

"Oh no," Khufu exclaimed, "not bouncy balls!"

45

Servants of the Prince

The shapes ricocheted down the hallway toward me in a mad blur. Urns smashed. Tables shattered. Statues teetered and fell. The creatures converged on me so quickly I couldn't even make out what they were. One slammed right into my face. Another into my gut. Two more took out my legs. They bowled me over and took me to the floor.

"No!" Khufu called.

I did my best to roll and kick and try to get away, but as I fought I just got more confused. If my mind wasn't playing tricks on me, the creatures pummeling me were about knee high. Instead of regular faces they had . . . rounded snouts? And, even stranger, they appeared to have bright blue skin.

"Stop it this instant!" Khufu said.

The attackers paused.

I squirmed out of their grip and struggled to get to my feet. Without thinking, I pushed up with my broken arm. Pain seared through me. I barely managed to stand. I paused, shocked motionless. The attackers were short, plump, standing on two legs, but were . . .

"Blue hippos?"

"You better believe it!" one of them said, just before he landed a jumping round house kick on my jaw. We all went down again, a chaos of limbs and snouts. Before I knew it, I was on my back. Pinned. One of the hippos, realizing my arm was damaged, twisted my wrist. The little brat! Several took turns jumping on my belly, knocking the wind out of me. One knelt on my chest. He cocked back his pudgy blue foot, ready to strike. He said, "This is going to hurt you more than it hurts me!"

I was pretty sure the little guy was right.

The prince shouted so loudly this time the corridor went still and silent. "Servants of the Prince, obey!"

The hippo's foot stopped just above my cheek. It stayed there, the tight wedge of hooved toes squeezed hard as a stone. The hippos still held me down, but they had all turned to stare at the prince.

"Don't harm him! I command you to release him!"

"Release him?" one of the hippos asked.

"Yes. He's one of the candidates!" Khufu exclaimed. "Can't you see that? He's not an enemy at all. Never use the bouncy-balls technique to attack him again. It's too dangerous."

"Yeah, but it's so much fun," another hippo said.

"Still, don't use it. You might hurt him. He's Ash, you ninnies!"

"This is Ash?" the hippo with his knuckles brushing my chin asked. He didn't sound convinced.

Another peered down at me. "Ash, the jerker of jackal tongues?"

"Yes, that's him." Khufu pushed the hippos away and helped me to his feet. "You were going to meet him inside."

The hippos stared up at us. "Can it be," one asked, poking me with a stubby finger, "that this is Ash, the bane of baboons?"

"He doesn't seem like much of a fighter," another one said.

"Hey, I've got a broken arm!" I protested.

The hippos ignored me. "Do you promise it, prince?" another one asked. "This is Ash, the antagonist of Ammut?"

"Yes, I swear it. We were just sparring together. I didn't expect you to attack him."

All the hippos seemed to understand their mistake at the same time. They flushed a vibrant shade of purple and began to mumble apologies. I tried to stay angry, but it was hard when the little guys were so cute. At least, they were cute when they weren't walloping me. They pulled both of us down the hallway now, chattering merrily as they did so.

Once inside the spacious series of connected rooms, Khufu said, "The others must be in the lower terraces. They'll be back in a minute. Let's just wait."

He asked the hippos to prepare mats on the terrace. He sent others to steal choice bits of food from the banquet tables. The hippos shot off in different directions, all of them with looks of determination on their blue faces. Several leaped right over the balcony edge and vanished.

Khufu's quarters were as sumptuous as you'd expect. Plush couches, ornate tables and chairs, cushions everywhere. Incense scented the air and, from somewhere I couldn't see, a musician plucked out a tune on a stringed instrument. The rooms blended into one another, many of them open to the wide terraces that overlooked the palace grounds. My whole village could've lived in here, but this was all for one boy. It was still hard to get used to.

"Let me show you something," Khufu said. He led me to one of the large balconies that provided an amazing view of the palace and the city beyond. "Have you seen *The Mistress of Light*?"

I stepped up to the railing and looked down into an enormous square plaza. In the center of it, floating just off the ground, was the largest ship I had ever seen, way larger than the barge that had brought me to the capital. It was magnificent, all smooth, flowing lines. The way it moved slightly with the air currents, pulling against the ropes that tethered it to the ground, made it look as light as a feather. It obviously wasn't very fragile, though, since people clambered all over it, moving supplies onboard, adjusting the rigging, and doing whatever the crew of such a vessel had to do to care for it. Scarab beetles crawled across the hull, but from where I stood, I couldn't make out what they were doing. Even though the sails were furled, I could see their shimmering, delicate suncloth rolled along the spars. Banks of oars jutted out from either side, at least a hundred of them. They weren't like normal oars that river ships used, though. They were delicately thin, with curving scoops that looked like the petals of a lotus flower.

"After the testing," Khufu said, "whoever becomes my shadow will take a trip up and down the Nile with me. We'll sail in *The Mistress of Light* and see all of Egypt, stop in at every city. It'll be a celebration of sorts."

Celebration? If that was the case, I wondered why he didn't sound more excited about it.

A little later, once we were seated and munching on the small food parcels the hippos had returned with, Khufu said, "I argued with my father."

"You did?" I asked. I couldn't imagine anyone arguing with Pharaoh Neferu.

"I said he should end the testing. You've done enough. All of you have."

I felt a slight inkling of hope. "What did he say?"

Khufu dropped the small meat-filled pastry he'd just picked up back onto the tray. "That tradition has to be honored. That the testing has to continue to the very end. No exceptions."

"Oh," I said.

Khufu's glance shifted away again. "I wish it didn't have to be this way. When I'm pharaoh . . . I mean, *if* I become pharaoh, I'll change the tradition. What's the use of ruling a nation if you can't change things for the better?"

I thought of the conversation I'd had with Sutekh. Suddenly, it seemed important to succeed, to be there for a prince who wanted to change things for the better.

I wanted to say something more, to tell him how much I agreed, but the words didn't come quickly enough. The sonorous voice of the palace guide announced the return of the others. With that, my private conversation with the prince was over.

46

A Tale of Two Boys

A few hours later, when I returned to the room I shared with Yazen, he was waiting for me. "Ash, there's something I must discuss with you."

"Can it wait till tomorrow?" I asked. "I'm dead tired."

His face was grave, his forehead lined with deep wrinkles. "No, it can't wait. I've just come from a meeting with the pharaoh. He has given the mentors leave to speak about a change in the testing tomorrow."

Suddenly, I was a bit less tired. "A change?"

Yazen pointed toward a chair, indicating that I should sit. This wasn't sounding good.

"So far you've competed with the others," he said. "Tomorrow you will not only compete with them. You'll also compete *against* them."

"What's the difference?" I asked.

Yazen exhaled. "I know that some of the candidates have been devious. They've managed to get away with it. The difference, Ash, is that tomorrow they don't have to hide their treachery."

"You mean that Sutekh and Kiya will be able to just attack us? They won't even have to hide it?"

"Yes. This tradition, Ash, was developed in a distant, harsh time. Candidates don't *have* to turn against each other, but"—he shook his head—"they often do. Tomorrow you can trust no one. You must think of yourself first, Ash. All the others will surely do the same."

"Not all the others," I said. "Gilli and Seret won't turn against me."

"How can you be sure?"

"We made a pact—Gilli and Seret and me—to help each other."

"But you cannot win together, Ash. There will be only one shadow for the prince. Your pact is at an end, I'm afraid."

"They're my friends!" I said. "I finally have friends and I trust them. If you had any friends, you'd know what I mean. You don't, though, do you? No, all you've ever had is me! Sometimes I wonder if this whole shadow thing is about me . . . or if it's about you." I hadn't actually ever wondered that, but the words just came out. Once I had said them, they fed my anger and frustration even more. "It's not your life that's on the line. It's all on me, and if I win you'll be famous, won't you? Mentor to the prince's shadow. That's what you care about. That's why you'd have me kill my own friends!"

Yazen stared at me, mouth open, face drooping, looking shocked like I'd never seen him before. I thought he was going to storm out of the room. He didn't. Instead, he covered the space between us in two long strides. He slid in beside me and wrapped his arms around me, like when I was a small child and needed comforting. I tried to push away, but he pulled me into his embrace. I had no intention of listening to yet another lesson, and yet the first thing he said— and the fact that he whispered it in a tone of voice I'd never heard before—disarmed me.

"I am not asking you to harm your friends, Ash," he said. "You couldn't do that even if you tried. You're too good a person to do that. You're pure of heart. That's the best thing about you. Not your fighting or knife throwing or any of your tricks. What makes you the son that I love is that you are kind and fair and honorable. You care about other people. In this world, Ash, those are rare, precious traits."

I twisted in his grip, not wanting to let my anger go easily.

"I know the testing is unfair," Yazen continued. "Believe me, I know. If I could take any of the burden from you, I would. If I could lay down my life for you to live, I would do it in a heartbeat. That would be an easier course than letting you face these trials again and again."

I made a half-hearted attempt to squirm away. I was listening, though.

"There are some things that we've never spoken about. Some we never can, such is the burden of our roles—both mine and yours. You should know that all my life I've been a soldier for Egypt. I was very good and that got noticed. You are not the first candidate I've mentored."

That got my attention.

"I never spoke of him. It hurt too much. Ash, for twelve years I raised a boy, one whose name I haven't said in years. I fed him and clothed him and taught him everything I could. All the time I hated that I would have to bring him here one day and release him to the demons. I thought many a time of fleeing with him, taking him to a foreign land to live out a long, safe life. But they would've found us. I knew that I was watched, always. The pharaoh commands; we obey."

Yazen drew back. "So I brought him to Memphis, and to his death on Day Five of the testing. That's tomorrow, Ash. I was overcome with anger and sadness and regret, but mostly with shame for the part I played in leading him to his death. I fled the city, vowing never to take part in this again. Yet here I am. Here you are. And here, again, is day five."

I couldn't grasp all of what he was telling me, but I knew it was big. He'd spent years struggling with things I'd not even imagined. "That was for Pharaoh Neferu's Shadow Testing?"

"It was. Another candidate passed the testing, and she became Neferu's shadow. Aniba was a good person, a skilled warrior and magician, but I'm sure she regretted the things done to win her post. She—"

"Wait," I interrupted. "Did you say Regret*ed*? *Was* a good person? Is she . . . dead? Is that why she hasn't . . . been around?"

Yazen looked uncomfortable. "That is not for me to discuss, especially not today of all days. Point is there was much to regret. And I know the pharaoh feels that way as well."

"But you're still part of it," I said. "All of you: the pharaoh, the gods, you." I didn't mean it as an accusation. It was a question. Why was he still part of it, if he despised it so much? He gave me an answer, one that I hadn't expected.

"I am still part of it because of you, Ash." He frowned and kneaded his forehead with his fingers. "When they brought you to me, I refused to accept you. I swore I would never mentor again. I wouldn't adopt another son, watch him grow, and then let him go. I couldn't. That's what I said." He inhaled a long breath. "The man who delivered you said many things to me, but in the end it was two things that made up my mind. One, he said that if I wouldn't do it you would go to another mentor, a person I knew and despised. That gave me pause, but I said so be it. Let him take up the burden. But the man did one last thing. He went to the basket in which you lay. He picked you up and pushed you into my arms. He pulled back the hood from your face and ordered me to look upon the boy who I wished to refuse. I looked at you and I saw . . . a boy I instantly longed to call my son. A boy I wanted to live, and thrive, to see grow into a man. A boy I was already proud of, for the courage in his tiny eyes." He looked at me, his own eyes red and tearful. "I could refuse the pharaoh, but I could not refuse you, Ash."

THE
TESTING
DAY FIVE

The Ruins of Katara-Nesur

The morning of the final test, we gathered together once more to wait for the attending gods. Though I'd spent all the testing days worrying, I felt even more worried today. Glancing around at the others' expressions, it seemed like we all did.

We shone in our armor, chest plates glinting, wrist guards and arm bands in place. We looked more like warriors—more like shadows of the prince—than we ever had. The armor fit each of us differently, as if it was molded to our different body shapes and sizes the moment it touched our skin. If not for the gravity of the day, we'd all have been prancing around, keen to show off our new look. Not today, though. We knew today would be our biggest challenge yet.

"Now, candidates," the pharaoh said, "you have only one more challenge to face. But it is to be the greatest challenge. I trust your mentors have prepared you for how this test is different from the rest?" He pursed his lips and looked us over.

One by one, we nodded.

"All right, then," Neferu said. "I'll say no more about it. Meet the god who will oversee your final testing . . ."

For the first time, the tester was a god I'd met already. Lord Thoth. Not him again! Hadn't he already tested me—kind of, at least—on the first day? What if he had some magical test in mind? Something about Divine Writing and scholarly studies and ancient spells and all that? I know he claimed I had special talent, but I was sure he was wrong. I'd been freakily lucky that first day. That was all there was to it.

"Candidates," Thoth said in that strange, clipped voice of his, "I see no need to dally any longer. This needs to be concluded, whatever the outcome."

Easy for you to say. You're not the one on the line here.

I didn't say that, of course. I didn't do anything other than glance briefly at Yazen. I tried to put a lifetime's worth of gratitude into that momentary gaze. It was all I had, but it wasn't enough. I knew it. More than ever I wanted to live. Not just for myself, though. Not just for the prince. But for Yazen.

We vanished before I even felt Thoth's touch. It was the quickest trip of all. In a blink, we were someplace else. A ruin. An abandoned palace cut into the side of a mountain. Slabs of broken stone, tumbled pillars, dry pools, structures with their roofs long caved in, walls blackened by fire. On one side of the palace rose jagged granite cliffs. On the other, a wide expanse stretched away from the ruins, a once fertile valley sectioned into pastures. I could still see the geometric order of the overgrown fields and the lanes between them. It was silent in the ruin, except for the wind.

"This place, Katara-Nesur, was once the capital of Egypt," Thoth said as he led us through the rubble. "This is where Egypt's two most powerful magicians— Teket and Djedi— battled one another. They were both incredibly gifted. I trained them myself. For a time, they were fast friends, but later Teket's nature twisted. It may have happened when Neferu chose Djedi instead of Teket as the royal magician, but I suspect the evil was hidden within him before that, a seed waiting for the right moment to grow. He became wicked, bitter, power-hungry."

The god stopped at the crumbled remains of a terrace wall. Propping one foot up on a stone, he inhaled deeply. His face had a wistful quality, as if he was remembering the glory that had once been Katara-Nesur. "Jealous that gods were set apart from humans and that all Egyptian magic came from Lord Ra's union with the sun, Teket began experimenting with another sort of magic, a dark form that didn't depend on the sun. He came to believe that his power could rival that of the gods. He quarreled with Neferu, and his rage turned murderous. Once, when both I and Lord Horus were away from the city, Teket snuck into the palace and attacked the pharaoh and his wife while they slept. Aniba, Neferu's shadow, defended them bravely. She held Teket back as best she could, but in the end the queen perished. And Aniba . . . Teket destroyed her with a powerful spell."

"Perished?" I asked. "Destroyed? Both of them? But Queen Heta . . ."

"Is the pharaoh's second wife," Thoth said. "His first wife was mother to Rami, who was just a babe when this happened. Heta is mother to Khufu. This is rarely spoken of, but you must understand the pains of the family you will hopefully serve."

Khufu looked down, suddenly interested in the texture of the stone at his feet.

All this time I had thought the royal family was perfect. I guess they weren't. Things had happened to them just like to anyone. Tragedies as well as all the pomp and circumstance of being royal.

"Because Aniba fought so bravely," the god said, "Djedi was able to arrive in time to save the pharaoh. He drove Teket from the palace and chased him through the sky on winged magical mounts. Teket—"

"Winged magical mounts?" Gilli repeated. "What are those?"

Thoth clicked his beak. He seemed annoyed at being interrupted, and then a bit confused. "Well, they were . . . a bit like lizards. But larger. Quite large. Massive, really. And a bit like birds. Though not with feathers. I mean to say . . . I'm not entirely sure what they were. I wasn't there, you see. May I continue?"

"Oh, yeah, please," Gilli said.

The god fluffed his plumage, and then resumed: "Teket, who was injured, sliced a hole in space-time and escaped. Djedi followed him through it, knowing

Teket had to be fully defeated or the world would never be safe. Neither of them was ever heard from again.

"Afterward, Neferu moved the capital to Memphis and had Katara-Nesur razed to the ground. He ordered for it to be forgotten. So great was his grief that this tragedy still hangs heavy on his heart.

"Though years pass, Neferu still hopes Djedi will one day return. We all share that hope. We also all share a fear that it won't be Djedi who returns, but Teket instead. If he has somehow survived, he will be terribly powerful by now. That is why we have come here, to the place of that original battle. If Teket returns, the royal family will be in grave danger, including Prince Khufu.

"Therefore on this, your last day of testing, I have a difficult task for you. First, you no longer need those . . ."

Thoth snapped his fingers. Something changed. For a moment I didn't know what. And then I realized that my armor had disappeared. I looked down. My spear and throwing knives had vanished as well. "Hey, what—"

The others were mumbling the same thing. Kiya looked around for her staff. The sword that had hung at Sutekh's side was nowhere to be seen. Gilli patted his chest with both hands, as if doing so would make his chest armor reappear. None of us had any weapons or any of the armor we'd earned up until this point.

"Today," Lord Thoth said, "you face a greater foe than can be defeated with wood or iron weapons. Instead, you will require an instrument of greater finesse."

Another snap of his fingers and something was in my hand: a slim, slightly curved sliver of metal with a bejeweled point. "A stylus," I whispered. Oh no, this was going to be a repeat of the first day of testing! Only this time, I was sure I wouldn't be nearly so lucky.

"We have to do spells?" Seret asked. She didn't exactly sound pleased. She stared at a custom-made stylus that attached directly to the point of one of her claws. She carved little shapes in the air, testing it.

"Yes, you have to do spells. Let me show you why."

Thoth's stylus was suddenly in his hand. He began to draw. His stylus point carved radiant blue hieroglyphs that hung in the air. His arm moved so quickly it blurred. In no time at all, the air crackled with the energy of row upon row of Divine Writing.

The characters didn't fade like mine had during the first day's testing. If they had, there was no way he could have drawn a spell this complicated. It went on and on.

Eventually, Thoth closed out the cartouche and pulled back. He slashed in the closing stroke. The glyphs swirled into each other, twisting and changing. Soon, they began to take shape. A person's shape, etched in glowing blue lines that quickly became solid. Light and energy formed into flesh, and soon a man dressed in a flowing robe stood before us. His face had strong, prominent features. At first, his eyes were closed, but the moment he was completely formed, they opened. He looked us over. A malicious gleam twinkled in his eyes. He grinned as he sized us up.

"This is a version of Teket," Thoth said. "He is only a spell, but he is gifted with the powers the magician once wielded. Think of him as if he were Teket himself, returned once more to wreak havoc."

The magician snapped out his wrist. A blue stylus appeared in his hand. He tilted back his head and let out a rumbling laugh. I didn't just hear it. I felt it. It made the ground beneath me vibrate. The next instant, the magician leaped into the air. He carved a spell above his head as he did so. It ignited and he went scorching up into the sky. He flew as if for the pure joy of it, looping and diving, shouting and laughing as he did so.

"But," I pointed out, "I haven't been trained in magic. Not really, I mean."

"That is unfortunate. The study of true magic takes years, but the world's villains often strike when you are least prepared." Thoth began to float away, pulling Prince Khufu along with him. He said, "We will watch from a safe distance. Candidates, defeat this evil one if you can. Your final test has now begun."

48

Collaborative Spell Casting

We all tensed for action, styluses held at the ready. I could feel the magic in mine, sizzling inside the metal, ready to ignite. There was power in it, and I itched to use it. But I wasn't sure what to do. The moment I began to compose a spell against the magician, Sutekh or Kiya would probably wallop me with a spell of their own. Everyone's eyes darted around. Even Gilli and Seret—both of whom I wanted to trust—looked at me nervously. None of us wanted to make the first move.

"Listen to me, everybody!" It was Sutekh. He pinched his stylus against his palm with his thumb and held his hands up. "Before you do anything, just listen! I know they've made it seem like we should fight each other at the same time as we fight the magician, but let's not do that. Let's work together. If we don't, we might all end up dead. That's not what's best for the prince."

"You expect us to believe that you only care about what's best for the prince?" Seret asked. Like all of us, her eyes jumped from person to person, and then back up into the sky, where the magician still carved loops in the air.

"Of course I care about the prince!" Sutekh said. "This is all for him, after all."

"Hey," I protested, "that's not what you said when—"

"Forget about what I said before! None of that matters now. What I'm saying is that if we attack him together, we have the best chance of defeating him."

Kiya crouched low, with her stylus at the ready. Pretty as ever; deadly as ever. "Yeah, and then who wins?" she asked.

"We all do," Sutekh said. "Let's finish this challenge together."

We all hesitated. I wanted for us to fight together, and suddenly it did seem like the thing that mattered most was getting through this together, even if

Sutekh or Kiya ended up as the prince's shadow. Maybe Sutekh was changing for the better. It certainly sounded like it. Still, I had to be sure. "Sutekh," I said, "you're saying things you never would've said before and you know it. What's made you change?"

Sutekh looked pained. "This test," he admitted. "I'm no good at magic. Never have been. I can't win this by myself, but I could help enough that we could win together. Come on! The magician's not going to just fly above us forever."

Kiya flipped her long locs back from her face. She spoke through gritted teeth. "You'd better not be lying."

"Wait!" Gilli said. "We're not going to trust him, are we?"

"Do you have a better idea?" Sutekh asked. "Think fast, because Teket is coming back."

He was right about that. A boom shook the air, announcing his return. The robed form was shooting toward us at an incredible speed.

"What do you want us to do, Sutekh?" snapped Seret, sounding angry that she was even asking the question.

"We make a spell together. All of us. We all draw

glyphs. Whatever comes to mind. Explosions and fire and arrows and stuff. One of us closes it in a cartouche. And one of us ignites it."

"And I suppose you want to be the one who ignites it!" Kiya spat. "Fat chance of that!"

The spell-magician slowed, drawing up and hovering in the air high above us. He made my skin crawl, just hanging there watching us. But he didn't attack. Instead, he only looked amused.

"No, I won't ignite it," Sutekh whispered. "You can ignite it, Kiya. Or you, Seret. Ash or Gilli. I don't care who does it, even if it means that person gets credit for the spell and becomes the prince's shadow. Let's just finish this. That's what matters."

He really meant it. He must have if he was willing to lose so that we could survive. He was actually doing the right thing. Maybe all the death and cheating and lying had finally gotten to him. Not a moment too soon, either. "Yes," I said, "let's finish it!"

Teket slowly descended to the ground, landing on his feet as if he'd just been out for a little stroll. He twirled his stylus, inviting us to fight. We were ready for it.

"Now!" Sutekh cried.

All of our styluses began writing at the same time, carving out glowing glyphs that crackled and popped with energy. I wrote like crazy, throwing any glyph I knew that seemed like a weapon into the spell. A sword. A knife. An angry rhino. A flaming monkey. An exploding turtle egg—hey, I was improvising! I didn't see what the others wrote, but we were making one massive confusion of a spell.

The magician drew back a step. Some of the arrogance fell from his face. He must've been reading it, seeing it for the incredible confusion that it was. He wouldn't be able to block it. It was going to work. I knew it.

And then we were done. I stepped back, out of breath, gazing at the wall of flickering glyphs in front of me. Gilli stood at one side. Seret and Kiya on the other. Sutekh was still working, putting the final strokes to the giant spell of Divine Writing. He wrote a few extra lines, small glyphs that I couldn't make out. Then he closed the cartouche. He stumbled away, gasping, "Ignite it!"

"This is my spell!" Kiya shouted. She shoved Seret to one side, me to the other. Then she pushed Gilli back, making him stumble. Her eyes found me and hesitated for a moment. She mouthed, *I'm sorry.* At least I think that's what she said. I didn't get a chance to make sure because she slashed the massive spell into life.

Nobody, I think, was more surprised than she was by what happened next.

49

Betrayal

Everything that we'd put into the spell burst into life: flaming monkeys, all sorts of weapons, something that looked like a two-headed hyena, claws that slashed the air, crocodile jaws. There were more things writhing in the spell than I could make out. It was a raging storm. I worried the parts of it would fight themselves instead of the magician. That didn't happen. But it also didn't attack Teket.

Instead, the whole glowing mass turned and flew at Kiya. One moment her face was bursting with exhilaration over her victory. The next, she disappeared in an explosion of magic so strong it knocked the rest of us off our feet. I flew head over heels and landed, skidding, on the sand. My ears pounded. I couldn't see. Sand filled my mouth, making me gag and cough. It felt like a hundred zebras had kicked me all at once. I lay until my breath came back and the roar in my ears died down. Then, painfully, I climbed to my feet.

Magical residue rippled in long, slithering ribbons in the air, mixing with a haze of dust that made it hard to see. Blinking, with one hand shading my eyes, I stumbled back to where Kiya had stood. She wasn't there anymore. The ground had been cratered by the explosion. I peered down into it. Nothing but blackened stone and sand.

"Kiya?"

Seret climbed to all fours. Her fur was charred and smoking. "What . . . what went wrong?"

"I don't know," Gilli said, limping in from the other direction, "but I think I know who does."

"I'll tell you what happened!" Sutekh shouted. He marched toward us through the shifting bands of magical smoke. His face was a grimace of anger. His stylus danced before him, writing a spell with amazing speed. So much for his claim that he was bad at magic! He slashed it to life before any of us could respond.

A barrage of glowing blue arrows scorched at us. I had enough time to draw the first few characters of a shield spell, but no more than that. The arrows would surely have taken us all out if Seret hadn't leaped forward. Roaring, she reared up in front of Gilli and me, her claws out.

"Seret, nooo!!!" I screamed.

The arrows slammed into her. For a moment she was captured in silhouette, her lioness shape caught in shadow in front of the magical blue light. Then she vanished.

I fell to my knees, miserable. I couldn't believe what had just happened. Seret gone? Dying to protect Gilli and me? It couldn't be true. "Not Seret . . ."

"Oh, yes," Sutekh said, his voice filled with triumph. "You stupid peasant! You're so easy to fool. All of you were."

Gilli pulled me back to my feet with one hand even as his other drew glyphs with his stylus. "Why, Sutekh?" he spat.

I tried to keep one eye on Teket as Gilli spoke. He still didn't attack. He just rose above the ground, smiling like a predator. I guess it made sense. Why should he bother with us? We were destroying each other for him!

"You even killed your own partner!" Gilli screamed.

"Because I don't just want to win. I want to be the last one standing. The only one. I want total victory." Sutekh stopped a little distance away. Like Gilli's, his stylus etched glyphs in the air. They weren't any one particular spell, just the pieces of one so that if he needed to attack he could do so with a few strokes. As soon as any of his glyphs began to fade, he drew new ones to replace them. "As for Kiya, what did she expect? I wasn't going to share being shadow with her. She knew the time would come for us to fight each other. I just beat her to it."

The spell-magician studied us with an amused expression on his blue face. The air began to blow around us, electric and buzzing.

"You did something to that spell," I yelled toward Sutekh.

"I added a few lines to turn it back to its sender. Clever, huh?" He grinned. "The only thing that annoys me is that Kiya got too greedy at the end. Shoving you three away was the only thing that saved you. The spell *should've* killed you all at once. Oh well, I'll just have to finish you off one at a time. And then I'll take him on by myself." He cocked his head to one side.

My eyes darted back toward the spell magician. Teket's bemused expression was now an all-out sneer. He rose above us as if he wanted a better view of the fight. I watched him a moment too long. Another mistake. I shouldn't have looked away from Sutekh at all.

Sutekh dashed off a few quick glyphs, then closed and released a spell. A massive blue hand formed before him, fingers spread wide. It looked like a giant's hand that had just been thrust up from beneath the earth. It surged toward us. I jumped left. Gilli jumped right. I rolled, spun, and came up facing the hand. I didn't even think. I just wrote. It was a simple glyph, but I finished and cast it. The spell's glowing images shot above the hand. They formed into a solid rectangle that I hoped was as heavy as stone. Just as the hand began to turn to swipe at me, the block dropped. It pinned the hand to the ground for the briefest moment, until the hand puffed into vapor. The block fell to the sand and vanished.

While I took care of the hand, Gilli ran for Sutekh, cursing him in colorful ways that I'd never imagined before. He threw lightning bolt spells, one after another. He was fast, seriously fast. Each time, the air cracked and the ground shook.

Sutekh dodged them, tossing back his own spells when he could. Gilli pressed his attack so hard I thought he might be winning. When Sutekh stumbled into the crater the exploding spell had made, I said, "Yes. You've got him!"

Gilli must have thought the same. He dashed up to the edge of the crater, a new spell ready to be slashed. In that moment, he didn't look small at all. He looked powerful and confident, with the tool he was born to use held high in his hand. He had just drawn back his stylus, when a glowing tentacle snapped up from the hole. It wrapped around his legs and yanked him into the pit.

Gilli was gone.

50

A Few Styluses Too Many

Sutekh climbed out of the crater. He dusted himself off. His eyes found me. "So it's just you and me—oh, and the magician. When it comes down to it, he'll be the hard part. He's smart, isn't he? Letting us fight each other until there's only one left." We both glanced at the grinning spell-magician who was moving closer to where we now stood. "Shame for you to come so far only to lose now. I'm faster than you. Try throwing anything you want at me. I'll beat it every time. So long as I have this"—he jiggled his stylus—"you're no match for me."

I had the sinking suspicion that he was right. I knew that Lord Thoth had thought there was something special about my glyphs, but I'd never truly believed it.

All I did was write things in my sloppy writing. I still felt I'd been lucky that any of them had worked. Even if I did have some talent, it was clear that Sutekh had more training. If I stood here exchanging spells with him, I'd eventually lose.

Think, Ash, I told myself. *Think! What would Yazen say if he were here?*

"Come on, try me," Sutekh said. He began pacing. "You want to go out fighting, don't you? Take your best shot."

My best shot. That was exactly what I needed. But what was my best shot in this case? I could sense that I almost knew. An idea was there, but it was just at the edge of my mind. I couldn't quite grasp it, especially with thoughts of Seret's and Gilli's deaths tormenting me. But I *had* to think of something. Not just for me. To honor them and make sure they didn't die for nothing.

"And do try to think of something more complex than a stone block."

I could see the tip of his stylus, tracing energy as he paced. He'd be able to block most of the things I could throw at him. So there had to be a better way than that. But what? And then I remembered something Yazen used to say. *Your opponent will always rely on the weapon that makes him strong.*

"All right," Sutekh said, "I've given you enough time. If you won't finish this, I will."

There was no more time to hesitate. The glyph I made was fairly simple. Just a few wavering lines for the object itself, and then the symbol for the number one thousand, which I hoped I remembered correctly from the mathematical equations Yazen had made me study.

Sutekh watched as the glyphs floated toward him, swirling as they changed shape, growing in number. By the time the cartouche hovered over him, it was clear what I'd made. Hundreds of styluses. They were each the exact size and shape of his. They bobbed in the air above him.

"This is the best you can do?" Sutekh guffawed. "Dancing styluses? You belong in the circus, not the palace."

That's when the styluses converged on him. They all rushed down, fast as arrows. He wrote a spell, casting a protective orb around him. The styluses stuck on it, just like he wanted. It was protection against magic, but I was betting it wouldn't work against a physical attack. I ran toward Sutekh and kicked through the orb, my foot passing right through it, right into Sutekh's gut. He hunched over, letting go of his stylus. It spun into the air with the others. They all rained down, clattering to the desert floor. Hundreds of them, falling all over each other. Sutekh snatched one up. The stylus melted away as he moved it. He tried another and then another, growing more frantic with each attempt. He scrabbled around on all fours, but he couldn't find the real stylus.

As Yazen said, *Your opponent will always rely on the weapon that makes him strong. If you cannot defeat him, disarm him instead.*

I stood with my stylus before me, sparking like the anger I felt. Sutekh, realizing his search was futile, looked up at me. For the first time, there was real fear on his face. There was no faking that look. He was beaten, and he knew it. Nearby, Teket began to laugh. The sound of it clattered through the air.

I might have killed Sutekh right then and there. I was angry enough to do it, and Teket wouldn't have stopped me. He deserved it, didn't he? He was a murderer, a cheat, a villain who would do anything to get what he wanted. And if he became the prince's shadow, he'd only get worse. There were thousands of reasons to wipe him from the face of the earth.

I drew back my hand to start writing. I could think of a lot of different weapons to make, or creatures that would devour him, or explosions that would do to him what he had done to my friends. But as I stood with his life at the mercy of my stylus I realized something. I hadn't wanted those spells to be used on my friends. And, truth be known, I didn't want to use them on Sutekh, regardless of how much I hated him at that moment.

"No," I said. "I'm not going to kill you. I'm not like you. Gilli wasn't either. Seret wasn't. They were my friends. You probably don't even know that means. But know this—you've lost, Sutekh. You'll have to live with that and with all the terrible things you did for nothing."

My spell had begun to fade. I reached down and plucked up Sutekh's stylus from among the fading spell ones. I cracked it over my knee and tossed the two pieces down on the ground. I looked toward Prince Khufu, who was still far away, watching from a higher section of the ruins. I knew he'd be as sad about Gilli and Seret as I was. They were his friends too.

He would understand what I was feeling.

As I turned to walk away, I realized Lord Thoth had been standing just behind me. He studied me for a long moment, his ibis eyes more intense than I'd ever seen them. "You have done well, Ash," he said. "You triumphed in more ways than one, and you have become the last remaining candidate. But this test is not over. Rally yourself. You must still face the magician."

51

Something Horrible

Set groaned, stepping out of his light portal. Not Katara-Nesur! It was the wrong location entirely. Such isolation and desolation. He had hoped to just unleash Ammut on the candidates and be done with it, but the Devouress of the Dead's appearance here would most certainly raise questions. She couldn't claim to have just been hanging out in the ruins having a picnic or something. If she appeared here there would be a full-on investigation.

Set was on dangerous ground, but what else could he do? He wanted the candidates dead, and Ammut was keen to oblige. Back in the foul caverns of her lair, the demon had blathered on about how she would tear the children limb from limb, rip them into pieces and grind

*them into a paste that she could spread on crackers. With
her eyes rolling about, her jagged confusion of teeth, and
her fetid breath, the old crocodile-lion-hippo had been
pretty convincing.*

*The god caught sight of Lord Thoth and the
candidates. They were a good distance away among the
ruins. He squinted, bringing the scene into focus.* But
what's this? *he wondered.* Only one remains? *That was
better news than he could've hoped for. The fools had
likely turned against each other. Typical.*

*And it got even better. Once Set understood what the
glowing blue shape was, he made a pleased sound low
in his throat.* Thoth, you old fool, *he thought,* you've
doomed them and you don't even know it. *With godly
clarity, he saw exactly what was happening and why.
Thoth was going to make the remaining boy fight a
spell-magician version of Teket.*

*For years, Thoth had been trying to find another
Djedi. Ever since the magician disappeared, Thoth had
been longing for another student of his skills. He was
blinded by his own pathetic hope that he might once
again mold a perfect student. But clearly the remaining
boy was no Djedi. And he certainly wasn't up to scratch
against Teket.* That guy had ambition, *Set thought*

wistfully. Real ambition. They could've done wonderful things together. Too bad he had to go and vanish . . .

In the distance, the glowing Teket floated up into the air. He carved out a spell with his stylus and ignited it. The glyphs in front of him formed into a throbbing red cloud. It grew, bulging and twisting, slowly taking shape.

Set stared openmouthed. Yes, he thought. Yes. Unleash something horrible!

What dropped from the air and landed in a cloud of dust was indeed something horrible. Something that looked like it could've been dragged up from the slimiest crevices of the underworld. It was also disgustingly fleshy, a massive, formless blob, wrinkled and blubbery. Hairs as tall as a boy's arms sprouted from it, as did red pimples and festering sores. It blinked open bulging black eyes. They turned and fixed on the boy. The thing opened its cavernous mouth. It squirmed forward, its whole body convulsing in waves. The boy turned and ran.

"Oh, this is delicious," Set whispered. He said it softly, but had to duck behind a rock when Thoth turned toward him. For an ibis, he had good ears. Set decided he'd better clear out. Why not? The boy didn't stand a chance against that beast. Set would rejoin the

other gods and be able to sit with them as they waited,
thus thoroughly assuring that the boy's demise couldn't
be blamed on him. Ammut wouldn't be happy, but he'd
bring her some fresh raw hearts to chew on. That always
calmed her down.

Set tiptoed away.

52

New Tricks, Old Tricks...
What Tricks?

I was running again, slipping in the rubble, jumping over debris, dodging around pillars. The slug monster thing Teket had created was enormous! It could've eaten an army, much less one boy. It was complete overkill, really, and it did nothing to improve my opinion of Teket. The beast squirmed like crazy, smashing through the ruins coming after me.

This was how magicians fought each other? Didn't seem very scholarly. I couldn't really say, though, and I couldn't ask anybody either. Thoth had rejoined Khufu where they continued to watch from a distance, far away from me and the danger. There was no Yazen to speak calm advice. No Seret. No Gilli. Not even Sutekh or Kiya. Just me.

Back on that first day of testing, I had used spells made up of simple glyphs to attack Ammut. It worked then. Maybe it would work again. I needed to defeat Teket, but I couldn't do that with this monster chasing me. What I needed, I decided, was a spell to take out Teket's spell.

I snapped around and tried to remember the glyphs I'd used against Ammut. What were they? A basket! That was the first one. I drew it. Next was ... a chicken. I began to draw, but a chicken wasn't quite right. I didn't want the thing trying to peck the monster to death. No, not chicken—an *eagle*! That was what I needed. I drew it, though I wasn't sure I'd made it eagle-y enough. The squiggly line that I called a viper was easy, but it took me a little longer to scratch out Ra as the rising sun. Even as I drew, I could see the beast coming closer, sickeningly huge.

As my first glyphs began to fade, I circled the spell into a cartouche and ignited it. To my delight, the spell formed just as it had before. The glowing basket looked magnificent. It hung in the air a moment, crackling with energy, and then it surged at the monster. The basket burst open and the winged serpents hissed their fury as they converged.

"Take that, slug!" I shouted.

I spoke too soon. The monster did take it. It opened its gigantic mouth and swallowed the lot of them. For a moment, I felt dizzy. The ground seemed to shift under me. The monster's eyes rolled back to me. It burped.

Teket, from his floating vantage point, threw back his head and laughed. At least someone was having a good time!

I leaped to the side as the creature surged at me again. I took off down a lane, hoping to lose the beast in the maze that had once been the town outside the palace. Several times, I stopped long enough to send new spells at the monster.

I sent anything at it I could think of. A magical spear? Nice idea, but the beast caught it in its mouth and snapped it like a twig. A pillar of fire? Impressive, but the slug squelched right over it with barely a sizzle. A three-headed lion? That was a weird glyph, but it worked. The cat bounded at the slug like it was going to tear it to pieces. Instead, it ran right into the monster's mouth. The trap slammed shut and that was that. No more three-headed lion. I gasped, feeling like I'd been punched in the chest. I was beginning to think there was nothing that thing couldn't eat.

I stumbled into a wide plaza, paved with enormous granite slabs. I could tell that they had once been painted wonderful colors. It must've been beautiful in the city's heyday, but that was before. Now, the artwork was faded, the stone weatherworn and eroded by sand. I paused. There was a bigger problem facing me than art appreciation. The plaza was a dead end. In front of me and on either side, collapsed pillars leaned in a great jumble, like a whole forest that had been uprooted by an earthquake. There was no way out, except for the way I'd come in, and that . . .

I spun around.

. . . was blocked by the foul creature that slid toward me. The monster's squirming wasn't so frantic now. It seemed to know I had no place to go.

I backed up, trying desperately to think. Yazen had more than one thing to say about dealing with an opponent's strength. He'd always said, *We are weakest in the ways that we are strongest. Remember that, and you'll be a match for anything.* I wasn't sure he'd say that if he saw this thing, but . . .

What was this monster's strength? It hadn't actually done anything except chase me around. And eat things. *That* was its talent. It could eat anything I threw at it. I'd never been very good at that. Sensitive stomach, you see. Yazen had scolded me so many times for . . .

". . . wasting a mountain of food," I whispered.

That gave me an idea. The glyph I drew had likely never been drawn before, and would likely never be drawn again. "Here, eat this!" I said, slashing the spell to life.

53

A Short Attempt at Negotiation

What did I drop in front of the monster? I sent it all the scraps of food I'd ever left on my plate over my entire life. Times a hundred. All the meat and chicken bones and fish heads. All the moldy bread and gloppy gruel and cement-like porridge. Every vegetable I'd ever slipped into my pocket while Yazen wasn't looking. I made sure it was all just as rotten and gross as I imagined it to be, one big mound of uneaten yuck.

Seeing it, the creature couldn't have been more pleased. Its eyes grew wide. Its mouth opened in an enormous grin, and it chowed down. It took it all in, every fly-speckled, fungus-sprouting drop.

It munched and crunched and slurped. When the entire mountain of rot was gone, the creature's mouth closed.

"There," I said, "you're full, aren't you?"

Apparently not. It began to inch toward me.

And then something happened.

The monster jerked to a halt. A tremor ran down its long body. A low, gurgling rumble came from inside it. Its eyes—that had a moment before seemed so ravenous—went blank. Another tremor shook the monster's blubber. It burped, which was really unfortunate for me, since I was standing right in front of it. The gas it expelled was awful, like no awful I'd ever smelled before. The only thing that kept me from passing out was the collapsed pillars I was leaning against. I'm sure I turned a serious shade of green.

The monster turned even greener. It had been hideous before, but now it was hideous *and* had one whopper of a stomachache. Inside of it, everything it had eaten—the mountain of rotten food, the three-headed lion, the flying snakes—must've blended together into a foul, gaseous stew. The monster realized it, too. Its eyes rolled down, as if the beast was trying to look inside itself. The grumbling, sloshing commotion grew louder every moment.

"Ate something that doesn't agree with you?" I asked, with mock concern.

That did it. The monster heaved itself around and began to squirm away. But it was too stuffed. It rolled over, belching and groaning. Its eyes twirled in circles and its mouth trembled each time putrid air blasted out of it. Just as I was sure it was about to explode, it vanished, leaving nothing behind but a cloud of swirling gas.

I punched the air triumphantly. "Yes! Gotcha, you—"

The spell-magician cut my celebration short. He drifted down from above and landed in the ruins. When he touched down, he seemed unsteady on his feet. He shook his head, blinked, and then looked at me. His blue features scowled. "You shouldn't have done that," he said. His voice was cold and strangely distant, as if he spoke from far away. "You were clever in defeating that other boy, I'll admit. I was starting to like you. Now I'll have to revise that."

Starting to like me? He had a funny way of showing it. "I've beaten you," I said, hoping against hope that it was true. I'd defeated his monster, hadn't I? That seemed reasonable grounds for calling it quits. "This is over. You lose."

He didn't agree. He shook his head. "We've only just begun, you and I."

"Why don't you leave me alone?" I said. "I never did anything to you. Just go back to where you came from."

The magician's scowl just got more disdainful. "This is where I came from. Egypt. This place, Katara-Nesur, is my home. It won't be long before I return for good. Believe me, I am making plans."

I did believe him. He seemed so real, so mean and powerful. "Why don't you just fade away? You're only a spell. None of this even means anything to you."

Raising a finger, the magician wagged it in the air at me, like a village elder chastising a naughty boy. "You are wrong. This place means everything to me. I did away with the queen and would've done the same with the pharaoh. I'll soon finish what I began. First, though, I'll dispose of you."

Faster than I'd ever written before, I drew the glyph for a spear and hurled it.

I thought I was fast, but the magician's stylus

moved in a blur. A glowing arm sprang up, caught the spear and flung it back at me. I ducked just in time. My next spell twirled through the air a moment later. A frying pan. Hey, I had to think fast! It wasn't the only random object I threw at him. Magical chairs, a statue of Anubis, an angry crocodile, a rain of toads. I just drew whatever came to mind. I couldn't touch the magician, though. No matter what appeared from my stylus, he didn't seem surprised. He just smacked it away. He was barely breaking a sweat, while I was quickly running out of ideas. Each time he defeated one of my spells, it got a little harder to conjure up a new one. I should've been getting better, right? But I was getting clumsier, more sluggish all the time.

When I paused, unsure what else to do, the magician composed his own spell. He smugly watched my face as another nightmare of a creature materialized. I'd never seen anything like it. It was like a lizard, but massive, with wings that unfurled and stirred up a cloud of dust. Its skin was plated and its snout long and savage looking. Long claws scratched at the paving stones. It looked at me with a reptilian coldness and blew a plume of smoke from its large nostrils. I didn't even know what type of creature it was, but I had the feeling I didn't want to be standing in front of it, if that smoke was anything to go by.

I began writing my own spell.

The creature opened its mouth. Tilting its head back, it spit a torrent of fire high into the air. What the heck was it?

I sparked my spell to life. Above me, another winged creature appeared. It was a bat. I know, not the most impressive beast, but I'd always loved watching them dart around in the early evening back at the village. It wasn't like those tiny desert bats that sleep in the crevices between rocks, though. The one I created was larger, with pretty good wings of its own. It didn't look to be a match for the magician's fire-breathing creature, but that was not what I had in mind.

"Bat, come to me!" I called.

The creature swept down. Its claws reached out. It grabbed me by the shoulders and hauled me into the air.

54

Battle in the Skies

The bat's wings fluttered furiously. Its hand-like claws pinched my shoulders, but I didn't complain. At least it had a good grip on me. The ground beneath us pitched and heaved as I swung about, making me queasy.

Below us, the fire-spitting lizard bellowed with rage. Teket floated onto its back, and the lizard slammed shut its wide expanse of wings. It surged up into the sky in a great thrust. No doubt about it, the thing was faster than my bat, more powerful and focused. The short distance we'd won by surprising the magician shrank fast. The beat of each massive wing ate away at the gap between us.

Thing was, I hadn't chosen a bat for its speed.

The bat suddenly zigged to the left. No warning,

just a sudden change of direction as a torrent of fire roared through the space we'd just occupied. *Yay, bats!* They may not be the mount of choice for long-distance speed, but boy, can they fly weird. Darting side to side, rising up only to pitch and drop unexpectedly, rolling over in the air, changing directions so fast it left my head spinning: that was what my bat was best at. Good thing, too, since the lizard kept shooting jets of flame at us. The bat sliced through them, so close I could feel the scorching heat of the flames.

You like fire, lizard? I thought. *I'll give you fire!*

That was easier said than done. With the wind whipping at me and the bat dodging about, I had a heck of a time drawing a legible glyph. I'd etch a few symbols out, only to watch them get snatched away as we changed direction. I needed something simple, straightforward. I drew a tiny sun and ignited it. A flaming ball appeared right in front of me. I stared at it, unsure how to handle it. But then the bat zagged to one side. Instinctively, I grabbed the ball. To my surprise, it didn't burn me. I knew it was hot, but maybe being my spell, it couldn't hurt me.

Holding the ball of flame in my hand, I waited for the right moment, one in which I wasn't getting yanked around and had a clear shot. When I got one, I threw. I aimed at the creature's head. The ball of flame scorched the air. *Yes!* Dead on target.

The lizard thought so, too. Only, it didn't mind as much as I'd hoped it would. The beast cocked its head and inhaled the fireball through one of its nostrils. A moment later, it opened its mouth and burped a puff of smoke. It roared its triumph so loud that the bat faltered. I thought my ears were going to burst. It began climbing, its wings like grasping claws as it came after us.

Right. Make a note of that, Ash. Balls of flame ineffective against fire-breathing monsters. Good to know. Won't try that again.

The bat rolled and dove. Through squinting eyelids, I watched the world rush up at us.

We skimmed across the top of the ruins, dipping into alleys, dodging around pillars. The lizard was right behind us, but it was too large to get in as low as we were. I'd have a good shot at it. If not with fire, what about water?

I managed another of my strange glyphs. I wasn't sure it was going to make sense, and, in a way, it didn't. What popped into the air next to me was a large, round fish, inflated like a balloon and completely filled with water. Its lips were pressed tightly together, holding the water in. Its skin was so thin I could see right through it. It looked at me expectantly. I pointed at the lizard and the magician. The fish took off. The lizard tried to pull up when it saw the fish coming, but he was too bulky to avoid it. The fish exploded in a cloud of water and hissing steam. It drenched both the lizard and the magician. I wished I could've laughed at the sight of them. Thing was, I was feeling more and more fatigue while they both looked more furious than ever.

The lizard stoked whatever furnace was at its heart. Its chest billowed as it sucked in air. This time, when it let loose a torrent of flame, it didn't let up. No matter how we dodged, the loops and twirls of flame followed. I smelled burning flesh and heard the crackle of something catching fire. The bat's wings were aflame. It flapped on bravely, but the flames only grew. The bat dipped to one side, then righted itself. Then dropped down. Its wing beats grew erratic. This bat wasn't going to last much longer. The fabric of the magic that held it together—and kept me in the air— was fading.

I scanned the ruins below, looking for someplace to land, someplace that would give me an advantage so that the lizard wouldn't just stomp on me or burn me to a crisp. In the end, it wasn't me that found a spot. The bat did.

We were at the edge of the city now. The bat flew straight toward the cliff wall of the mountain behind the old ruin. It dipped toward a crevice in the wall, a cave mouth. It set me down in it and rose up. Hovering in the air a moment, it looked me right in the eyes. Though its face was that of a rodent, composed of magic, the eyes that looked back at me were familiar. They were . . . mine. I was suddenly terribly sad, watching it burn, knowing it was all my fault.

The bat turned and flew back toward the oncoming lizard, blazing a smoke-blackened trail. The two creatures collided. They became a flaming, writhing mass, grappling with each other. The magician was flung away. The two spell-creatures plummeted toward the earth. I knew when they hit because the explosion made the ground shake and threw up a great cloud of smoke . . . and ash.

55

My Spell-Self

Even if it was only a spell, that was one brave bat.

Misery washed through me, a sadness as great as if I'd lost an old friend or a beloved relative. It was as bad as losing Seret and Gilli. I stumbled back into the shadows of the cave, barely able to stay on my feet. Why was I so tired? It was a different sort of tired than just physical fatigue. It wasn't my muscles that were giving out. I felt drained from the inside, like thestuff of my spirit had been sucked away. The feeling had been growing in me, but now it was undeniable, from the moment the bat crashed to the ground.

"Boy!" the magician's voice boomed. "Come out into the light. Let us conclude this." He drifted into view and landed at the mouth of the cave.

I stayed in the shadows. I felt like I was on the verge of understanding something, but I needed a few more moments to figure it out.

When the bat died, a piece of me did, too. A piece of my soul.

It had been part of me. That was why its eyes had been like mine. The three-headed lion, the water-balloon fish, the bat. I'd been so foolish! Yes, they were powerful spells, but each time one of them was defeated, it made me weaker.

"Come now, I'm losing patience," the magician said.

It had to be the same for the magician. That was why he'd looked so shaken when the slug died. That creature had been part of him as well. A foul, hideous part. Now, with the flying lizard also dead, he must be weakened too. But I couldn't count on him being as weak as I was.

Waving my stylus, I tried to conjure up the energy to make another spell. It barely glowed at all. My magic was nearly spent. There was no way I'd be able to spark up another large spell. I had no idea what to do.

Images of Seret's golden eyes came to me. And Gilli's laugh. Even Sutekh's smirk and Kiya's beautiful, ice-cold face. Memories of things Yazen had revealed the night before.

A bunch of different emotions dropped on me at the same time. All the days of testing. All the moments of near death. All the worrying and wondering, the hoping and fearing. The toll of the magic. The feeling of loss for the spells I'd created. The soul-deep tiredness. The wish—which I couldn't deny—that this was all just over. One way or another, just over.

"Boy, if you do not come to me, I will come in after you. I'll destroy you like a rat in the dark. Is that what you wish for?"

I shook my head. No, that wasn't the way I was going to finish this. If this was going to end, better that I step out to face it instead of staying hidden in some cave. My friends—and Yazen—deserved better than that from me. I steadied myself, took a deep breath, and tried to remember all the things I had to be proud of.

As I started forward, I drew a small spell. I wasn't sure where the idea came from. Maybe it was just my way of acknowledging that all the spells I'd sent at the magician were parts of me, little bits of my spirit. Why not, for my last spell, give all of myself?

My glyphs got a little stronger as I approached the light, drawing from Ra's energy. I closed the spell and struck life into it. I watched as a spell version of myself stepped away from me. Just like Thoth had made a spell-magician, I had created a spell-Ash. It was just like me, my size and shape and with my mannerisms. Since the magic in it was so weak, it didn't even glow. That made it look more like a regular person. My spell-self walked toward the waiting magician, with me following. My body felt empty. The edges of my vision blurred. I had to fight to stay conscious.

As my spell-self approached the mouth of the tunnel, the magician asked, "Ah, so you've finally found courage, have you?"

And it was only then, when I could see Teket through my fading vision, that I knew what I was going to do.

My spell-self stepped calmly into the light of the sun at the exact moment that I moved my real physical body forward into a run. I ran with all the energy I had left—and some that I didn't even know I had left.

I smashed through my spell self, sprinting toward him, astonishing the magician.

Recovering from his surprise, he began to draw a spell.

I cocked back my fist and swung for his jaw. Before I knew whether or not I'd hit it, the world went black.

THE
DAY AFTER

56

Waking from Darkness

"**A**sh, can you hear me?"

The voice spoke softly. I could hear it, yes, but I wasn't sure I wanted to. It was disturbing me, reaching into the deepest sleep I'd ever been in.

"It's time to wake up, Ash."

I was in a dark, silent comforting place. I wanted to stay there, to linger in the nothingness. To *not* be.

"Come on, Ash, open your eyes. I know you can do it."

I recognized the voice. I'd heard it before. She kept speaking. Each word pulled me up from the depths a little more. My eyes fluttered open. The face that came slowly into focus was Lady Mafdet's. She leaned over me, her large mongoose eyes wide with concern.

"There you are!" Her whiskers twitched. "I knew you'd come back to us. Everyone, the prince's shadow has returned!"

Sitting up and looking around at the pharaoh and the collection of gods crammed into a small room did a lot to wake me up. They surrounded the bed on which I lay. For a time, their words of praise—"Congratulations!" and "Well done, lad!" and "Very impressive!"—rained down on me without making any sense. Lord Sobek let out a low, guttural rumble, which I think was his way of expressing approval. Lady Nekhbet was so moved, she draped one of her vulture necklaces over my head. For once, Lady Isis's face tilted into a full-on grin.

And there was Yazen. He smiled at me, looking happier than I'd ever seen him. He had tears in his eyes, but they were clearly happy tears.

Pharaoh Neferu called for someone to fetch Prince Khufu. "He sat vigil with you until he collapsed from exhaustion," he explained. "I think it's time to wake him up as well."

It gradually dawned on me that I was alive. In a shaky voice, I asked, "Is it over?"

Lord Thoth shouldered through the others. "Yes,

Ash, it is. I'm not surprised you don't remember, though. By the end, you were very weak. As close to death as any mortal can come. You nearly killed yourself. I myself put the breath of life back into you." He gestured to the other gods. "We all sat vigil beside you, feeding energy back into you. Too many of your spells had your essence in them. You figured that out, didn't you?"

I nodded.

"Divine Writing is something we do in partnership with Lord Ra. He makes magic possible in Egypt, but all spells also feed off your soul energy. The more complicated the spell, the more of your soul is needed to animate it. When you create thinking spells you do so at an even greater risk, since they draw more deeply from your soul. What you did at the end was unconventional, but effective. That spell version of yourself was a perfect decoy. It used the last drop of your magical energy, but you, Ash, were clever enough to strike your final blow with a simpler weapon—your fist."

"So . . . I got him?"

"You did." Thoth's small eyes twinkled with amusement. "You socked that old magician something good. Knocked him out. You fell into a deep unconsciousness, but you struck the final blow, Ash. Teket fell at your hand. That's why I'm giving you this."

Suddenly, there was a small, rectangular box in his hand. It was metal, ornate and bejeweled. He set it on the bed beside me and held up a gold chain with a key dangling from it. He draped it around my neck. "This key unlocks this box. The box contains the stylus that helped you triumph. It's yours, Ash. In the years to come, I hope to teach you how to really use it."

A feeling of relief bloomed in my chest. It was like I'd been holding my breath for days without knowing it and had just remembered how to breathe. I'd made it. The testing was over, and I'd never have to do it again, and that meant that . . .

Before I could get too excited, something occurred to me that squeezed the joy right out of me. "I made it," I said, "but the others didn't."

Lord Thoth drew back. "Ah, yes, there is that. Pharaoh Neferu, would you like to explain?"

The pharaoh moved around the cot. Princess Sia followed him, watching me with curious eyes. I hadn't seen her since the night of the banquet, when her laughter sounded like birdsong and music dancing together. The Pharaoh sat beside me, pulled his daughter close to him, and placed his hand over mine. "Ash, I'm afraid I've kept a secret from you and the other candidates."

"What do you mean?"

"What I mean is that I've made a change to the shadow testing tradition, the first change in hundreds of years. In all that time, candidates have died in great numbers. Most often, those who made it to the final day turned on each other. When this happened on the final day of my shadow's testing, I hated it. Children that I had come to know and admire were slaughtered before my eyes. It haunted me, and it haunted my shadow as well. I vowed then that I would change things. When the time for Rami's testing came, I bowed to pressure and let the tradition stand. But watching his candidates perish just brought back all the pain. This time, I stood my ground. Sia here had a hand in that. She asked me, 'What use is being pharaoh if you don't get to change things for the better?'"

He said this with a smile and a wink at his daughter. There was a twinkle of humor in his eyes that I'd never seen before.

"Pharaoh, what did you change?" I asked.

"I had Lord Thoth weave spells around each of the candidates on the first day. It did nothing up until the exact moment a candidate was about to die. In that instant, the boy or girl was transported to a safe place in the palace. They've been there, hidden, ever since. It was a secret only Thoth and I knew about."

I heard the pharaoh, but it took a moment for the words to sink in. "You mean nobody actually died?"

The pharaoh smiled. "Thanks to Sia, no. They didn't."

The princess looked away and hid her eyes behind her hand, suddenly shy about being the center of attention. *Wow*, I thought. What was she, like, eight years old? She'd already changed the traditions of Egypt for the better and saving lives in the process!

"Your friends are waiting outside," Pharaoh Neferu said. "Very much alive, and very keen to see you."

That was the best news I'd ever heard. A feeling of relief and joy like I'd never known before washed over me. I wanted to jump up right then and rush out to see them, but I had another question, one I was almost too scared to ask. "And . . . am I Prince Khufu's shadow?"

The voice that answered was as drippy as ever. "Don't be rash," Lord Set said. He stared at me, tiny flames in his eyes. His snout trembled with barely contained emotion. But just what emotion, I couldn't tell. If he was excited for me he had a strange way of showing it. "You are not the prince's shadow."

He said it like a statement of hard, cold fact. Full stop. That's all there was to it. Lord Horus agreed, but in a very different way. "Lord Set is correct. You're not the prince's shadow until you are officially named so at tonight's ceremony."

"That's just a formality," Pharaoh Neferu said. He placed his hands on my shoulders and grinned at me. "The tests are complete. Lords and ladies, do we all agree that the candidate has met every challenge with triumph?"

Various heads, human and animal, nodded. Set grumbled something I couldn't hear. Nobody paid him any attention.

"If none speak against him," the pharaoh continued, "I pronounce Ash to have passed all his tests."

I slipped the keychain to the stylus box over my head.

"You have every right to be elated. Tonight . . ." The pharaoh paused. Then, grinning, he winked at me. "We'll let the festivities begin in earnest!"

57

A Close Call

As Yazen, the pharaoh, princess, and gods stepped out of the room talking about all the things that needed to be done for the ceremony, Set was the last of them to walk to the door. He paused in the door-frame. He stood there a moment, until the footfalls and chatting of the other gods faded. His snout slowly turned back to face me and he fixed me with a most disturbing expression. His tiny eyes bored into me, flames sparking in them. I could feel it physically, like the touch of his eyes was slowly burning my skin. He pulled the door shut and strolled back to me.

"Ash," he said. "Now everybody loves Ash, don't they?"

I hesitated, unsure what to make of his tone. It was

sickly sweet on the surface, but something sinister writhed just beneath his words.

"Well, don't they!?" he snapped.

I flinched and stammered a non-answer.

"The other gods think you're so clever." He reached the edge of the bed. He looked unreasonably tall, and the light in the room seemed to have dimmed. His features, viewed from below, were dark and shadowy. "*You* think you're so clever. Are you? Well, are you!?"

"No," I managed. "I'm just . . . um—"

"You're just 'um'? Yes, that's it. You're not clever. Do you know what you are?"

Man, this guy had a lot of questions.

In a low, venomous voice, he said, "A peasant. You may have fooled the others, but I've got a feeling that you're a troublesome boy. Do you know what I do to troublesome peasant boys?"

"Scare them to death?" I offered sheepishly.

"I'll show you what I do."

Something really weird happened then. Set's face changed. His snout went soft. Softer than usual, I mean. It stretched and drooped. His mouth grew wide with a smile. I mean *wide*. Like three or four times wider than it should have been. He leaned over me, opening his mouth as he did so. I got a look into the depths of his insides. But it wasn't a normal tongue and teeth and throat. His insides went on forever, like a massive cavern far down in the underworld. He was about to swallow me whole.

The door opened. "Ash, you made it!" someone said in a light and lively voice. Prince Khufu. He drew up, obviously surprised to find the god in the room. "Lord Set," he said, bowing his head, "sorry for intruding. We thought Ash was alone."

Yazen walked just behind him, staff in hand. "Many apologies, my lord. Should we give you a moment more with the boy?"

That almost got a scream out of me. Were they crazy? Didn't they see that he was about to eat me? Just look at the jaws on him! I glanced back at him.

Lord Set's snout had snapped back into place. Small, rubbery, kinda odd looking. Not scary, though. He changed his gape-mouthed grimace into a gentle yawn, stretching his arms and back as he did so. Turning, he greeted Yazen with a smile. "Yes, indeed, here he is. Our young hero. Ash, shadow to the prince!"

He said that last part with such enthusiasm that I almost doubted he'd been about to eat me. He was an upright, dignified, godly version of himself again. Clearing his throat, he said, "I was just having a word with the boy. Congratulating him, you understand."

"Of course, Lord Set," Yazen said. "We've come to take the prince's shadow to the tailors. After that he'll need to visit the baths, to have his feet scrubbed and be oiled and sprinkled with gold dust. And there's the ceremonial cleansing."

"Yes, yes," Set said. He glanced at me again, looking—to me, at least—like he was considering just gobbling me down despite the audience.

"Forgive me for mentioning it," Khufu said, "but aren't all the gods gathering in the temple of Ra for a post-testing debriefing?"

"I know that," Set snapped. He sniffed and turned, snout raised. "I was just going." With that, he strolled from the room.

58

Seizing the Moment

Prince Rami came upon Lord Set just as the god kicked his beetle to life. Set tried to ignore the youth. He slipped his visor over his eyes and tugged on his crocodile-skin gloves. Rami wasn't going to let him get away that easily, though. He shouted and gesticulated, trying to be heard over the roar of the beetle's wings.

"I'm in no mood for it, prince," Set snapped. "So your brother gets a bloody shadow! What do I care?"

Rami had a good few things to say to that, but he couldn't even hear himself over the sputter of Set's beetle. He kicked the insect in the backside. Twice. Once to shut it off. A second time out of spite. The commotion of the insect's wings faded, and the prince could finally hear himself. ". . . bungled everything. Each and every day of *the testing! All those opportunities. Failure after failure. You promised so much, and yet you delivered nothing. Nothing!"*

One of Set's arms flashed out with blinding speed. His fist clamped around the prince's neck, pinching off his speech. And his capacity to breathe. "Keep your complaints to yourself. You came to me, remember? I did what I could. The others, they . . ." He gestured vaguely toward the palace with his free hand. ". . . Conspired against me. The nerve of them: Neferu and Thoth. They love their little secrets, don't they? Keep everyone else in the dark, thinking the testing was as deadly as it should be. The nerve! And all that work I put in. All of it wasted."

Rami clawed at the god's iron grip, his face red and frantic. He tried to gesture, to indicate that he couldn't breathe, but the god wasn't paying attention to him.

Set gnashed his teeth together, his snout tense with exasperation. "You have no idea how close I came to eating Ash whole. I would've done it, but his friends *arrived just in time to spoil it." He said the word* friends *as if it were something unpleasant he'd stepped in.*

Rami began to thrash, a full-bodied crazy dance, writhing and jerking and flailing his arms. Set turned to him. Mildly confused, as if he wasn't sure how he had come to have the boy's neck in his clenched fist, he let go. The prince fell to the paving stones, gasping for air.

"Sorry about that," Set said. "You just caught me at a trying moment. It's just that I was so close to closing the deal. One gulp. That's all I needed."

"I've got . . . an idea," Rami said, sucking for breath. "In preparation for the ceremony, Ash has to go through all that ritual purification stuff, and then he's supposed to stay in his room, alone, until summoned for the ceremony."

"I know all this!" Set snapped.

"He'll be alone! You could get him. Lord Thoth's spells are no longer protecting him."

"That's tempting, but not possible. I'll be with the other gods all afternoon. Official duties, you know. As if things weren't bad enough, Horus has summoned several of the demons from the testing. He wants to question them to see if I gave them any special instructions. Can you believe that? The nerve. Not that Ammut's much for answering questions anyway."

"Wait," Rami said. "Ammut is here, in the palace?"

"She is in one of the royal waiting rooms. What of it?"

It took Rami a moment to answer. He couldn't believe that Set didn't see the plan that he suddenly saw so clearly. He pressed his hands together and tapped them against his lips, thinking. He said, "Lord Set, all is not lost. Remember what you told me about always being ready to seize the moment? I think an opportunity just presented itself."

59

Times of Change

Needless to say, the others didn't believe that one of the High Council gods had been about to make a snack of me. No matter how I tried to describe it, they shrugged it off.

"Set's not exactly a treat to be around," Khufu said, "but he's not about to hurt my shadow, now is he? That wouldn't make any sense."

"I know, but—"

Yazen pulled me into a one-armed hug. He mussed my hair playfully. "You've had a traumatic week. It's no wonder a god as powerful as Set would seem menacing."

"Yeah, but—"

"Maybe you hit your head when you passed out,"

Khufu offered. I couldn't help rolling my eyes. "What?" he asked. "It's nothing to be embarrassed about."

I gave up. They weren't listening. They were too excited that the testing was over, and were sure that I should be, too.

Gilli and Seret joined us. Perfectly healthy, totally alive. "I thought I was done for," Gilli said. "And then—poof!—I wasn't done for after all. Neat trick."

"A lifesaver," Seret added. "All the others are here, too. After you are announced as the shadow prince, the rest of us will be announced with our different posts, too. Warrior. Magician. Priest. You name it."

"All the others?" I asked.

"Yeah," Seret said, knowing what I was really asking, "even Sutekh and Kiya. I know, they should be punished, but nobody seems to know that but us! Adults and gods, why do they never *see* anything?" She tugged on her whiskers thoughtfully. "So . . . there's a downside. We'll still have to keep an eye out for those two."

"There are other downsides," Gilli said, "like Ash being the prince's shadow instead of me!" He put on a face of mock jealousy. He didn't hold it long. "You know what, though? It doesn't really matter. I'm alive, and I'm going to start training as a magician!"

"I'm not surprised," I said. "The way you threw lightning bolts at Sutekh!" I smiled. "I was impressed."

"And I'm joining the Royal Guard!" Seret added. "Turns out the testing wasn't just about who would become the shadow. We've all been given special assignments based on how we performed in different battles."

"What are Sutekh and Kiya going to do?"

"Sutekh is starting officer training in the air force," Gilli said. He pursed his lips. "Hopefully, he'll be flying off somewhere far away on one of the warships. Kiya's been assigned to some top secret project. Nobody knows exactly what it is, but they're sending her north. To Giza." He shrugged. "It's a building project, or something—"

"Anyway," Khufu cut in, "don't worry about them!" He grabbed my arm and tugged me from the cot. "There's too much fun stuff to do!"

They pulled me out of the room and through the palace, detailing all the wonderful things that the coming days would offer. The official ceremony tonight, the banquet after it, the days of games and festivals to come. Khufu and I would soon be taking a trip up and down the length of the Nile, all over

Egypt, in the royal sunbarge, *The Mistress of Light*. The trip was to show off the prince. And me, too, I guessed. We'd be stopping at cities and monuments and temples, meeting all sorts of dignitaries and gods. I'd be seeing all of Egypt's wonders firsthand, actually gazing on things that I'd only ever dreamed about back in the village.

"We'll get up to all sorts of adventures," Khufu said.

Truth was, it wasn't that hard to forget about Set. They were probably right. I'd misunderstood him, thinking something was scary when really, it was probably just weird. Swept along by my friends' enthusiasm, I joined in their high spirits. I carried the stylus, locked in its case, to the prince's quarters.

Some of my cheer disappeared during the preparations, though. The scrubbing I received in the baths was fierce. Apparently, it was really, *really* important that I be spotless, enough so that the bath attendants attacked me with hard-bristled brushes, scouring every inch of my skin. Embarrassing? You bet. Ever had someone clean between your toes? Polish your toenails? Clean out your earwax?

I'll admit that the way they made my skin golden

was pretty cool. An attendant had me stand beneath a large, drooping flower. He batted its stem and fine flakes of gold pollen rained down on me. As they touched my skin, the flakes melted into it, covering me in a golden hue. Not bad, unless you're allergic to pollen—which I am. Sneezing fits ensued.

Other attendants draped a silky, shimmering tunic over my shoulders, fastening it in place with a silver belt with a large, reddish jewel at the buckle. Carnelian, they informed me. Incredibly valuable and rare. I snorted, thinking of Sobek and his palace built of the stuff.

After that, they draped me in jewelry: bracelets and rings and necklaces, enough to weigh down a camel. There was so much of it I couldn't see my keychain anymore, but I could feel it pressing against my chest. I hoped this was just for tonight. How would I ever defend the prince if I had to wear this stuff all the time?

I stood in front of a polished bronze mirror. I barely recognized myself. It was partly because of the gold and silk and jewelry. Not to mention being clean instead of dusty, sweaty, and drenched in canal muck.

But it was more than that. I looked—and felt—

proud and confident, in a way I couldn't have imagined just a few days ago. I was still just barely twelve, still a bit thin, still with small feet, still a village kid at heart, but I liked what I saw in my eyes, in my high cheekbones and full lips. I looked Egyptian, and I was a part of something grand. Maybe I always had been, but now, finally, I believed it.

As I returned to the room Yazen and I shared, my golden skin tingled. My head swam with the scent of perfume, making me dizzy enough that I wobbled as I walked in my bejeweled new sandals. I did note that I could hear better. That may have been because of the earwax thing. Hadn't cleaned those guys out in a while. Yazen, Khufu, Gilli, and Seret were waiting for me, along with the blue hippos.

"Can that be him?" a high-pitched voice asked.

"No, it can't be," another answered. "This boy is clean. Ash was . . . well, you smelled his feet, didn't you?"

As I stood teetering in a haze of perfume, the little guys approached me, waddling on their short, stout legs. Gazing up, one of them asked, "Is this really Ash, the scourge of scorpions?"

"Ash, the foe of feisty fishes?"

"Ash, the babysitter of buzzards?"

"Ash, the terror of Teket?"

"That's him, all right," Khufu said.

"Amazing what a bath can do," the first hippo said. "Did they polish your eyeballs yet?"

"My eyeballs!?" For a horrible moment, I thought he was serious. After what I'd been through, I wouldn't put it past them. I snapped my head around, expecting to see attendants converging on me holding whatever frightful tools they used to polish eyeballs.

Khufu burst out laughing, Gilli, Seret, and Yazen and all the hippos along with him. Apparently, I was to be the day's source of amusement. I was even fair game for hippo humor!

Once the hilarity died down, the first hippo got serious again. "Are you sure you're ready to protect the prince from harm?"

"Yeah, I think so," I answered.

Squinting at me suspiciously, the second hippo asked, "Really? All by yourself?"

I began to answer in the affirmative, but Khufu elbowed me in the ribs. Pursing his lips, he dipped his head to the side, gesturing toward the hippos. I finally caught on.

Turning back to the hippos, I said respectfully, "I will protect the prince, but with your assistance, of course. You've done such a fine job so far. I'm sure there's a lot you could teach me."

That did the trick. The first hippo made a satisfied humph. The others nodded and nudged each other. Apparently, I'd said what they wanted to hear. They moved off, chatting animatedly.

Though I was supposed to be alone before the ceremony, Khufu declared that they were staying to keep me company. It was great to see Yazen, Seret, and Gilli so happy. Khufu dismissed the palace guards from the doors. We all chatted and joked. We munched on the coconut cakes the servants had set out. We acted out key moments from the testing, finding nothing but humor in events that had before seemed deadly serious. As the time passed, I grew more and more at ease. I was going to be the prince's shadow. I had friends. I had Yazen. Maybe someday soon I'd even get my parents back. Things were about as good as they could get.

Later, I sat beside Yazen. A little distance away, Khufu, Seret and Gilli took turns wrestling with the hippos. I cradled the caracal kitten in my lap. It purred softly as I stroked it.

"And what name have you chosen for your friend?" Yazen asked. He let go of his staff, reached over and scratched under the kitten's chin.

"I don't know. I forgot to think of one."

"All right, but don't wait too long. All good companions deserve a name. This little one, I believe, will be a loyal friend to you." Yazen inhaled a deep breath and grew thoughtful. "In a few hours you will step into the role you've prepared for all your life."

"Yazen," I asked, "with all the stuff I went through, with all the tests, does it mean I'm really ready to be the prince's shadow?"

"Of course," Yazen said. "It will be a grand adventure. You will see and do many things, I'm sure. You'll have to come visit me sometimes and tell me of your escapades."

I looked up from the kitten. "Visit you?"

"You didn't think I'd be staying here with you, did you? *You* are the prince's shadow, Ash. Not me. I am just a humble mentor who had a part in helping you become who you are. That's all the honor I need, and palace life is not for me. When you leave on your journey in *The Mistress of Light*, I'll depart as well. But I won't be flying high in the sky. I'll just walk the slow road back to the village. For me, our old life will remain my future life. Ash . . . don't look sad!"

I fought not to, but sadness washed over me. I'd been thinking constantly about becoming the prince's shadow, and possibly finding my parents, but I hadn't considered all the things I'd be leaving behind in the process. The thought of not having Yazen around, with his wise words and steady support . . . The thought of him living back in the village without me, involved in the lives of all the people who had watched me grow . . . The thought of beginning a life without him, surrounded only by new people and things . . .

My eyes went moist. Embarrassed, I had to wipe away the tears before they fell.

"Ash . . . ," Yazen whispered, leaning in close. "My adopted son. Times of change bring sadness. I feel that, too. Every step of the walk home I'll miss you. Every time I cook a meal I'll probably make extra for you. No doubt I'll wake up every morning and go to your room, thinking to wake you. The house will be desolate without you in it. I know that already."

Was he *trying* to make me more miserable?

"Look at me," Yazen said. He nudged my chin until I looked up, tearful, into his dark face, lined with age. His eyes were kind and steady, as was his voice. "You see, Ash, that is the way of life. We miss people and places in direct proportion to how much we love them. I will miss you very, very much. I hope you feel the same about me. That way, we can both know how much we mean to each other. And when we next again meet, we'll just have to make sure that every moment counts." He added, with a grin, "I'll be sure to say hello to Merk, Dowser, and Setka for you."

That almost got a smile out of me. I'd forgotten all about those guys.

Yazen was kind enough to wipe my eyes free of tears as Khufu, Seret, and Gilli, having surrendered to the hippos, walked back over to us. Khufu plopped down beside us, thankfully not noticing my wet eyes. He grabbed a sweet and popped it in his mouth.

All of a sudden, Seret's smooth lioness stride halted. She wrinkled her nose. "Ew. What's that smell?"

Gilli sniffed the air. "What smell?"

"It smells like . . . rotten meat . . . and fish . . . and the crust people collect between their toes. And other horrible things as well."

We all stared at her.

"What? I'm a lioness! I've got a good nose. And you

humans are stinky, believe me. This is something different, though."

One of the hippos asked, "What stinks?"

"You smell it, too?" Khufu asked.

The hippo that had spoken rolled his bulbous eyes. Glancing at Seret, he said, "Humans!"

Human I might be, but I caught the scent of something foul, too. It was faint at first, but as the others talked I inhaled, trying to place it. I'd smelled this reek before. It was . . .

The door at the other end of the room suddenly slammed open. The lumbering figure that stepped through it was one I'd hoped never to see again.

60

The Demon's Revenge

Ammut.

The bulky demon scanned the room. Her crocodile eyes took everybody in with a reptilian coldness. How was it possible? She was a creature of the Duat, a thing banished to the dark caverns of death. How could *she* be here, free, wandering about the palace?

It was so unfathomable I couldn't think beyond it. Nobody could. Except for Ammut. She had pretty clear plans.

She bellowed, a roar that shook the room. Her hippo legs kicked into motion. Her lion claws churned and ripped at the air. She ran straight at me. As she crossed the room, she batted away one blue hippo after another. She shoved a table at Seret, who leaped to avoid it. Then Ammut grabbed for me. It all happened so fast I didn't have time to react, except to snap my head back as her claws flew under my chin, hooking angrily around my necklaces. She grabbed them in her fists and pulled.

If it wasn't for Yazen, Ammut would've yanked me right into her jaws.

Yazen lunged in, bringing his staff up between us, and lifted the pile of chains up over my head. Released, I flew backward, landing in a sprawl on the floor. Ammut stumbled back, and Yazen followed through on his attack. His staff had always been his weapon of choice, and he twirled the slim length of ebony in blurred circles toward the demon. He hit Ammut first on one side, and then whirled around and smacked her on the other. For a time, Ammut's claws were tangled in the loops of chains. She could do nothing but back away, swatting at Yazen's staff and yowling with rage.

Yazen jabbed her in the belly, and then swiped his staff down between the demon's feet. She tripped and went down. Looking at me, my mentor snapped, "Run! Call for the guards. Tell the gods what's happening here!"

"But what about you?" I shouted.

"You are the prince's shadow. Defend him! Get the guards!"

I tugged Khufu into motion and called to Seret. She sprang to us. Gilli was already at the smashed door, beckoning to us. I was almost through it, but I couldn't help looking back at Yazen.

That's why I saw what happened. The most awful thing I'd ever witnessed.

Ammut had made it back on her feet. She tossed her arms wide, flinging the necklaces into the air. The glimmering chains and pendants flew out in all directions. Several of them landed on Yazen. As he swatted them out of the way, Ammut closed the distance between them, slashing. One of her claws caught Yazen's chin. The blow yanked his head around, tossing him off-balance. The hippos leaped at her, climbing on her large frame and punching with all their might. But she focused only on Yazen. She tore his staff out of his hands and raked her claws across his chest. Yazen cried out in pain and fell to the floor.

I tried to run to him, but Seret grabbed me. "No, Ash!" she said. "You have no weapons. There's nothing you can do against Ammut."

I fought to get free of her grip.

Gilli said, "Yazen wouldn't want you to throw yourself at her without a plan. We have to think."

"Your stylus!" Khufu called. "You beat her with magic before. You could—"

He cut himself off when he saw the way my hand clutched at my chest and came away empty. He knew as well as I did what that meant. Ammut had yanked the necklace off. The key was somewhere in the turmoil of the room. I had no idea where. Without it, I'd never be able to get the stylus out of the locked box.

The demon stood over Yazen's crumpled form. She roared and stamped. She smacked a hippo out of midair and sent it somersaulting away. Another one, she caught in her jaws and devoured. She liked the taste, apparently. She began to scoop them into her mouth, devouring them one by one. No matter what happened to their comrades, the hippos continued to leap at her. Soon, there was only one left, a stunned, injured one that picked himself off the floor, shaking his head to clear it.

Ammut then reached one of her lion claws down for Yazen.

"You guys find the key," Seret whispered. Her golden eyes stared intensely at the demon. "Get the stylus and use it."

"And what are you going to do?

"This . . ." Her lean muscles tensed. She bounded across the room and attacked Ammut. Snarling, she went in slashing with both claws. I'd never imagined she could be so fierce. Her claws were lightning fast. Her bared teeth looked savage. The way she exchanged blows with Ammut, I almost thought she'd be able to drive her away for good.

"Come on," I said, "there's no time to waste!" We began searching. I scurried around the room, kicking through the debris, lifting necklaces and flinging them away. So many necklaces, but all of them useless to me, except for the one with the key. I tried not panic about Yazen. *He's going to be all right*, I kept telling myself. I would save him *and* protect the prince.

I crawled under a table and over a broken chair. I sifted through the shards of a shattered urn. Where was it? Come on, key! As I went, I ripped the bracelets from my arms. They were slowing me down. My broken arm hurt when I put pressure on it, but I didn't care. I would've tossed the cast away if I could. The carnelian belt buckle jabbed me in the abdomen. I tore that off too and flung it.

Then I saw it. The key. It lay a little distance away, on the floor near where the belt landed. I sprinted toward it, grabbed it up, and turned back toward the others. Khufu was on the other side of the room, a whole span of clutter between us. He held the locked box in his hands. He tossed it to Gilli, who tucked it under an arm and ran toward me. For the first time since Ammut arrived, I felt a flare of hope.

Seret's scream snapped my head around. She was crawling away from Ammut, limping, her shoulder striped with bright red gashes. There was such pain in her eyes. It got worse with each wincing step. The demon followed her, shoving her way through tables and chairs, backing the lioness up against the wall.

"Hey, demon! Where you going? We got unfinished business."

It was the injured hippo. He stood, snout held high, hands on his hips. "Turn around and face a hippo. Or are you scared?" His high-pitched voice dripped with sarcasm. No doubt about it, he was a spunky little guy.

The demon turned from Seret. The little hippo didn't hesitate. He ran forward, vaulted into a series of snappy flips and cartwheels, and then sailed through the air right at Ammut, his pudgy foot leading the way. It was an amazing aerial kick, perfectly executed. It was the type of kick that would've knocked the brawniest soldier unconscious. Only . . . Ammut wasn't a soldier. She was a demon, with the jaws to prove it. She simply opened her mouth and snapped the hippo out of midair. She held the little guy a moment, and then tossed her head back. In one gulp, the hippo vanished down her throat. And that was it.

Yazen was down.

Seret was down.

Now, the last of the hippos had been consumed.

"Noooooo!!!!!!" Gilli dropped the locked box and flew at Ammut. He was fearless, enraged, thinking nothing about himself as he cursed the demon for eating the hippos. Ammut swiped him into the air with one of her lion claws. He crashed into the wall and lay crumpled beside Seret.

"Noooooo!!!!!!" It was Prince Khufu's turn. He tore into the demon with his fists, pounding her lion belly. He kicked her shins and stomped on her hippo toes.

I ran for the dropped box, leaping over the clutter, slipping and falling and getting up.

Ammut towered above Khufu, her claws upraised, her jaws hanging above his head. She grabbed him, almost gently, by the shoulders. She lifted him up, staring down her snout at him. I thought he was done for. But I wasn't going to let him go without a fight.

Reaching the box, I fumbled with the key. I got it facing the right way and slammed it into the lock. I turned, heard it click and . . .

Ammut grabbed me. She lifted me by a lion claw and spun me around. For the second time in my life, I got a close-up view of Ammut's toothy jaws. The demon held both the prince and me in midair. She looked at us from one to the other, considering which of us to eat first. By the twinkle in her bulbous eyes, it was clear she was enjoying the moment. Khufu thrashed and kicked. I just held still. She'd beat me. I could still see the box on the floor, the key in it and the lid just slightly ajar. So near, and yet totally beyond my reach.

Ammut lifted me high. Her snout levered open, toothy and foul. Her rank breath rushed up into my face. Apparently, she'd made her choice. I was going down her throat first.

Or . . . not exactly first.

I could see beyond the jagged confusion of her teeth, past the slithery wetness of her tongue, down the enormously wide cavern of her throat . . . the tiny faces of the hippos. They looked up at me all crammed together with the most miserable defeated expression. But they weren't defeated . . . yet.

"Hippos!" I shouted. "Bouncy balls!"

They didn't understand what I meant. They just looked at me with numb incomprehension. *Come on!*

Ammut almost had me in her mouth. The hippos had to act fast! I turned to Khufu. I didn't think he could see them the way I could, but he must've understood me. He piped right up.

"Servants of the Prince!" he shouted. "I command you. Do bouncy balls!"

I looked back in at the hippos. Something sparked. Their eyes went wide. Their tiny squished faces took on looks of great concentration. Their foreheads twitched and their blue skin turned purplish. Then things got wild.

61

Bouncy Balls

A hippo drew up his legs and kicked off of one side of Ammut's belly. Another did the same. Soon they were zipping to one side, banging into the belly-wall, then zinging back. The rest followed. In an instant, they were all in motion, ricocheting about in the cauldron of the demon's big belly.

Ammut grunted. She groaned. She threw us to the ground and cradled her large lion belly. Under her paws, her torso bulged and contorted.

The hippos inside her bounced faster and faster. Ammut's belly jiggled and jumped. Khufu and I both backed slowly away. It was a good thing we did, too.

Just when it seemed that the commotion inside her couldn't get any more frantic, Ammut let out a piteous wail. Honestly, despite all she'd tried to do to us, I felt sorry for her. She sounded like a frightened child.

Of course, she was a demon, which was why when she exploded all that was left of her was a noxious green cloud. She was back in the underworld. Little blue hippos erupted through the gas, flying in all directions. They caromed off the walls and ceiling. They crashed through the chairs and tables. One smashed the only remaining unbroken urn. Another came at me with such speed only sheer instinct made me duck to avoid it.

And then, as quickly as it had all begun, the room went silent. I looked at Khufu. He looked at me. One by one, the hippos rose, rubbing their sore heads. They complained of bumps and bruises, which I was pretty sure meant they were just fine.

"She's gone," Khufu whispered.

"Yeah, she is," Gilli said, standing up and getting his bearings. "Right back to whatever cavern she came from."

Khufu ran to check on Seret. "Are you all right?" he asked her, looking at her wounds.

"I think so," she answered, weakly.

Looking at where Yazen lay, I knew I couldn't ask

him the same question. With dread in my heart, I pulled away the debris that covered him. His tunic was dark with blood.

"Yazen?"

I knelt down and placed my good hand on his chest, trying to feel if he was breathing. I couldn't tell. My hand trembled too much. My heartbeat pounded in my ears. This moment was even more frightening than all the things that had come before. I'd never seen Yazen so limp and still, not even in his deepest sleep.

My breath caught in my throat as I thought the unthinkable. I began to say his name again, but stopped. What if I said it, but he couldn't hear me? What if he never heard me again? What if the only person—the only parent—I'd ever truly known was dead? In that moment, I'd never felt more afraid.

Guards rushed in. Burly men with long spears, they fanned out throughout the room. "Prince Khufu, are you all right?" one of them called. His eyes scanned every corner of the room. "Where is the enemy?"

The pharaoh and Lords Horus and Thoth arrived to hear the answer. Set and Prince Rami as well, both of them wearing expressions that were hard to read. Surprised? Disappointed? Annoyed? I couldn't tell.

When he answered, Khufu sounded strangely grown-up. "Yes, Captain. I'm okay, but this lioness needs a physician. And that man is gravely hurt." Khufu indicated Yazen, and then looked at his father. For a moment I thought he'd run to him. I think I would have, if he'd been my father. But Khufu stayed composed. I guess that's something they teach princes to do.

"Of course," Pharaoh Neferu said. He turned around, spotting the just-arriving physicians. "Healers, see to this man. Give him your full attention. Hear me? Keep him alive." He made the last sentence a command, one with the power of a pharaoh.

The physicians went to work, Thoth with them.

Other guards arrived. Khufu reassured them, "The enemy has been defeated. It was Ammut."

Lord Horus gazed about the wrecked room. "The Devouress of the Dead? She was here for questioning, but how could she have gotten free?"

"That's what I'd like to know," Khufu said. I couldn't be sure, but I'd swear that his gaze snapped over to Rami. The pharaoh gathered Khufu into his arms and hugged him. "This is madness. Unforgivable. We can expect no better from Ammut, but whoever freed her from the holding cell must be found and punished. This was an act of treason!"

Lord Horus began to say something, but Set beat him to it. Stepping forward, he said, "Your Majesty, leave this question to me. I'll investigate the matter thoroughly. Interrogate Ammut. Follow all leads until I get to the bottom of just how this dreadful attack occurred."

Pharaoh Neferu looked unsure. "Thank you, Lord Set, but—"

"I'll accept no buts," Set continued. "It's a point of honor for me. My duties take me through the Duat more often than most other gods. Who better than me to find the culprit that no doubt lurks down there right now? I insist. Unless . . ." He hesitated, the horny tufts on his head drooping slightly. ". . . you have reason to doubt me?"

Ha! I thought. *Yeah, there's reason to doubt you!* I almost blurted out as much, but I wasn't sure what I'd say. I was suspicious of Set? I was, but I couldn't really have said what I suspected. That he didn't like me? That was hardly a crime. Was I going to mention the way he scowled at me, those flames that appeared in his eyes, that he wrinkled his snout when he looked at me? I'd sound silly if I said any of that. And what good was claiming that he almost ate me? He hadn't ended up doing it, and nobody else saw a thing.

No, there was really no way for me to pipe up about Lord Set. So I didn't.

I still hoped that Pharaoh Neferu would express doubts of his own, but that hope vanished when he said, "Of course not, Lord Set. We all know the many ways you labor for the good of Egypt. If you wish for this assignment, it is yours."

Turning away from Lord Set's smug face, I saw something I had thought I might never see again. Yazen, with his eyes open. He was alive! I rushed over to him as the physicians were placing him gently onto a stretcher. He couldn't talk, but he could smile, and he did. Lord Thoth stood above him. He slipped his stylus into his belt. "Your mentor will heal," the god said. "Scarred, perhaps, but for the second time in as many days I've breathed life into a body close to death."

I'd never heard better news.

62

Out of the Shadows and into the Light

"**L**ord Thoth's magic is strong," Horus said. "But . . . you both appear to be unarmed. Just how did you defeat such a powerful demon?"

He asked the question in such a serious tone, with his falcon eyes on me so intensely that I had every intention of answering him. But when the words *bouncy balls* came into my mind, I couldn't spit them out. Instead, I giggled.

Khufu tried to say the words that I couldn't. "Bo . . . bo . . . bouncy . . ." That was as far as he got. He guffawed so hard he snorted. That made Seret and Gilli lose it. Seret was wincing in pain as the physicians doctored her wounds, but she couldn't help laughing. We each tried to explain, but failed utterly.

The pharaoh and the gods watched us in astonishment. "Apparently," Horus said dryly, "they defeated the Devouress of the Dead with a good joke. I just wish one of them could tell us what it was."

By the time attendants came to say it was time to head to the ceremony, we still didn't have ahold of ourselves.

"We will discuss what happened later," Pharaoh Neferu said. "Right now we have a ceremony to attend. The people are gathered. Khufu, Ash. They await you." He frowned. "Only . . . look at the state of you. I don't know that we can present you to the court looking like that."

Glancing down at myself, I had to admit he had a point. My skin was still golden, but all that carefully placed jewelry was now strewn about the room. Blood stained my tunic. The fabric was tattered and torn. Khufu didn't look much better. He was sweat-stained and streaked with Seret's blood. Despite that—or maybe because of it—he seemed confident in a way I hadn't noticed in him before.

Pharaoh Neferu turned to Thoth, asking if he might work an illusion on us. Khufu interrupted.

"Father," he said, "I would like us to stay as we are.

We look this way because we were attacked. Together, Ash, Seret, Gilli, and I—and Yazen and the Servants of the Prince—fought back a powerful demon together. Why not show that to the people? Already, my shadow has had a hand in my fate. Isn't that worth declaring tonight?"

The pharaoh studied his son for a long moment. "Khufu, you look different to me, in more ways than just those ragged clothes," he said, a hint of amusement on his lips. "So be it. Go, let the people see you as you are."

Lady Isis spoke then. "If I may . . ." She moved close to me and said, "Ash, I have a gift for you. Will you accept it?"

"Um . . . yeah," I said.

She raised a hand and traced her fingertip across the skin around my eye. Her touch was hot and cold at the same time. It left my skin tingling. She lifted a hand mirror from the bedside table and showed me my reflection. There, etched around my eye in twinkling gray lines, was a symbol.

"An Eye of Isis," the goddess said. "My son's is similar, but this is the original." She winked. "This means that when you are protecting the prince and are in grave danger or in need of help I will know it. I will aid you if I can."

"That's quite a gift," Pharaoh Neferu said. Under his breath, he added, "I think thanks are in order."

Thank her I did! I stumbled over my words until the whole room was laughing, me included.

As we left the room, the physician's assistants lifted Yazen and carried him away. He smiled as he passed out of sight. Seret, with her shoulder being bandaged, waved weakly. Gilli called, "Don't trip during the ceremony, or anything embarrassing like that!"

Khufu and I tried to maintain suitable decorum. It was hard. We were both giddy. Happy at being alive, at everyone being safe, at having sent the demon back to the underworld. At being friends, for that was definitely what we were. I couldn't believe I'd only known Khufu for a week. I remembered the first time I saw him. Back then, I couldn't imagine what I might have in common with him. Now, I realized I'd give my life to protect him. Thing was, I felt sure he'd do the same for me.

The pharaoh and the gods left us in the care of a court official, who looked shocked at our appearance. There wasn't time to explain, though. Instead, he herded us up onto the rear of the dais. From it, we would step into view of the crowd gathered below us in the great plaza as the pharaoh announced us. We stayed hidden. I couldn't see the audience that must have stretched out below the dais, but I could feel their presence, the hum in the air of many expectant people.

"Remember what Gilli said," Khufu whispered.

"Just watch your own feet," I said, smiling.

And then came the moment. The pharaoh said our names. An attendant nudged me. I stepped forward. Slowly, the ranks of people in the audience below came into view. It was incredible. I'd never seen so many people before. Rich people draped in jewels. Lords and ladies. Foreign dignitaries. Gods and magical creatures in all their various forms and guises. Humble people far into the distance. I could barely take in the whole scene. But I knew one thing for sure. They were all looking at me. I made sure I didn't trip.

I glanced over at Khufu. He made a fist, and—just faintly—punched the air. With my good arm, I did the same. Together, we stepped forward, out of the shadows and into the light.

Glossary of the Gods in *The Shadow Prince*

HORUS is the son of Osiris and Isis, the divine child of the holy family triad. He is one of many gods associated with the falcon. His name means "He Who Is Above" and "He Who Is Distant." The falcon had been worshipped from earliest times as a cosmic deity whose body represents the heavens and whose eyes represent the sun and the moon. Horus is depicted as a falcon wearing a crown with a cobra or the Double Crown of Egypt. The hooded cobra (uraeus), which the gods and pharaohs wore on their foreheads, symbolizes light and royalty. It is there to protect the person from harm.

ISIS represents the power of love to overcome death. She brought her husband and brother, Osiris, back to life and saved her son Horus from certain death. She is portrayed wearing the hieroglyph for "throne" on her head, and she sometimes wears a solar disc between cow horns. She is also often depicted mourning the death of her husband and nursing their son.

MAFDET is an early goddess of justice who pronounced judgment and meted out execution swiftly. Her name means "She Who Runs" for the speed with which she dispensed justice. She is the earliest feline deity in Egypt, predating both Bastet and Sekhmet. She protected people from venomous bites, especially from scorpions. Her sharp claws are likened to the tip of the harpoon of the pharaoh that protects him from his enemies in the underworld. Because of this, Mafdet is the protector of the pharaoh, his chambers, his tomb and other sacred places.

NEKHBET is portrayed as a vulture and is the principle goddess of Upper Egypt. In early times, she was the goddess and protector of royal children, but in later periods she became the protector of all young children and expectant mothers. Her southern counterpart is the cobra goddess Wadjet. The two are referred to as "The Two Ladies" and shown together on the crowns of a unified Egypt.

RA is the sun god and is considered the central and original power of creation. The daily rising and setting sun offered tangible evidence of the sun's power to fall into the western sky and be reborn each morning in the eastern sky. Ra brought Maat, the principle of truth and balanced justice, to the Egyptians. This became the cornerstone of the Egyptian civilization.

SET is the god of darkness, drought, and chaos. He is the opponent of everything good and life-giving. In some legends, Set is the adversary of Ra, but in others, he is Ra's protector. As the god of disorder, Set is placed in opposition to Horus, the god who rules the land with order and stability. Seth is an animal-headed deity with a curved head, tall square-topped ears and an erect, arrow-like tail. The animal he represents has not been identified.

SOBEK is the "Lord of the Waters" and the god of the Nile who brings fertility to the land. He is thought to have risen from the primordial waters of Nun to create the world. One creation myth states he did so by laying eggs on Nun's banks. He is also believed to have made the Nile from his sweat. Sobek is most often represented as a deity with the head of an alligator.

THOTH is a moon god and the patron of the arts, hieroglyphics, science, speech, and wisdom. He is the protector of scribes and is credited as the author of the Book of the Dead and the writer of all knowledge. It is said that he organized the Egyptian government and religion, and he is responsible for delivering all the final verdicts at the trials of dead souls. Along with all of these feats, Thoth is considered a great magician, knowing "all that is hidden under the heavenly vault."

Resources:
egyptian-gods.org
historymuseum.ca
ancient.eu
ancientegypt.co.uk
ancientegyptonline.co.uk

Acknowledgments

I am grateful to Stacy Whitman and Tu Books for embracing this novel, and especially to my editor, Elise McMullen-Ciotti, whose hard work and creatively supportive editorial pen made this a much better book.

About the Author

David **Anthony Durham** was born in New York to a Caribbean family and raised primarily in the Mid-Atlantic area. He holds an MFA in creative writing from the University of Maryland, and teaches at the Stonecoast MFA Program and the University of Nevada, Reno. David is the author of seven books for grown-ups. *The Shadow Prince* is his first book for middle-grade readers.